"Nate." W⋯⋯⋯⋯d into his arms.

He held her like she had not been held since that night.

"I—I did not know if you were alive," she rasped.

"I made it through," he said. "Much has happened since."

She clung to him. "I never expected to see you again." She loosened her grip so she might look into his eyes. "You are the Marquess of Hale."

He gave a dry laugh. "Believe me, I never expected to be. You are a widow?"

She nodded. "Cards I did not even realize were in the deck."

He touched her cheek. "But are you well? How do you fare?"

"I am well," she responded. "Never better than right now." He was alive. She melted into his arms again.

The musicians sounded a chord, loud enough to reach their ears.

Nate pulled away. "The first dance. I fear I must go. I promised..."

"Of course." She released him. "Will you call on me tomorrow? I am on Clarges Street. Do you know it?"

"Yes," he responded. "I am nearby on Half Moon Street."

So close. The street just behind hers.

The music started again.

He looked toward the sound. "I must go."

She reached in to embrace him once more before he pulled away again and left.

Author Note

I belong to an authors' group called Regency Fiction Writers, formerly The Beau Monde, whose members offer educational workshops on various topics about the Regency era. In 2020 my friend Louisa Cornell gave a workshop called Gay in Regency England, which was worthy of an accredited college course. Although this book is a completely heterosexual reunion and secret-baby romance between my hero and heroine, Nate and Eliza, it also touches upon the issue of being gay during that era, when it was considered a crime punishable by hanging. Thanks to Louisa, I've been able to make that piece of the story as historically accurate as possible.

DIANE GASTON

—

Secretly Bound to the Marquess

Recycling programs for this product may not exist in your area.

ISBN-13: 978-1-335-72350-5

Secretly Bound to the Marquess

Copyright © 2022 by Diane Perkins

For questions and comments about the quality of this book, please contact us at CustomerService@Harlequin.com.

Harlequin Enterprises ULC
22 Adelaide St. West, 41st Floor
Toronto, Ontario M5H 4E3, Canada
www.Harlequin.com

Printed in U.S.A.

Diane Gaston's dream job was always to write romance novels. One day she dared to pursue that dream and has never looked back. Her books have won romance's highest honors: the RITA® Award, the National Readers' Choice Award, the HOLT Medallion, the Golden Quill and the Golden Heart® Award. She lives in Virginia with her husband and three very ordinary house cats. Diane loves to hear from readers and friends. Visit her website at dianegaston.com.

Books by Diane Gaston

Harlequin Historical

The Lord's Highland Temptation
Secretly Bound to the Marquess

Captains of Waterloo

Her Gallant Captain at Waterloo
Lord Grantwell's Christmas Wish

The Governess Swap

A Lady Becomes a Governess
Shipwrecked with the Captain

The Society of Wicked Gentlemen

A Pregnant Courtesan for the Rake

The Scandalous Summerfields

Bound by Duty
Bound by One Scandalous Night
Bound by a Scandalous Secret
Bound by Their Secret Passion

Visit the Author Profile page
at Harlequin.com for more titles.

To *my* Elizabeth, my always supportive
and wonderful daughter-in-law

Chapter One

Surrey, England—1810

The muddy soup of the country road grabbed at Eliza Varden's half-boots like fingers from the nether world. Impeding her progress. Mocking her.

She wanted to run.

Get away. Leave Henry, the Viscount Varden, her new husband, her closest confidant, her best friend.

After what she'd done.

And what he'd told her.

Oh, what he'd told her! It bore no thinking about. A betrayal. An unexpected, acutely painful betrayal. She dared not think about it. How could she? She must simply get away and never go back.

She wanted to wail, to rend her clothing, tear out her hair, but what good would that do? There was still what Henry had hidden from her. The truth. The truth he'd hidden from her even when he was in school.

Her cloak was soaked through with rain falling like a biblical deluge, whipping around her like an incarnation of her inner turmoil. The wind chilled her to her bones, its cold coming almost as a relief, quelling the flames of disappointment and rage inside her, giving her the strength to trudge on.

One foot in front of the other. That was all she must do. Her boots slipped again for the hundredth time. She managed to regain her balance when the pounding of horse's hooves some distance behind her broke into the din of the incessant rain.

A man's voice called, 'Madam!'

Was she discovered? How was she to explain why Lady Varden was slogging along a muddy road in the pouring rain?

Hiding her face with her hood as best she could, she turned to see who it was.

A man on horseback emerged from the grey curtain of rain. She kept walking.

He pulled up alongside of her. 'Madam. Miss. Where are you bound? May I help you?'

'No!' she cried.

Nothing could help, except perhaps that he leave her alone.

'Here now,' he persisted. 'You cannot keep walking. My horse will carry us both. Let me take you to wherever you are bound.'

'No!' she cried again.

She tried to hurry away from him, but, like a gleeful trickster, the mud slipped under her boots and made her fall to her knees. The man jumped off his horse and rushed over to her.

He grasped her arm and helped her to her feet. 'Are you hurt?'

'No,' she snapped. 'Please let me continue on my way.'

'I merely wish to help you.' He still held her arm. 'I will take you—'

She pulled away.

He stepped back. 'You have nothing to fear from me, I

assure you. You are soaked and cold, I expect. And it must be fatiguing to walk in this mud. My horse can carry two. We will take you wherever you are bound.'

She stole only the slightest glance at him, enough to see he was tall and muscular. And no one she knew, thank the heavens. None the less she kept her head down. She'd lied that she was unhurt. Her fall had shaken her and her legs suddenly felt as if they could no longer keep her upright.

She nodded her assent.

Before she could attempt to move, he picked her up in strong arms and carried her to his waiting horse.

He placed her on his horse's back and mounted behind her.

'Where are you bound?' he asked.

She certainly could not tell him she was running away from her new husband, back to her parents' estate.

'Witley,' she said finally. Another lie.

'Witley?' the man repeated. 'Where is Witley? Can you direct me?'

'Past Milford,' she replied.

'That must be at least ten miles.' His voice was stunned. 'You were intending to walk that distance?'

'As you saw.'

Had she gone mad? She'd no wish to go to Witley when her parents' house was no more than three miles away. She merely did not want him to know where she was bound.

'Not far out of my way, then,' he murmured, apparently accepting her statement as true.

They continued down the road that would eventually lead to Witley—after it passed the road to the house in which she'd lived her whole life.

Until marrying Henry, that was.

At least her companion was not chatty. The poor horse, though, seemed to struggle under the addition of her weight. Her mind whirled with how to convince this man to leave her on the road again. He could certainly reach an inn if unimpeded by her weight and she'd no doubt she could finish her trek even in the rain and mud, now she'd rested against his strong chest.

'I am rested,' she said to him. 'I could walk now.'

He scoffed. 'Don't be daft. I'm not leaving you in the pouring rain.'

They rode past farm fields, but the landscape was so obscured she was unsure precisely how far they'd come. Had they left Henry's land and entered her family's property? If not now then soon, she supposed. The mud of the road worsened with each step. The poor horse. The mud was as treacherous on the horse's hooves as it had been on her boots. How could she bear causing such a lovely horse to break a leg on top of everything else?

Abruptly the horse turned off the road.

Eliza peeked out from her sodden hood, trying to see where they were. 'Why are you leaving the road?' she asked.

'I see shelter,' he told her. 'At this pace we cannot count on reaching a village soon. I need to rest my horse. We can wait out the rain in a dry place.'

When they reached the structures, Eliza recognised them immediately. This was one of the huts on her father's estate. The estate manager kept it supplied for just such an instance, when inclement weather might force the farm workers to wait out a storm. It was also a place she and Henry had often played as children.

Her companion dismounted and opened the wooden boards that were cobbled together to make a stable door. Eliza knew he would find the stable dry and supplied with clean hay.

The horse followed him inside. Eliza slid off the horse's back.

The man immediately gathered a fistful of hay and

began wiping the wet off his horse. Eliza went to the trunk set against the far wall and brought him a dry rag to better do the job.

He looked at her in surprise but took the rag and continued to dry the horse.

'You might as well remove the saddle, too,' she said.

He glanced at her. 'I thought to open the cabin for you first, then continue to tend to the horse.'

She shrugged. 'No. Take care of him.'

'Pegasus.' The man's voice softened. 'His name is Pegasus.'

While he removed his bags and lifted off the saddle, she took a horse blanket from the trunk and brought it to him. He nodded gratefully and draped it over the horse.

He stroked the horse's neck. 'Do not fret, Pegasus. I'll find you some water to drink as soon as I can.' He picked up his bags and slung them over his shoulder. 'Do you wish to wait here where it is dry while I see if we can open the hut?' he asked her.

'I'll come with you,' she said.

Eliza knew where the key to the padlock was hidden, but if she showed him, there would be questions about why she knew. She did not want to reveal anything about herself.

Outside in the rain, he removed his gloves and stuffed them into a pocket. He took out his folding knife and worked on the padlock that secured the door. While he worked at it, she found a bucket and filled it from a water trough.

She lifted it up for him to see. 'For your horse.' She turned back to the stall.

By the time she returned, he'd opened the lock. They entered together.

It took several minutes for her eyes to adjust to the relative darkness. She'd not been in the cabin for years, but it could have been yesterday. Nothing was changed. Not the table and chairs where she and Henry had played cards. Not the cot in the corner or the small scullery.

Her companion dropped his saddlebags on the floor and took off his hat—a shako. He shrugged out of his topcoat, beneath which was the red coat and sash of an army officer. She released a breath. A soldier was an uncommon sight in her village. He was not someone who would know her. He must merely be passing through.

It would be safe for her to show her face.

He hung his topcoat over one of the chairs and gestured to the fireplace. 'I'll start a fire.'

As she expected, there were stacks of wood, kindling and tinder near the fireplace. There would also be a tinderbox and a candle on the mantel. While he used the tinderbox to light the candle, she went to the counter in the scullery and picked up the oil lamp she knew would be there.

He used the candle flame to check the flue and reached inside the chimney to open it, then he set about laying the wood on the grate. The tinder caught fire immediately. When the kindling caught, he placed some larger logs on the fire.

When he turned around, Eliza handed him the oil lamp.

His brows rose in surprise. 'Very good.'

He lit the lamp and its flame illuminated the whole room.

For the first time, Eliza fully saw his face. A handsome face framed by dark curly hair that glistened from the rain. His brows were thick, his eyes an assessing brown. A nose that must have been broken at one time. A strong jaw. Expressive lips. Her sisters would have swooned over such a face. He was also tall, at least a half a foot taller than Henry. And herself.

He stared back at her and the moment stretched until a

flash of lightning brightened the room, followed almost immediately by a loud clap of thunder.

He turned towards the window. 'I am afraid we will be here a while.'

She still thought she could make it to her parents' house. What would two miles be, even in the rain?

Lightning struck again. Leaving would be dangerous.

'May I help you with your cloak?' he asked.

She had to decide. Stay or leave. She suspected he would follow her if she left now, putting him and his lovely horse at risk of the lightning as well. She really had no choice, did she?

Stay, then.

She unclasped her cloak. 'I can manage.' She slipped it off her shoulders and draped it over the other wooden chair. She took off her gloves and placed them on the table.

Wind rattled the windows and Eliza shivered from the chill. Her dress was nearly as sodden as her cloak. Her feet were freezing.

Without seeming too obvious, she wandered over to the trunk near the cot and opened it. She pretended to rummage through it, but she well knew what was there. 'There are blankets.' She lifted them out. 'And dry clothes.'

She set aside the blankets and reached into the trunk again. 'A couple of dry shirts and breeches.' She inclined her head to another part of the room. 'There is also a pump for water over there. We only need some rainwater for priming it. Then I can make some tea.'

'There is tea?' He was surprised.

'Tea and a kettle and other kitchen wares.' But she was revealing too much. 'I found them while you were lighting the fire.'

He nodded approvingly and inclined his head towards the trunk. 'We should remove our wet clothes and change into dry ones. Hang our clothes near the fire to dry.'

She stared at him. To do so would necessitate staying longer than she'd hoped. It would protect her identity, though, in case he was somehow connected to someone in the village.

She turned her back to him. 'You will need to undo my buttons.'

The touch of his fingers on her nearly bare skin aroused sensations inside her, an awareness that she was alone with a man in this one-room cabin, although she and Henry had often been alone in similar spaces.

He stepped back when done. 'I'll venture outside for some water for the pump.'

Good. She'd have privacy to dress. And some distance from him to cool the heat of his hands.

He flung his topcoat over his shoulders and, taking a jug with him, ventured outside into the still steady sheet of rain.

Once outside, Robert Nathanial Thorne, Captain in the 30th Regiment of Foot, leaned against the closed door of the hut and let the rain cool his face and extinguish the sudden flames of awareness—awareness that he was alone with a beautiful young woman in very intimate circumstances.

When he'd plucked her out of the mud, she'd been little more than a mystery. A lone woman walking in such a deluge? For ten miles? He'd noticed her gloves, though, fine kid embroidered with flowers. Her cloak was of equally fine cloth, such as worn by a lady, not a village girl or housemaid. Then he'd learned she knew and cared for horses and, when in the cabin, was useful and resourceful. She'd still been a mere mystery then—why was a lady, albeit a useful one, to be found traipsing through the rain and mud?

Then she'd removed her cloak and the fire and lamplight illuminated her face. He'd been momentarily devoid of breath.

She was beautiful.

Her eyes were startlingly light. Grey? Green? He had not been able to tell, but they were framed by dark, delicately arched brows. Her hair was dark, as well, but there was not enough light to reveal its precise colour. Her skin, as pale as cream, was flushed by the cold and her full lips were pink enough to have been tinted.

All that aside, it was the aura of despair that called to him most strongly, making him yearn to take her in his arms and comfort her. Nate knew despair. He knew loneliness and loss and all of it seemed reflected in her eyes.

At least her despair made him forget his own. He'd been perilously close to wallowing in his own self-pity on that rainy, solitary road, particularly after his rare obligatory and bleak visit to his uncle.

He wiped the rain from his face and listened to the rumbling of distant thunder. The weather was not going to clear sufficiently for them to proceed safely in daylight. They must spend the night here. Together. And no matter how he burned inside, he would not add to the lady's problems by ungentlemanly behaviour.

Inhaling deeply, Nate pushed himself away from the door and stepped over to the stable to check on Pegasus. The horse nickered at the sight of him, but the tension was absent from the animal's muscles and he blinked lazily at Nate. Nate found the cloth again and wiped the mud from Pegasus's hooves before replacing the hay that the horse had consumed.

'You'll fare well here, my old friend?' Nate asked aloud.

Pegasus nudged him and blew out some air in reply.

'I will check on you later.'

He picked up the jug and again ventured out into the downpour to fill it with water, which was in plentiful supply.

Hoping he had allowed her enough time to don the dry clothes, he opened the door to the cabin and carried the jug and his bags inside.

The woman gave him the most fleeting of glances. 'I put a shirt and breeches on top of the trunk for you. Stockings, too.'

She was a sight to behold, hair tangled, wearing the man's shirt over her shift and the breeches underneath. She'd put the rough stockings on her feet. Though her underclothes were likely still damp, she'd be warm enough in the strange outfit so unbefitting a lady. She returned his gaze and held it and he felt snared by her allure.

He forced himself to turn away, putting the jug on the counter near the pump and dropping his saddlebags on the floor. He removed his topcoat and draped it over the table as she had done with her cloak.

He must undress in front of her, but he hesitated.

'I'll prime the pump and draw some water for tea,' she said, crossing the room and turning her back to him.

He quickly walked to a corner of the room and peeled off his wet coat, waistcoat and shirt. He put on the dry shirt before removing his boots, stockings and trousers, replacing them with the dry breeches and rough stockings much like the ones she wore. By the time she'd drawn the water for tea, he was dressed.

He gathered his wet clothes in his arms. 'How fortunate to find dry clothing here.'

'Someone supplied it well.' She walked past him to put the kettle on the fire.

He moved the second chair closer to the fire, as she

had done, and hung his uniform coat, trousers and stockings over it.

'I'll clean the mud from our boots,' he said. 'They can dry in front of the fire.'

Afterwards he pulled the cot closer to the warmth of the fire. Soon they sat on it like a bench, each wrapped in a blanket, sipping tea from tin cups.

Finally completely warm.

He turned to her. 'I should make myself known to you. I am—'

A panicked look came over her face and she held up her hand. 'Please do not! I do not want to tell you who I am and I do not want to know who you are.'

He was unprepared for such a vehement reply. What had he stumbled into?

'You had better explain why,' he responded in a stern tone. 'Because I have no wish to be accused of abduction or something equally as sinister when my only thought was to help you.'

She shot him a flaming glance. 'You gave me little choice!'

'Choice?' he retorted. 'What sort of man would I be if I had simply ridden by you?'

She bowed her head and spoke in a small voice. 'Forgive me. I am not ungrateful.'

He leaned towards her. 'Are you in trouble? If there is something I can do—'

'No trouble,' she said quickly. Defensively, he thought. 'I am merely…' she paused '…unhappy.' She waved her hand as if it was a trifling matter.

He caught her hand and touched the ring on her finger. A wedding ring. Some inner part of him registered disappointment. 'Should I fear the wrath of some jealous husband bursting in upon us?'

She pulled away. 'He does not know I am gone. I made certain of it.' She immediately looked regretful, as if she'd said too much. Just as quickly her expression changed to something like contempt. 'Jealousy,' he thought he heard her say under her breath. 'Not very likely.'

He took a sip of his tea. 'Why not jealousy?'

She tossed him a scathing look. 'Never mind.'

Oh, no. He was not about to leave these tantalising clues to the mystery unquestioned. He lifted his brows.

'I will not tell you,' she snapped, refusing his challenge, then in a low, despairing voice. 'I cannot.'

As she retreated into silence, he fancied her descending into a misery that poured upon her like the rain.

He spoke again, taking a lighter tone. 'May we not exchange given names, then? No harm in that, is there? Then I will not have to say, *Hey, you* when speaking to you.' Or *my lady*, which he suspected she would not wish him to guess.

She did not answer him.

'May I tell you my given name, then?' he persisted.

Reluctantly she nodded.

He turned to her and extended his hand. 'I am called Nate.'

She hesitated before accepting his hand to shake but still did not speak. He was not insensible to the softness of her skin, nor the unexpected steadiness of her hand. He released her and she wrapped her fingers around her cup of tea and brought its rim to her mouth.

He continued to face her, cocking his head in expectation.

'Eliza,' she said finally.

He took a sip of tea to cover his amused smile. She'd done what he'd asked of her. 'Eliza,' he repeated.

She averted her gaze and involved herself in drinking the tea as if that kept a barrier between them. He continued to watch her, sensing some deep disappointment inside her. When she blinked away tears he was certain of it.

'I think you had better tell me what troubles you,' he said in a soothing voice. 'I am involved now. Inadvertently, I admit, but I was the one to find you on the road. That involves me. What harm can it do to tell me if I do not know who you are and you do not know who I am?'

'I cannot speak of it!' she said. 'I will not.'

'And I cannot force you,' he continued in those modulated tones. 'But whatever it is, it is causing you great distress. You must face it. Running away will not help.'

Nate learned this at six years old. No amount of running away, or pretending, or denying, made trouble go away. Something would always bring it back and knock you down again. The only thing that worked was facing it. And living through it.

She tossed him a side glance, equally as scathing as those before. 'How would you know?'

Oh, that was a joke if ever there was one. Of course he knew. 'I assure you I have had a great many distressing events in my life. I do indeed know.'

She gave a derisive laugh. 'Not like this.'

'Very well, perhaps not the precise thing, but I will wager no less devastating.' What could hers be? A row with her husband? No, something worse. 'Why not tell me?' he persisted. 'After the rain, you will never see me again. I am bound for Portsmouth, for a ship to Portugal.'

Realisation dawned on her face. She understood he was headed for war, he supposed, and he thought he saw sympathy there, but she quickly turned her head away.

He took another sip of tea. The fire crackled pleasingly and warmth filled the room. Why should it suddenly matter to him that she tell him whatever was so crushing she had to flee during a torrent? How often had he sat with others while feeling separate and alone; why did he feel he could not do so with her?

He'd undoubtedly see hard combat as Wellington's armies sought to push the French from the Iberian Peninsula, but hard combat suited him. After all, he was the perfect soldier.

It mattered to no one if he lived or died. Not even to himself.

So why did it matter that this lady confided in him? Why did he feel connected to her when he prided himself on having no attachments to anyone? Was it all a mere fancy that her misery called to him? Had he not conquered his?

He could help her conquer hers, he knew. He simply did not know why he wanted to.

Chapter Two

Lightning flashed again and immediately after, a rolling clap of thunder. Rain pattered on the roof and the fire crackled and popped in the fireplace.

Nate took another sip of tea.

He glanced at her profile, worthy of a Classical Roman cameo. There was no denying her beauty aroused the male in him, but this was more. Something deeper that pricked at something inside him he usually kept so carefully buried. Having just left his uncle's house had not helped. His uncle was the antithesis of a true family connection. Oh, the man had paid for his schooling and had purchased his commission, but out of obligation, nothing more. Even as a child it had been plain to Nate that his uncle cared nothing for him. Nate returned that sense of obligation, hence his visit.

He'd have been better off travelling straight to Portugal, though. His uncle had been as unwelcoming as if Nate had been an infestation of woodworm. Such an icy reception always weakened the walls Nate erected over his own feelings. Perhaps that was why this woman's despair affected him so.

But he did not need to reach into the depths to convince her he'd endured hardship. He could start with Martinique.

'I am lately from the West Indies,' he said. 'The island of Martinique. We'd taken it from the French and my regiment was garrisoned there. Battle is a deadly thing, but it was my job, so expected, you see?'

She shot him a uninterested glance, but at least she was listening.

He went on. 'Afterwards, though. Afterwards men died from fever. Hundreds of them. One was a friend.'

Such a rarity for Nate to call anyone friend. The few he'd had as a schoolboy eventually returned to their families or befriended other boys with families. In the army, friends moved from regiment to regiment. Or died in battle. Or, like Woodman, died from yellow fever. Skin turning yellow. Eyes red. Vomit black. Finally delirium and the relief of death.

He would not share the description with her. 'Death from yellow fever is not a pretty one, I assure you. There is terrible suffering before death finally comes.' He could not keep the memory from the tone of his voice, though.

Her voice turned soft, her eyes sympathetic. 'How terrible.'

Not so completely wrapped up in her own misery, then.

He frowned. 'There was nothing anyone could do for it. Least of all me. All I could do was wait to catch the fever myself. Instead, I chose to purchase a captaincy in another regiment. I am on my way to join them now.'

She nodded, then slid him another glance. 'Was that not running away?'

That took him aback. Clever of her.

And not inaccurate. 'I would call it making a better choice. But the point is I faced the problem and figured a way out.'

'How do you know I am not making a better choice?' she asked.

She was quick-witted. He could not help but admire

that. 'I do not know. But charging out in a raging rainstorm does suggest flight, does it not?'

She averted her gaze.

He was beginning to like her more and more. Clever. Useful. Quick-witted and not missish. Even her steadfast obstinance had an admirable side. All the more reason to help her.

Except helping her seemed to mean opening himself to his own pain. Already he could feel the cracks inside him widen from the coldness of his uncle, from the memory of his friend's agonising death. And most of all from her obvious despair.

Wait. He'd faced the pain before. He could do so again.

He glanced at her as she set her empty cup of tea aside. Her eyes glistened with tears. His throat tightened in response.

It had been a lifetime since he'd last wept.

Since his parents died. 'I will tell you more about myself,' he said, pushing the words out. 'About when I was six years old, when typhus hit our village and spread quickly until it seemed like everyone was ill. My parents, too.' He swallowed, momentarily becoming that six-year-old boy again. 'I watched my mother and father die of fever within hours of each other.'

She glanced at him and the horror of it showed in her eyes.

He closed his eyes and again saw their mottled skin, heard their cries as they, too, descended into delirium. His eyes stung with unspent tears.

He cleared his throat and continued. 'I was the son of a younger son of a younger son. There were no close relatives willing to take me in. There was my uncle, but he wanted nothing to do with me. He did, however, pay for my schooling and my commission in the army, but that was mostly to be rid of me.'

Nate turned to her, but she quickly averted her eyes.

His chest ached and breathing became difficult. How shocking that the memories could flood him with so much emotion after all these years. As if no time had passed. Grief. Fear. Loneliness. He remembered, when alone at school, when everything he'd known and loved was gone, he'd lectured himself, echoing his father's voice. 'Buck up! Be strong! You have only yourself now. You can do it.'

Only at this moment that strength seemed an illusion.

He attempted a wan smile. 'So, you see, I have known pain.'

She was fully listening, at least. 'Surely the teachers at the school took care of you.'

He laughed. 'The teachers had no inclination to coddle a weak, unhappy boy. I was on my own.'

'What of friends?' Was she trying to talk him out of how hard this was?

'Friends always went home to their families.'

'That was a terrible way to grow up!' she said with feeling.

They lapsed into silence.

Had he made a mistake? Had he merely succeeded in opening himself to his own pain, rather than attending to hers?

Finally she spoke and her voice became clipped. 'That is all very sad for you. Very sad and I am sorry for it. But I am still not going to tell you anything about me.'

Ah, this sparked of a challenge. Never say he baulked at a challenge. Besides, focussing on her seemed the only way to seal up those cracks inside him again.

'You force me to guess, then,' he said.

'Guess all you like,' she responded. 'I am not speaking of it.'

He reached over and grasped her left hand. Her wedding ring, a gold band clustered with diamonds, glittered in the firelight. 'Something about your husband.'

She snatched her hand back and tucked it under her arm.

It was about her husband, then. 'Your husband would not be jealous, you said. Perhaps it is you who are jealous. Perhaps he is unfaithful—'

Her eyes flashed, but she quickly set her chin.

He'd hit the mark. 'I see. Another woman.'

To his surprise she scoffed. Not the husband who was unfaithful? Had it been she who was unfaithful? 'Another man, then.'

She paled and averted her face.

Obviously he'd touched on the truth, but he still did not know what it was.

Infidelity. Not a woman. A man. But no jealous husband. It made no sense—

Until it did.

He lowered his voice. 'Not a woman, but a man. Your husband has been unfaithful to you with a man.'

She turned back to him. 'How could you guess such a thing?'

'It seemed the only explanation,' he said.

She looked askance. 'You do not sound appalled or shocked.'

He shrugged. 'Some men are born that way.'

He rose to pour her another cup of tea and sat beside her again, handing it to her.

Eliza wrapped her fingers around the tin cup, its heat comfortingly real. Never in a million years should anyone have guessed why she'd fled from her husband. She'd never suspected such a thing, why should anyone else?

The captain—Nate—spoke again, his voice matter of fact. 'It was not that unusual in a boys' school. There were always those boys with special friendships. Eventually one saw something or heard something and began to understand theirs was something more than friendship.'

How could he sound so casual about it? 'Did it not alarm you?'

He shrugged. 'Perhaps a little at first. Some of the other boys taunted and teased them, but some of them were kind to me, kinder than their tormentors. I could not dislike them. So I and the other boys simply ignored it.'

'But is it not unnatural?' she asked. 'A sin?'

'Some say so.' He rose and poured himself some tea. 'However, men loving men have been around since ancient times.'

'Yes. In ancient Greece and Rome,' she agreed. 'I have read that.'

'Nisus and Euryalus in the *Aeneid*.' He sat beside her again. 'They were soldiers. I've seen great tenderness between some men in the army. It would be difficult to condemn them.'

'You approve of this?' she asked, surprised.

He lifted a shoulder. 'My approval or disapproval means nothing. I do not think such men can change. They just are as they are and have done so throughout history. I surmise it is natural for them.'

Natural for Henry, then. Known by Henry since childhood, perhaps.

He faced her. 'It is, however, highly condemned by most people and very much against the law. Punishable by hanging or the pillory, which is why those men must keep it secret at all costs.'

She shuddered. 'Punishable by hanging.' She did not want Henry to die, did she?

He abandoned his instructional lecture and changed the subject. 'So, tell me about your husband.'

She squeezed her cup. 'My husband.'

She ought to say no more. Keep the secret, like she'd

kept all the secrets in her life, but this cabin, lit by the fire-place, darkness and rain surrounding them, seemed apart from everything and everyone else. This was a moment in time between strangers who would go their separate ways, who would never know who the other was. Her secrets would travel no further than the safety of these walls.

She put down her cup of tea and began again, forcing out the words. 'My husband confessed to me today that he loved another. That he loved a man and had loved him for years and would continue to love him.'

'So you ran away because of that?' he asked.

'Not because of that!' Although she could see why he'd think so. 'Because he did not tell me before marrying me. He claimed to be my friend and yet he hid this from me. For years.'

He gave her a direct look. 'So you ran away because he kept something secret that might otherwise be punished by death or the pillory?'

'You do not understand!' she protested. 'I would have kept his secret. He knows very well I can keep secrets. But there were never any secrets between us—I thought. I trusted him. Why could he not trust me?'

'Then he knows you left for Witley.' He continued to look her in the eye.

'Of course not!' She huffed.

'Then you have kept something secret from him.'

She averted her gaze. 'He will know where I've gone. I will send word to him when I am ready.' She faced him again. 'Can you not see? He should have told me before marrying me.'

The challenge in his eyes softened. 'He should have told you. I agree. Should have given you a choice.'

'Yes!' That was it! Henry had not given her a choice. This captain did understand—at least that part of it.

'Would you have married him had you known?' he asked.

Would she? How much of a choice had there been, truly?

She glanced away. 'It was either marry him or marry the old widower my father had selected for me.'

'Or choose neither of them,' he offered. 'Was that not another choice? You are still young. Why marry at all?'

She laughed drily. If he only knew...

Well, why not tell him? He did not know her or her father or who the old widower was.

'Oh, I had to marry,' she said, her voice bitter. 'My father was in terrible debt. Ruinous debt. Terrible enough to ruin the futures of my sisters and brother. My father offered marriage to me in payment.'

The soldier's eyes flashed.

She went on. 'Then H—my husband, I mean—offered to marry me instead. And pay my father's debts. And help my sisters and brother. My—my best friend rescued me. I was so happy.' But she'd thought theirs would be a real marriage. Henry ought to have warned her. Then she would not have humiliated herself so.

But she could not think of that.

She drank the rest of her tea and rose to put her cup in the scullery.

When she returned to sit by him again, she could not help but continue her story. 'I've known my husband my whole life. We grew up together, so I have met his friend. Many times. He used to visit on university holidays.' She'd seen nothing unusual in Henry's friendship with Ryland. 'His friend married a year ago.' She shook her head in confusion. 'Why would he do that? Why would either of them marry?'

Was that why Henry married her? Because Ryland had married?

He took both her hands then and met her gaze. 'Think of life from their vantage point. They must hide their true nature. Hide who they love. If they reveal themselves they face hanging or the pillory and the ruin of their entire family. That is a very heavy price to pay for loving someone.'

She did not want Henry to hang. Or be placed in the pillory to be abused and scorned. Or for her sisters and brother to be ruined by the scandal. All she'd wanted was— was—things she believed about marriage when speaking her wedding vows. Impossible now.

'What of the wives, though?' she said bitterly. 'What of them?'

'Some may never know,' he said. 'Some men are able to perform the duties of a marriage. Others cannot, I suppose.'

'My husband.' This was so hard to say. 'My husband— cannot perform.'

Or would not.

'I waited weeks for him to come to my bed, but he didn't. At first I was so busy with learning to be—' she'd almost said *learning to be Viscountess Varden* '—learning to run a house, I'd not thought much of it. After all, we were friends since childhood. It was awkward to think of us in any other way.' She'd been determined they overcome this, though. To have a real marriage.

So she'd dressed in her most alluring clothes and gone to him…

'I—I tried to seduce him, but he—he pushed me away.' The memory of his face, the look of revulsion on it, made her eyes sting with tears. She wiped them away with the sleeve of her shirt. 'He said he could not be unfaithful to his friend. It was then he told me. Only then.' When she'd been half naked with him, trying to make him touch her, kiss her.

The captain then did something so unexpected. He wrapped his arms around her and held her close and murmured words of comfort. The floodgates of her tears burst open.

She sobbed. 'I thought I was lucky to marry my best

friend. I thought we would be happy.' She shuddered. 'I thought I would have children. But it will never be. Never be.'

He stroked her hair. 'Now. Now. It is difficult. Very difficult for you, I know. I know.'

She cried sloppy, ugly tears, dampening his shirt. She cried until no tears were left and still he held her. Finally she was able to breathe normally again.

She pulled away. 'Forgive me. I am not usually such a watering pot.' She sniffed and wiped her face with her sleeve again.

He gazed at her, his expression still sympathetic. 'No need to apologise.'

He rose again and poured her another cup of tea, weakened now to be no more than flavoured water. She sipped gratefully and quickly regained her composure.

She took a deep breath and released it. 'So you see how it is.'

'A very unhappy state of affairs,' he admitted to her in that low, soft, soothing voice that helped set herself to rights. 'So you ran away.'

'I told you I am not running away!' she cried.

He nodded in a placating way.

She peered at him. 'How can I stay?'

She looked into the captain's eyes, their light brown reminding her of warm gingerbread. She saw sympathy in them, not only for her, but for Henry, as well. He did not condemn Henry's nature, but could he not see? It was not Henry's nature that made her flee. It was that Henry had hidden it from her. He'd never trusted her, obviously. And he'd never made it her choice to marry him or not, knowing what was ahead. He had never trusted her to accept him for who he was.

The captain spoke, his voice soft. 'He was once your friend, you said. Is he not the same man as before? The same man who was your friend?'

She shook her head. 'I do not know. I never really knew him, did I?'

'Not all of him, certainly,' he agreed. 'Not this one thing, but how could he tell you? To tell you would be risking exposure and death.'

'You do not understand.' She withdrew. 'He did not trust me.' Eliza hugged her bended knees and hid her face. How was she to trust Henry now? 'We were *close* friends. He—he knew everything about me. About my family. He should have known he could trust me. That I would never say anything to cause his death.'

Nate reached over and brushed a strand of her hair off her face. 'Perhaps he was that afraid.'

How could she explain to this captain? Because Henry could not trust her, because he'd never confided his true self and what would be the nature of his marriage to her, Henry had let her humiliate herself in front of him.

She glanced at the captain, now taking a sip of his tea. Look how *he'd* trusted her with his painful life story just so she would tell what was disturbing her. So he could help her. What other motive could Nate have had except to help her? He did not know who she was. They would part and never see each other again. He had no obligation at all to help her.

But it had helped to tell him about Henry. Her captain had been right about that. He'd helped her understand. He'd helped her grasp what the real issue disturbing her was.

Trust.

How could she trust Henry from now on, knowing what he'd withheld from her?

How remarkable. She trusted this captain even more than she'd ever trusted Henry. Or anyone.

Chapter Three

Nate picked up his cup of tea, tepid now, and drank its contents.

He'd been speaking calmly to her, but inside him something raw and painful had been unleashed and he struggled to keep it at bay. He'd launched himself back in time and was no longer the soldier bound for war, but that six-year-old boy again, watching his parents' last agonised breaths, that lonely boy sent to school who'd so envied the boys who'd had someone to love them.

No, he could not disapprove of a man loving a man, not when he'd felt so starved of anyone for whom his existence mattered. He must push these emotions away, though, as he'd done when he'd been alone at six years old. That was the only way to survive. Push through whatever life threw at him, whether it be schoolboy pains of cruel tutors or bullying older boys—or death. Death on the battlefield. Death of hundreds of soldiers from fever. Death of a rare friend.

Of Mother and Father.

He'd mastered this once. By God, he could do so again.

As could she, the beautiful, despairing Eliza. He glanced at her, hiding her face, hugging her knees, just as he'd done so many times when he'd first arrived at school. He could show her.

It was the one way he could help her. 'Do you believe your husband's treatment of you will change now?'

She lifted her head and gave him a suspicious look. 'What do you mean his treatment of me?'

'I mean before he married you. If he was kind and considerate before, will he be so again?' he clarified.

'He was always kind and considerate.' She lowered her head again.

Nate envied that type of friendship. 'He will be the same man he was before.' The essence of a person did not change. 'He only hid that one part of him.'

She looked up at him again. 'But perhaps I have changed. How am I to trust him now, knowing he kept his very essence from me? And will he trust me, knowing I wanted to seduce him?'

She had a point.

Nate took another tack. 'What do you imagine will happen, now you've run away?'

She shuddered, as if she'd not considered anything beyond running. Her eyes filled with alarm. 'Will it anger him, do you mean? Will he take revenge? My family depend upon him. Without his assistance and control, my parents' debts will grow again. And my sisters. They will have no chances to make a good match without his providing a dowry. And my brother—' She broke off.

Nate felt a pang of pain. She had all those people in her life. A family. Sisters. A husband who was once a friend. He had no one.

'How lucky you are—' his voice rasped with emotion '—to have family to care about. To have a lifelong friend willing to marry you. What I would give for a brother. Or sister. Or to have my parents still living.'

She looked pained, but he could not tell if it was sympathy for him or pain from the situation that she must face.

He had to change the subject, though. It was too painful for him. 'People will ask why you left him. What will you say?'

She stared at him. 'I've not thought of what to say.'

'If you told the truth—'

Her face paled. 'Henry might be hanged.'

A flash of lightning lit the room and thunder followed on its heels. They both jumped in surprise. This storm was unremitting, as if fuelled by the turmoil inside both of them. Surely streams would be swollen, roads flooded. Perhaps even death awaited, if one ventured out in it.

Her eyes were wide and glistening as she held his gaze. He felt a powerful urge to enfold her in his arms again— and have her arms hold him. The urge was more than carnal, more than anything he'd experienced with any other woman.

How was he to resist when they were trapped together for the whole night?

He rose. 'I am going to check on Pegasus.'

She unfolded her legs and stood. 'I'll go with you.'

His intent was to put distance between them. Cool his ardour. He was about to protest but could not make himself refuse her company. They put on their still-wet boots. He lit the lantern and donned his topcoat. She wrapped her cloak around her and they stepped out in the rain, dashing over to the small stable.

Pegasus whinnied at their entry.

'There, there, old friend,' Nate murmured. 'How are you faring?'

Pegasus blew out a breath and bobbed his head as if in reply. Nate stroked his neck. The stable was damp and cold, but still reasonably dry. Pegasus had munched on the hay Nate had provided for him, but the water trough was almost dry.

'I'll get him some more water,' Nate said.

Eliza had joined him at the horse's head, touching the animal briefly. 'He is a fine horse.'

Nate laughed. 'Hear that, Pegasus? She thinks you are fine.'

Pegasus was quite ordinary, a common bay with only a tiny spot of white on his forehead. He was descended from the horses first brought to the West Indies by Christopher Columbus. Sturdy, but nothing like the elegant steeds other officers had brought with them to the islands from England.

She handed the horse some dry hay. 'You *are* fine, Pegasus.'

Complimenting his horse? Was she trying to be irresistible?

Nate walked out to get some fresh water. When he returned she was mucking out the stable.

He could not believe his eyes. 'What are you doing?'

She merely gestured to the floor.

He quickly poured the water in Pegasus's water bucket. 'I'll do that.'

She handed him the rake.

As he finished she approached him with another horse blanket in her arms. 'Should we put this over Pegasus?'

'Where did you find that?' he asked.

'In a chest.' She gestured to a wooden box he'd not even noticed.

'Yes. Yes,' he responded. 'It will keep him warm.' The chill of the stable was already seeping into Nate's bones.

Together they put the blanket on Pegasus and soon were dashing through the rain back to the cabin, pleasantly warm in comparison.

Nate threw another log on the fire and crouched low to poke at the burning logs.

'Shall I make more tea?' she asked.

'Please.'

She pressed her hand to her stomach.

'Are you hungry?' He stood. 'I have some bread and cheese in my bag.'

'Yes!'

Her grateful smile made Nate's insides leap. Did she realise her allure? It was nearly irresistible.

Nate had had his share of women, willing tavern maids mostly. He'd had a brief affair in the islands with a free woman, a widow, but that ended, as they both knew it would, when his regiment was sent elsewhere. He'd liked her. Liked all the women he'd bedded. He'd liked talking to them as well as bedding them. He'd liked the companionship, but he'd always felt as if he were reaching for something more, something that eluded him thus far.

A connection.

Odd that he should feel connected to the mysterious Eliza—because of her pain.

Or was he fooling himself entirely? Using that kindred sense of pain to excuse his basest masculine instincts?

He walked over to his bags and unfastened the leather strap of one, drawing out the bread and cheese he'd purchased at the inn that morning and wrapped in an oil cloth which kept it reasonably dry.

Soon they were seated on the cot again, hot cups of weak tea in hand, nibbling on the bread and cheese set between them, trying to make it seem like a full meal.

'You know your way around horses,' he said, breaking the silence and attempting to quell the growing heat in his loins.

Her smile almost erupted again. 'My passion as a girl. I would have spent all my days on horseback or in the stables if I'd been allowed.'

He took a bite of bread and swallowed it. 'Does your husband like riding as well?'

Her smile fled completely, but she nodded. 'We used to ride together. I had a horse I loved. Had her since a child.

My father sold her to pay a debt. My husband found her and returned her to me as a wedding present.'

'That was kind of him,' Nate said.

She winced as if freshly in pain, but her expression quickly hardened. 'Is it kindness? Or mere means to keep me mollified?'

What could it be besides kindness? Although when your world turns upside down, you question everything you thought you knew. Such as, could the reason there is no one to love you be because you are unlovable?

No. No, he protested anew. Such things are random. Your measure—even at age six—is how you face up to it.

'Do you play cards, Eliza? Whist? Piquet?' he asked.

'I detest gambling,' she responded with vehemence. 'Besides infidelity, card playing is one of my parents' favourite vices.'

'For amusement, then,' he clarified. 'Not for money.'

She turned to him. 'I do hope you are not suggesting a game of piquet with soggy cards.'

He laughed. 'I have no cards. I, too, am not fond of gambling.' Why risk what little you have? He stared at the bit of cheese that sat on the oil cloth spread out between them. Leave it, he thought. For her. He lifted his gaze to her. 'I was compiling an analogy.'

'An analogy?' she asked sounding puzzled.

'An analogy,' he repeated, then cleared his throat. 'Life dealt you a rotten hand of cards, Eliza. There is no doubt about that.'

She looked down into her teacup. 'No doubt at all.'

'But it is how you play the hand that counts.'

Her gaze rose again.

He went on. 'Right now you are folding and allowing all the other players to determine the final outcome of the game without you. Have you not had players do that?

Throw down their cards and leave the game entirely? I have. Perhaps your sisters or your brother?'

She nodded grudgingly.

'If you stay in the game, though, play the cards you are dealt, you might come out with some winnings.'

Her eyes narrowed. 'If the hand is so rotten, loss would be the only possible result.'

'Ah, yes,' he admitted. 'But if you play the hand, you might lose less. Others might make mistakes. You might come out of it with enough coin to play another hand, one where the cards would be better.'

She sighed. 'I fear that is precisely how my mother and father increased their debts.'

The captain shrugged and lifted the oilcloth to give her the last piece of cheese. Eliza's fingers touched his for a moment as she reached for it. She'd left the last piece for him, but it would be churlish of her to refuse yet this new generosity.

'Thank you,' she said simply.

Her gratitude spanned more than over a small piece of cheese, of course. He'd rescued her from the storm, both outside and inside her. Not that she no longer felt her insides twisting over Henry's betrayal, but at least her anger over it had eased somewhat. For the moment at least.

The captain stood, folding his oilcloth as he walked back to his bags and put it in one of the pockets. She watched him.

He seemed to take each step as if daring the space before him to impede him. It sent an unexpected flutter within her.

She turned away.

Could she tackle the world as this captain said she should? As he had. Like a card game to be won? No. Not a card game. A battle. But her battle must be fought entirely in secret. Well, she had much practice in keeping secrets.

Henry knew that. He should have known he could trust her with his greatest one. He should have known she would never speak of it to anyone, that she could never risk he might be hanged.

The captain spoke as if their conversation about Henry had not stopped ages ago. 'You know, it seems to me that your marriage is not unlike so many who marry for reasons other than love.'

She met his gaze. 'Except even those marriages produce children. My husband made it clear that will not happen.'

That was an anguish she was not sure she could overcome, a joy she would never experience.

And the captain seemed to have no response.

He strode over to the window and peered outside. 'The rain is easing, but it is dark out. Even if it stops we cannot go on.' He turned to her. 'We are here for the night.'

'For the night?' It should upset her, to spend the night alone with this stranger. Instead, the tension in her muscles eased. She felt…relieved. She also felt safe, secure in the presence of this man.

'You will be missed, I fear.' He frowned.

She shook her head. 'I gave very clear instructions not to be disturbed until morning. No one will disobey my wishes, not even Hen—my husband.' She'd almost said his name.

Although if she had spoken Henry's name, indeed, if she'd revealed her complete identity, she somehow believed her captain could be trusted not to betray her. Or Henry.

He exuded strength, in character as well as in body, perhaps was the most admirable man she'd ever met. Ironic that in the world she inhabited, he would be too low for notice. Though her parents had been on the edge of ruin and their behaviour anything but admirable, they would never have allowed such a son of a younger son of a younger son to court her. Not elevated enough.

She shook herself. Not that courting ever held much appeal. She'd not dared to be romantic about it, not when her father had squandered her dowry and had been willing to sell her to settle his debt. She could envision her sisters becoming all starry-eyed over Captain Nate, though. So tall and handsome. And strong. She could imagine them wanting to dance with him and could see how his intensity would make dancing with him a thrill.

A wave of sadness washed over her, sadness for youthful dreams that suddenly seemed like nightmares.

At least she'd be able to ensure her sisters and brother could have dreams—if she stayed with Henry. The despair that had made her flee that afternoon returned and she gulped in air to remain composed.

The captain walked back to the cot. She blinked rapidly, hoping he would not notice.

'You must have the cot, of course,' he said. 'I will sleep on the floor.'

More chivalry.

He put more logs on the fire, then took his blanket and sat on the floor, leaning against a wall. Only a shadow now he was out of the light, she could almost fancy she'd conjured him up out of her desperate need. She felt alone again, even more alone than before, because now she could not even flee to her parents' estate. The captain had convinced her she must go back to Henry and live the biggest secret of them all.

The day's exhaustion caught up to her. She closed her eyes and sleep came faster than she would have believed it could.

Henry smiled when Eliza approached. She floated towards him, her heart pounding, the filmy fabric of her morning dress wafting around her, clinging to her body, transparent enough to reveal every curve, the rose red of her nipples, the flush of excitement tingeing her skin. She came closer, not speaking, but reaching for him.

A look of horror crossed his face and he pushed her away. She flew backwards into a dark tunnel, but the face receding before her was not Henry's, but the captain's...

She jolted awake.

So this was to haunt her nights as well as her days? The memory of Henry's rejection? The humiliation of her pushing herself on him? To make love to her. To fulfil the promise of the marriage bed.

She'd thought Henry merely shy, merely having difficulty transitioning from friends to husband and wife. She'd thought perhaps she'd not been alluring enough, so she'd dressed to seduce him. No undergarments. As near as naked could be while covered with cloth. He could not mistake her for his childhood friend then, could he?

Had this been what fuelled her anger? What made her flee? By not confiding in her about his attachment to his friend Ryland, he'd led her to this humiliation.

She winced at the memory. She'd fled to her bedchamber through the connecting door to his. He'd followed her. She'd curled up on her bed, covering her body and her shame, as he explained why he did not wish to bed her. He loved another, pledged fidelity to another, the man he'd known since they were both at school together, then university.

Like the Captain had said. Happens sometimes.

Henry had insisted he loved her. As his dear friend and he'd gladly saved her from the old widower her father wanted her to marry; he'd gladly paid her family's debts and would gladly take care of her family as if it were his own.

She'd screamed at him to leave her alone, for the whole household to leave her alone. He retreated. And she ran.

Eliza sat up in the cot and hugged her knees, just as

she'd done in her bedchamber. She ached inside for that young wife so eager to experience all that marriage could offer. She ached for what she would never know. No man would ever hold her, gaze upon her body. No man would ever warm her bed and show her what transpired between husband and wife. She'd heard of its pleasures, shockingly from some of the maids, but also surmised the pleasure because her parents seemed to seek it out in one affair after another.

She wanted nothing to do with that sort of loving, though. She'd wanted a *husband* to love her, to want to bed her, to give her children. She'd wanted a true marriage.

She rocked, back and forth.

'Eliza?' The Captain's voice came from his dark corner.

She heard him rise and move towards her until he was close enough she felt his warmth. His steadiness.

He brushed her tangled hair from her cheek. 'You are awake.'

She lifted her face. 'I had a bad dream. Of my husband's face when I tried to seduce him. He will never bed me. Never give me children. I tried. I repulse him.'

He sat next to her and put his arm around her as he'd done before. 'I am sorry for it, Eliza. It is so much less than what you deserve.' He touched her hair again. 'A woman so beautiful—'

She pulled away to look at him. 'You think I am beautiful?'

He averted his gaze before meeting hers again. 'Quite.' He no longer touched her, though.

She looked into his eyes. 'No one ever told me that before.'

A warmth spread like honey inside her. It jarred her.

It was because she could confide in him, she told herself. Even about her humiliation. It was safe. *He* was safe.

'The thing is,' she went on, 'I will never know that pleasure between man and woman.'

His hand dropped. 'You… You could take a lover—'

She shook her head. 'Never! My parents—well—they have lover after lover. I will not do that.' So much drama. Lovers angry and threatening. Her mother wailing if one left her before she could leave him. Her father pushing away women whom he had once happily bedded. 'So I'll never know.'

He gathered her in his arms again, letting her feel his warmth, his strength. She placed a hand against his strong chest and felt the beating of his heart. He stroked her hair, like her nurse once did when she fell or skinned a knee, but it did not feel at all like that. Desire rushed through her. She became acutely aware that the cloth of Nate's shirt was the only thing between her hand and his bare skin.

Would he? Would he?

She brought her lips close to his ear. 'Nate,' she whispered. 'Would you show me? Show me how it is between a man and a woman? Just this once?'

Chapter Four

Nate inhaled a quick breath.

Yes. This was what he desired. What he'd been trying to talk himself out of ever since realising her despair, her loneliness, so kindred with his inner self. His yearning to be connected to her. To matter to her when he did not matter to anyone else.

Lofty words. Perhaps it was his body merely craving hers, so beautiful, so perfect.

He gazed into her pleading eyes. Could he deny her anything?

'Are you certain?' he asked.

She nodded. 'I want it to be with you. No one else. To be a part of this—this—oasis.'

He knew what she meant. The cabin. The rain. They were alone, as if no one else existed, as if suspended in time. There would never again be a moment like this one for either of them.

He cupped her cheek with his hand and leaned towards her, touching his lips to hers. She was still for a moment, like a statue, but then seemed to relax, her lips softening beneath his.

He savoured the taste of her, the warmth of her, and wanted more, but he ended the kiss. 'We will go slow, because this is your first time.' How was he to accomplish this when his body pulsed with arousal? 'I will tell you or show you what to do.'

She nodded, her face flushed, her breathing quickened.

He stood and, taking her hand, helped her rise as well.

'First, let me undress you. That is where we will start.' He faced her and gently lifted the man's shirt over her head.

'My stays next?' she asked tentatively, turning her back to him.

The strings of her stays were still damp. He frowned at the idea that she'd remained in damp clothes that whole time. It was difficult to untie the strings and loosen them enough so that the undergarment could be lifted over her head. Nate laid it near the fire, hoping it would dry by morning.

She turned to face him again.

'Next your shift,' he said, his voice rasping.

He started to lift the thin, silky fabric, but her hand stopped him halfway and she gripped the fabric in her fist. 'My husband did not like to see—'

He unbent her fingers and the fabric fell from her hands. 'There is no husband.' He slowly lifted the shift again. 'No one else. No world outside.'

She gazed at him with an expression somewhere between wonder and anxiety.

'There is Pegasus, of course,' she said, trying to smile.

He grinned. 'There is Pegasus. We will allow him to stay in the stable, however.'

He lifted her shift over her head, leaving her naked except for the breeches they both wore and the thick woollen stockings. He could not help but gaze at her. Her skin glowed in the firelight, as if she were some ethereal being. Her breasts were full and high, her nipples a dusky rose in contrast. She was thin, lithe, but nothing like delicate.

'Oh, please.' Her tone was strained. 'Tell me I do not repulse you.'

'Repulse me?' He forced his eyes away from her naked beauty. 'You are lovely.'

Her body relaxed.

'Are you ready for me to remove your breeches?' he asked, something he'd never before said to a woman, he thought incongruously.

She seemed to steel herself, but she nodded.

He untied the rope she'd used around her waist to hold the breeches up and they slipped to the floor. He gazed at the most intimate part of her.

Now knowing she needed reassurance, he said, 'More loveliness, Eliza. You are very pleasing to my eye.'

She expelled a breath.

'Now sit and I'll remove your stockings.'

She sat on the cot and he knelt in front of her, so intimately close to her. He ran his hands down her shapely legs and thin ankles to remove the stockings.

She gasped as he did so.

He stood again, his gaze still unable to leave her. 'Next I undress. Or,' he said daringly, 'you can undress me.'

'I'll undress you,' she murmured.

She stood and, like a good student, lifted off his shirt as he'd done hers. She did not gaze directly at him, though. Instead she worked at unbuttoning the breeches he wore until they, too, slipped to the floor. He stepped out of them and kicked them aside.

She stepped back and dared to look at him. To his surprise, it was his turn to worry if he was pleasing, aroused as he was.

She lifted her gaze to his and smiled, amusement in her eyes. 'Lovely,' she said.

He laughed and sat on the cot while she removed his

stockings, as close to his arousal as he'd been to her most intimate place.

When she was finished, he grasped her hand. 'Now sit with me.'

She sat next to him and he turned her face to his and kissed her again, merely letting his lips rest lightly against hers. His body in full arousal somehow decided to agree that it was fine not to rush.

They had all night.

Eliza's heart beat wildly. How marvellous it felt to be sitting next to him, to feel his skin against hers where their legs touched. Should she feel trepidation of what was to come? She did a little, but also excitement. Anticipation. How glad she was that she was with him, that it was he who would show her what should transpire in the marriage bed.

His hand swept the hair away from her face. 'Do you know how it is done?' His voice was non-judgemental.

She understood why he would ask. He knew she was a maiden and maidens were not supposed to know such things.

'I—I know a little,' she responded. 'I grew up on a farm. And—and some of the maids explained it to me.'

'I will try to put you at ease,' he said. 'But you must tell me at any point if you want me to stop or if I do anything that you do not like.'

At the moment she could not imagine disliking anything he did.

He went on. 'Let us lie down together and I will stroke your skin. It will calm you.'

She lay down on her side and he half sat, facing her. He gently touched her face and let his fingers move down her neck to her shoulder and arm. It did not exactly calm her, although her body felt languorous.

'Lie on your back,' he murmured.

Her excitement grew. Would this be it?

But he continued to stroke her, circling her breasts, placing his hand flat against her abdomen. Then he touched her breasts, gently at first, then more firmly, and sensation rushed to her most private place. An ache, not precisely a pain, but something as equally urgent to relieve. She arched her back in response.

He stopped. 'Does this displease you?'

She shook her head.

'Shall I go on, then?' he asked.

She nodded. 'Yes. Go on. Please.'

It was a good thing she wished to go on. Nate's heart was at war with his body. His body was powerfully aroused, painfully so, urging him to take her fast and hard and relieve the desire almost too acute to bear.

But his heart wanted to do only what was right for her. If this was to be her only time of lovemaking, he wanted it to be wonderful for her.

And, if truthful to himself, his heart wanted this time with her to never end, to never come to that inevitable parting after their pleasure peaked. At the moment, they were connected—not in that physical way that was to come— but in the haze of this sensuality, in her awakening. Nate knew the connection could not last. He knew in the end he would be alone again.

His hands explored her breasts, relishing the silkiness of her skin, the rougher texture of her nipples. His hands pressed against her flesh and his body screamed at him to fulfil its urgent plea.

But he girded himself and slowed down again, stroking her face, looking into her eyes, savouring the wonder and pleasure and need he saw there.

He leaned down and kissed her, one hand moving to her breast. If her lips at his first kiss seemed maidenly, they now responded, pressing into his, as hungry for him as he was for her.

Her lips parted and he let his tongue explore her mouth. Its warmth. Its moistness. Her tongue responded in kind and engaged in a little duel with his.

His need grew.

But she was not yet ready. He was not yet ready to have this moment end. He broke away and pressed his lips against the tender skin below her ear, sliding his lips even lower, down her neck to her chest, to her breast where he traced her nipple with his tongue.

She made an agonised sound.

He stopped and looked into her face. 'Should I stop?' he asked, though he wanted more. Much more.

'No. No,' she rasped. 'Don't stop. Never felt—'

She didn't finish her sentence and he let himself savour the taste of her, the primal pleasure of his mouth on her breast.

She had not really touched him before, but now her fingers dug into his hair, keeping him at her breast. She then clutched at his back as if to make him mount her, although he knew she was in the throes of passion and did not yet know precisely what her body wanted.

He must move on, for both their sakes.

He lifted his head. 'I am going to touch you next,' he murmured. 'Help you to be ready.'

His hand slid down to that part of her he knew was aching for him but would feel pain if he were not careful. He gentled his touch, fingering her, easing her open.

She writhed in response and cried, 'Don't stop. Don't stop.'

'Are you ready?' he managed to say.

'Yes.' Her response was breathless.

He rose over her and she opened herself to him. His body now had him under the lash, insisting he plunge into her, relieve the agonising need, but he knew this part of lovemaking would be new to her and he wanted her to savour the building pleasure it would create.

He entered her a little at a time, so that her body relaxed enough to accommodate him. He gave a final thrust, she gasped and he forced himself to stop, but not withdraw.

'Are you hurt?' he asked.

'No!' she murmured. 'Yes. A little. Never mind. Don't stop!'

He pushed again and her body accepted all of him. The connection he felt to her intensified tenfold. He stroked slowly inside her until her body caught his rhythm and moved with him. As if they were one, truly one.

He was not alone.

But his body's need betrayed him, leaving only what was primitive inside him. He moved faster.

All thinking stopped.

Eliza had tried to press into memory every moment of this, every sensation, every thought. Most of all she wanted to remember this—this joining of bodies, this joining of movement. Even that tiny moment of pain she wanted to remember, but it was so fleeting as other sensations took over. The feel of him moving inside her and her moving with him. The ache building inside her, more urgent with each thrust.

She felt the change in him, the change from restraint to surrender as his thrusts came faster and deeper. Suddenly she changed, too, and need took over, a need like she'd never felt before, one impossible to neglect. She kept pace with him and the sensation, so pleasant before, took on a new urgency, a new intensity, building, building…

Pleasure itself burst inside her, unlike any she'd experienced before. She cried out, tensing, not wanting to move again. He did not stop, though, moving even more vigorously while she was consumed by her own delight.

He, too, cried out and another new sensation appeared. He seemed to quiver and she knew he was spilling a part of him inside her.

And then it was done. All that sparkling jubilation fading into languor. His body relaxed heavily on her a moment before he slid to her side, still breathing hard.

She rolled on her side, and he faced her. 'Did I hurt you, Eliza?'

She laughed softly. 'No,' she said. 'Just the opposite.'

His features relaxed. 'Good. I did not want to hurt you.'

Who else in her life had worried that they'd placed their pleasure before her pain?

She gazed at him, committing to memory his face, his eyes, discordantly warm with pleasure, but still tinged with pain. She would never forget this captain. Nate. Her captain. Never.

He kissed her again. A sad kiss, she thought. But she would not be sad—not yet. He'd given her what she'd asked for. She now knew what lovemaking was about.

It was so much more than she suspected. The physical sensations and pleasure were new, exciting and memorable enough, but there was also the sense of merging with him, as if by sharing this as well as all the rest they'd shared with each other had connected them completely. To be so at one with him felt wonderful. To be at one with him. Her captain. She could not wish it any other way, with any other man.

She settled next to him, moulding her naked body to his.

'Thank you, Nate,' she whispered.

His answer was only to hold her closer.

She fell asleep that way.

Eliza woke to a mere sliver of dawn lightening the window. Nate's arm was around her, but they faced each other. He looked almost boyish in sleep. What must it have been like for him to lose his parents at such a young age? As difficult as her parents were, Eliza could not imagine her childhood without them or without her brother and sisters. To be so alone.

She glanced at the window again. Their night together was over.

Suddenly the loneliness she imagined Nate had felt filled her, as well. Because she would part from him. How she wished she could stay with him, join with him again in that intimate way. That could never be, though. Would she be able to bear it?

Face it, like he said she must do?

At least she would have the memory of their lovemaking. That was something. The memory of him. What a profound gift he'd given her. What could she give him in return? Nothing could compare.

She would at least show him strength, a strength she did not feel at the moment. He'd taught her she must be strong enough to face whatever life threw at her. She'd at least show him she would try.

What would she have done if he had not picked her up in the torrent of the storm?

She would be grateful to him for ever.

And she would never, ever forget him.

Nate relished feeling warm and rested and sated as he opened his eyes to Eliza smiling at him.

'It is morning,' she said.

He groaned. 'Time to face it.'

'Time to face it,' she repeated, her voice low.

He ached inside. Already the loneliness was creeping in. Because he must part from her. He must not give in to it, however. That would not help either one of them.

He forced himself to look into her eyes. 'We will get through it, Eliza. Because we must.'

'Yes.' She set her chin. 'We'll bear it.'

He warmed at her little show of strength. Perhaps he had helped her, although it saddened him that she was returning to a marriage that could not offer her all that she desired. He would give her everything if he could.

How absurd was that? He would never see her again. Even if he survived the war—which he did not expect to do—he'd never mix in the society of wealth and privilege he believed she belonged to.

Today they would be saying goodbye and he would be alone again.

They rose and gathered their clothes, still damp, but wearable. He helped her on with her stays and buttoned her dress. He committed to memory the feel of her soft, smooth skin against his fingers. They finished dressing in silence, each lost in their own thoughts, he supposed.

Once dressed, he moved the cot back to the wall. 'We should put the place to rights.'

She carried one blanket to the pump and rinsed the spot of blood from it. He tended to the fireplace. There was really no way they could remove all evidence that the cabin had been used, though. He'd leave some coin to cover their use of it.

Too soon they stepped outside into a morning of clear skies and fresh breezes, as if the world had been created anew.

The world was changed for him, somehow, even though she was another person he'd loved and lost. He could at least imagine her alive and well and living in comfort, family around her.

Pegasus greeted him excitedly, bright-eyed and acting eager to be on the road.

As he picked up the saddle, Eliza spoke. 'Nate?'

'Mmm?' he responded, placing the saddle on the horse.

'I do not wish to go to Witley.'

He looked over at her. 'Where shall I take you?'

'Nowhere,' she said. 'I am going back to my husband's estate. It is not far, especially if I cross the fields.'

He must part with her now? Not several miles down the road? More time together?

She lifted her chin. 'We—we should say goodbye here. I am going to do what you said. Go back. Face it. Face *him*. But I will never, ever forget you. Or this night.'

He felt anguished inside, not ready to part. 'Are you certain?' He hesitated. 'I could take you back—'

'No. No,' she insisted. 'There is no need to burden Pegasus that way. And someone might see. Believe me, I know the way back very well. I even knew of this cabin.'

She knew of the cabin…

She went on. 'We played in it when I was younger. If anyone sees me, I will say I took shelter here. They will believe me.'

That explained why she always produced what they needed. She'd known it was there.

He opened his mouth, so many questions on the tip of his tongue.

She put up a hand. 'Do not ask me more. I—I do not want to say anything further. I want our—our time together to be…separate from everything else. A magical place and time known only to my heart.'

He nodded. That was indeed what their time together must be.

When Pegasus was all saddled, they walked out into the dawning day again. To say goodbye.

They embraced and he placed his lips on hers.

Eliza clung to him for a moment. 'Please take care of yourself, my captain. Stay safe.' She was remembering he was bound for war, he thought. 'And thank you. For everything.'

He kissed her again. One last time.

After mounting Pegasus, Nate rode away from her, not looking back.

Alone once more.

Chapter Five

Mayfair, London, 1817—seven years later

The carriage pulled up in front of an elegant town house on Charles Street as Eliza looked on in dismay. The windows were awash with light and the cacophony of voices echoed in the street.

A ball.

Eliza drew in a breath. How had her sister talked her into attending a ball?

'Here we are!' Joanna said brightly.

A footman opened the carriage door and Joanna's husband disembarked first.

Eliza slid towards the carriage door. 'I do not know that I am ready for this.' The footman raised his hand to help her out.

'Do not be foolish, Lizzy. Of course you are,' Joanna snapped.

Her husband urged them on. 'Ladies, let us not tarry.'

Eliza climbed out of the carriage, her sister behind her.

Her sister Joanna had married well, thanks to the come-out Henry had financed for her. Her husband, Francis Bentham, would be Viscount Bentham some day. Even better, he was a man of fine character and, from what Eliza could determine, devoted to her sister.

He offered them each an arm and they walked together through the doorway into the hall already crowded with guests. Bentham was almost immediately pulled aside by another gentleman and the two ladies were momentarily alone.

Eliza leaned towards Joanna's ear. 'I know I am not ready.'

'Nonsense.' Joanna pulled her forward. 'You are out of mourning. You must re-join society some time.'

Out of mourning.

Formally, that was true. It had been more than a year ago when Henry's horse had returned without him from his morning ride and a frantic search discovered Henry's broken body. Death certainly changed Eliza's life in that instant. His cousin inherited, but Henry, her dear friend Henry, had left her a large income, a town house in Mayfair and a small property and house outside Sandleigh, the village near what was now the new Viscount Varden's estate. Poor Natalie, only five years old at the time, had been through a bewildering set of losses in one year, not only her beloved papa, but her home—Varden House— and almost all the servants in it. It had badly shaken the child and made her cling to her mother like never before.

Dear Natalie. She was the gift Eliza was not certain she deserved, the gift her captain had unknowingly given her. How lucky Eliza had been that Henry accepted the child with great enthusiasm, although Eliza had wondered at the time if that was because having a child, like having a wife, protected his secret. Since learning he'd kept his secret from her, she'd begun to doubt his every motive. *Everyone's* motive. And Henry, in turn, had kept a distance between them, one caused, she believed, by her one attempt at seducing him.

But Henry *had* been truly devoted to Natalie. Doted

on her. Indulged her. Never gave Natalie one second not knowing she was loved. Natalie lost a wonderful father, Eliza had to admit, although she herself felt as if she'd lost Henry years before. On the day of Natalie's conception. After that day things had never quite been the same between them, although Henry never failed to be kind and generous.

Still, she did miss him.

Eliza had no wish to come to town. Unlike her dear daughter, Eliza found the change in her life to her liking, even as she mourned her husband. Eliza now made the choices for her and Natalie, no one else. She quite liked that independence.

Unfortunately, though, it meant she must take care of financial matters herself and that brought her to town, to confer with Henry's man of business. She'd brought Natalie and her governess with her. Eliza did not want to chance how a long separation from her mother might affect Natalie. Perhaps London's shops and attractions would distract Natalie from her grief. Perhaps her daughter would actually enjoy herself.

Another consolation of coming to town was the chance to see her sisters, whom Eliza missed dearly. Her sisters, on the other hand, considered this visit their opportunity to return her to society whose bustle and drama she never missed.

Like the bustle and din now in Lord Locksworth's hall. Eliza could barely breathe.

'Really, Jo,' she said. 'I believe I will go home. I am sure the carriage has not moved away.'

Indeed their carriage had waited in a long line of elegant vehicles before reaching the front of the house. It had probably moved inches since they disembarked.

'Oh, no, you will not!' Joanna pushed her towards the

footman waiting to take her cloak. 'Susan will flog me if you do not appear and, you know, Lord and Lady Locksworth particularly asked her to urge you to come.'

The Marquess and Marchioness of Locksworth were their sister Susan's parents-in-law. Their youngest son, the Lord Jeffrey Everly, was a rising Member of Parliament and this ball was, in part, a means of furthering his political ambitions. Apparently Henry, who'd been well thought of in the Lords, had been of great assistance to Lord Jeffrey. Henry had also been of great assistance in introducing him to Susan.

'Oh, very well.' Feeling trapped, Eliza let the footman take her cloak.

Joanna smiled in approval. 'Let us go up to the ballroom.'

Joanna's husband re-joined them. 'My apologies, ladies. Old friends.' He offered them each an arm. 'Shall we?'

Progress was slow as they made their way up the stairs to the doorway of the ballroom. When it was their turn, it was Eliza who was to be announced first.

'Elizabeth, Viscountess Varden,' the butler intoned. Eliza was no longer *the* Viscountess Varden, though. Announcing her by her given name distinguished her from the new viscountess.

She stepped inside the room to greet the host and hostess.

'Elizabeth, my dear girl.' Lord Locksworth clasped her hands warmly.

Lady Locksworth smiled. 'We are delighted you've come.'

'It was kind of you to invite me,' Eliza responded.

She shook hands with their eldest son and his wife, but no sooner had she done so than Susan ran up to her, pulling her away.

Susan gushed, 'Oh, Lizzie, I was so afraid you would not come. I am so glad to see you.'

Joanna joined them. 'Believe me, she tried to get out of it. I made her come.'

Susan air-kissed Joanna's cheek. 'I knew I could count on you.' She took Eliza's arm. 'Come, there are so many of your friends here who are eager to see you.'

The next few moments were a whirl of greetings, some genuinely friendly in their sentiments, some perfunctory. Some were people Eliza had missed during her year of mourning, although she did not much miss the crush of people, the scents and sounds of occasions such as this. The musicians were tuning their instruments at the far end of the room—two rooms, actually, opened up into one space large enough for dancing. In no time, both Susan and Joanna were lured away by their particular friends and Eliza seized the chance to go in search of something to drink.

She picked up a glass of champagne from the tray of a circulating footman and took a sip.

A voice sounded at her ear. 'Well. Well. Good evening, Lady Varden.'

She turned to see Baron Lymond, glass in hand, smirking at her. Lymond had been a schoolmate of Henry's, she knew. One Henry had always disliked. She suspected the feelings had been mutual.

'So you are a widow, after all.' He smirked.

She smiled in return. 'Thank you for your kind condolences.'

Joanna rushed up to her, unwittingly saving her from Lymond's continued company. 'I thought we'd lost you!' she said breathlessly. 'Susan's been ringing a peal over my head for leaving your side. I told her—'

Susan joined her. 'I have not been ringing a peal!'

Eliza shook her head. 'I assure you I just went in search of champagne.'

Susan glanced at the doorway. 'Oh, there is the new Lord Hale. Jeffrey will be pleased he's come. He unexpectedly inherited, you know, after his uncle died and two of his cousins. Apparently they had to look far down the family line for the heir. Do you remember old Lord Hale, Lizzie?'

'Vaguely.' A man in his seventies, she recalled. His death might have been expected, but his two sons, as well? How incredibly sad.

Joanna craned her neck to see. 'He is with that odious Lord Crafton. Crafton's daughter, too. Sweet girl, though.'

The odious Lord Crafton. How apt a description. And her sisters did not even know Lord Crafton was the widower their father tried to force Eliza to marry.

'The Marquess of Hale,' the butler announced. 'The Earl of Crafton. Lady Sibyl Bussey—'

Joanna and Susan went on talking about other guests while Eliza simply hoped she could avoid Crafton. The rare times she and Henry had come to town and attended society events Lord Crafton had been quite chilly towards them. Perhaps he would still be as eager to avoid her as she was to avoid him.

Susan broke into her own conversation. 'Oh, here is Jeffrey.'

Susan's husband was a compact man, only an inch or two taller than Susan and full of energy. Susan beamed at him, as besotted with him now as she'd been four years before when they'd married.

'My dear,' he said. 'I knew I would find you with your sisters.' He turned to greet Joanna and then Eliza. 'How are you faring, Lizzie? It is good to see you here.'

Before she could answer, he turned to a man beside him. 'Susan, love, may I present Lord Hale. I believe you have not met him yet.'

'Lord Hale.' Susan presented her hand.

'And my wife's sisters,' Jeffrey went on. 'Elizabeth, Lady Varden, and Mrs Bentham.'

Eliza looked up at the gentleman.

And froze.

'Nate,' she mouthed.

Her captain. Here.

His eyes widened before he recovered. 'Lady Varden.' He bowed. 'Mrs Bentham.'

No one seemed to notice the look of stunned recognition that passed between them.

Jeffrey continued talking. 'Wish you could have met Lord Varden, Hale. Died over a year ago. Tragic accident. Fine man.'

Nate's brows rose slightly. Perhaps the others missed that, too, but Eliza did not.

Jeffrey took Nate by the arm. 'Come. There are more people you should meet.'

All the sounds in the room turned into a whir. Eliza's vision blurred. Her sisters kept talking. About Lord Hale. She could not make out their words. All the air in the room seemed to have vanished. Did she appear as if she was about to faint? Eliza did not want anyone to notice.

She managed to get a word in with Susan and Joanna. 'If you do not mind, I believe I will visit the retiring room. Please stay and enjoy your friends. I'll find you.'

Joanna peered at her. 'You won't leave, will you?'

She made herself smile. 'I won't leave. I simply have to visit the retiring room.'

Susan asked, 'Do you want me to go with you?'

'Heavens, no!' Eliza replied. 'I know where it is.'

In earlier days she and Henry had attended balls in this house. She knew the house well.

She made herself walk slowly out of the ballroom, but her heart was pounding as if she'd run the length of Piccadilly.

Nate, her captain, was here.

He was alive.

And, by her glimpse of him, unharmed.

She hadn't known. After each battle, she'd perused the lists of officers wounded and killed, fearing she might find him, though she had scant evidence of precisely what his name would be. After the Battle of Salamanca, she found record of the death of a major with the given name of Nathan. Could that have been Nate? It was the wrong regiment, but could he have changed regiments? Been promoted? How would she ever know for sure?

She knew now.

He was alive.

He was here.

She fled, not to the ladies' retiring room, but to the far end of the hallway into the servants' stairway where she could hopefully snatch a moment alone. To collect herself.

The stairwell was cooler, darker and smelled of the rush light that barely illuminated the space. She did not care.

He was alive. He was here.

The door opened. 'Eliza?'

The rush light lit his face, making it so like that night in the cabin in the storm she felt her knees go weak.

'Nate.' Without thinking she rushed into his arms.

He held her as she had not been held since that night. 'I—I did not know if you were alive,' she rasped.

'I made it through,' he said. 'Much has happened since.'

She clung to him. 'I never expected to see you again.' She loosened her grip so she might look into his eyes. 'You are the Marquess of Hale.'

He gave a dry laugh. 'Believe me, I never expected to be. You are a widow?'

She nodded. 'Cards I did not even realise were in the deck.'

He touched her cheek. 'But are you well? How do you fare?'

'I am well,' she responded. 'Never better than right now.'
He was alive.

She melted into his arms again.

The musicians sounded a chord, loud enough to reach
their ears.

Nate pulled away. 'The first dance. I fear I must go. I
promised…'

'Of course.' She released him. 'Will you call on me tomorrow? I am on Clarges Street. Do you know it?'

'Yes,' he responded. 'I am nearby on Half Moon Street.'

So close. The street just behind hers. 'Midway between
Piccadilly and Curzon. My door knocker is the face of
Dionysus.'

The music started again.

He looked towards the sound. 'I must go.'

She reached in to embrace him once more before he
pulled away again and left.

It was only then that she remembered her daughter.
Their daughter. How was she to tell him about Natalie?
Goodness! He would know immediately if Eliza merely
mentioned her name.

Nate's thoughts swirled as he hurried back to the ballroom. All his senses were afire at the encounter. Seeing
her again. *Holding* her. *Eliza.*

How often he'd thought of her. Before battle and after,
and in the tedium between. Had he helped her at all? How
had she fared with her husband? Had she stayed with him?

When he inherited his uncle's title and was required to
join its social set, a part of him had looked for her at each
event. Would she and her husband show up at a ball or
soirée? Of course he did not know for certain if she was
of the aristocracy, although he'd always assumed she was.
She'd had the demeanour of a lady but could have merely
been the wife of a wealthy country gentlemen.

Merely the wife of a wealthy country gentleman? Nate had to laugh at himself. A *mere* country gentleman had certainly been vastly more elevated than a penniless army officer dependent on that status only due to his uncle's begrudging sense of duty.

He searched the ballroom and quickly found Lady Sibyl, whose furrowed brow cleared when she saw him approach.

'My apologies.' He offered his arm. 'I was out in the hallway when I heard the music.'

She smiled. 'I knew you would not forget me.'

He led her to the dance floor where other couples had already taken their places. Nate had promised her the first dance.

He'd met Lady Sibyl the previous January when the *ton* was abuzz with the attack on the Prince Regent. Nate had never anticipated inheriting his uncle's title. Indeed, he'd never anticipated surviving the war. But this new life of his was surprisingly lonely and filled with a great deal of nonsense. Lady Sibyl was pleasant and companionable and her father accepting of a new member of the House of Lords. He appreciated their willingness to introduce him to the more obscure nuances of Mayfair society. Lady Sibyl particularly seemed to sail those waters with ease. Nate had wondered why she hadn't married yet. She would be the perfect aristocratic wife.

When he touched hands with her in the dance, though, he realised she did not stir him like Eliza had in their brief reunion. She had never stirred him, even though he'd spent a great deal of time in her company. Was his reaction to Eliza simply due to the drama—and intimacy—of his first meeting with her? And of this second surprise meeting?

Nate stood across from Lady Sibyl in the line of dancers and tried not to let his distraction show as Lady Locksworth progressed down the line. He certainly noticed when Eliza slipped back in the ballroom. His eye seemed to catch her wherever she was in the room during and after the dance.

'You seem preoccupied this night, Hale,' Lady Sibyl said after the set was done and he'd brought her a glass of champagne.

'Do I?' He *was* preoccupied. With Eliza. 'Forgive me. I do not mean to be impolite.'

She smiled, as she so often did. 'Believe me, I would not presume to complain. I simply noticed.'

One of her friends called to her and he slipped away from her company, retreating to the hallway. He stood by the stairway and leaned on the banister. As other guests passed him by, he was tempted to retreat to the servants' stairwell again where he'd found Eliza, but he might be in the way of the bustle of servants now using the stairs. He and Eliza had been lucky not to encounter anyone.

Right now, though, he simply wished to have a moment alone.

There was so much about gaining a title that Nate abhorred. Enduring the crowd of a ball was one. To use the same analogy he'd used to Eliza that storm-filled night— one which she obviously remembered—any sane person would welcome the cards dealt him by earning his uncle's title. Money. Security. Status. But being the Marquess of Hale also meant giving up himself. He became his title, not Robert Nathanial Thorne, Major in the 30th Regiment of Foot. Not Nate.

That storm-filled night with Eliza when he'd yearned to matter to somebody, he'd mattered to her. *He'd* mattered to her. Now it was his title that mattered. To the House of Lords. To society. To the many people his property supported. To Lady Sibyl, even.

Any bearer of the title mattered. The *title*, not him.

Seeing Eliza again—holding her—caused that old

yearning to return. To matter to someone. Of course, then she'd been a young woman in great distress and confusion and he, nearly as despairing. He had been in a unique position to help her.

All was different now.

'Lord Hale.'

As if his thoughts had conjured her, there she was again, descending the stairs in the company of her sister, the hostess's daughter-in-law.

It was her sister who'd spoken. 'What are you doing here all by yourself? Has my family been neglecting you?'

'Lady Jeffrey.' He bowed. 'I am not neglected, I assure you.' His gaze travelled to Eliza, but he quickly brought it back to her sister. 'May I escort you back to the ballroom?'

Lady Jeffrey took his arm and Eliza walked at her other side. 'I know you are fairly new to all of this,' Lady Jeffrey said. He'd been through one Season but had attended few society events. 'Please allow me to help in any way possible.'

'Very gracious, ma'am,' he responded. 'I am out of practice for a ball, it is true.'

She inclined her head towards her sister. 'So is Lizzy. She's just out of mourning. This is her first ball in a long time.'

'Is it, Lady Varden?' He turned to Eliza.

'Yes, it is,' she murmured.

As they entered the room another dance was announced.

Dancing was one reason Nate disliked society balls. He always felt as though he was playing a role in a Covent Garden farce when he danced, although, he, like all his schoolmates, had been given all the proper dance lessons. Nate had taken care not to ask for more than two dances with Lady Sibyl, the second being the supper dance. Those were the only ones he'd intended to dance, but now he stood with two ladies who apparently were without partners. Lord Hale would be expected to be gracious enough to remedy that.

'Lady Jeffrey, are you engaged for this dance?' he asked.

'I am,' she responded, 'if my husband comes to find me, but my sister is free, are you not, Lizzie?'

Eliza blushed. 'I—'

'May I have this dance, then, Lady Varden?'

She nodded.

It happened to be a waltz, which meant Nate could touch her, face her, twirl with her.

They did not speak. Nate's hand was at her waist; hers on his shoulder. They were never not touching as the music quickened and slowed. Though hardly able to attend to the first dance and to his partner, this one held him captive. He was not some actor on stage. He, *Nate*, danced. The rest of the ballroom faded away and there was only Eliza, dancing with him.

Too soon the music stopped and he had to release her. He led her back to her sister, but before they reached her, Eliza clasped his arm. 'Tomorrow? You will call?'

He dared a direct gaze at her. 'I will call.'

Chapter Six

Susan's husband had just left her side when Nate delivered Eliza to her. She stood with Joanna.

'Well, that was a surprise,' she said to Eliza. 'But at least you had an opportunity to dance.'

Eliza was puzzled. 'Why a surprise?'

'Goodness, Lizzie,' Joanna broke in. 'He rarely dances. Except with Lady Sibyl. Everyone knows he will ask her to marry him, if he has not already.'

This news should not make Eliza's spirits plummet, but it did. 'Lady Sibyl? Lord Crafton's daughter?'

Susan leaned closer. 'No announcement has been made, but it is expected. He is seen with her everywhere. And with her father, of course.'

Eliza took a breath.

Nate had a right to marry. So what if the woman was Crafton's daughter? Eliza had no hold on him. It had been seven years, after all. Still, the joy of the dance a few moments ago vanished. 'I do not know Lady Sibyl. How is she regarded?'

'She's a pleasant girl. Well liked. Adequate dowry. She was much sought after in her first Season or two. I suspect she was waiting for a better title, though,' Susan replied.

'Hale is a big step up,' Joanna added.

Eliza's gaze found Lady Sibyl across the room just as Nate walked up to her. She greeted him with obvious pleasure. She did appear to be an agreeable companion. Beautiful, as well, with shining blonde hair and a graceful figure.

Eliza blinked away tears. What had she been thinking? That one night of begging him to make love to her meant he'd pined for her as she'd pined for him?

How often had she recalled the memory of his lovemaking? And when she'd gaze upon her daughter, she'd seen the fruits of that lovemaking and felt like he'd given her a miracle.

She'd kept her captain alive in her imagination, even after she'd feared he'd been killed. Seeing him now made it seem like the Nate of her fantasies had become real and that he would soon hold her again. Kiss her. Join his body with hers.

But to know he was courting another woman—Lord Crafton's daughter, of all people? That irony was particularly painful, but it also opened her eyes. Seven years had passed. Seven years in which they'd both lived their lives. Seven years could change a person. She'd certainly changed. She'd become stronger than that naive girl he'd met all those years ago. Less trusting. She'd learned to manage her own life and she liked it that way. She was dependent upon no one. She was also fiercely protective of her daughter who had already endured too much hardship. What effect would it have on Natalie if she somehow learned her beloved papa was not her real father?

Nate must have changed as well. How could he not? He'd been through war. He'd inherited a title. He was now a man of importance, of responsibility. She must face that the romantic fantasy she'd built around him all these years was merely fantasy, not real. For all Eliza knew he could have considered that night together a mere tryst, the sort a soldier or any man travelling would exploit. She'd begged him for lovemaking, had she not? What made her think it meant anything to him?

But then he remembered her, sought her out at the ball, returned her embrace—

But perhaps he was only glad to see her once again.

She glanced over at him, leaning down to hear something Lady Sibyl said. They made a lovely couple, she had to admit. Lady Sibyl was elegantly dressed with perfectly coiffed hair and a lovely smile. Who was Eliza to spoil his happiness with such a woman?

His wisdom and kindness had been too vitally important to her, that night and all the years since. He was the chief architect of the good parts of life. Most importantly he'd fathered her child, but he'd also taught her to accept Henry for who he was and to accept her marriage for what it provided, not for what it lacked. In a way Nate was even responsible for the happiness of her sisters. If she had left Henry, he never would have financed their come-outs. Or kept her parents out of debt.

She glanced at her sisters, happily gossiping with each other. Eliza would not for the world spoil their happiness. Nor would she spoil Nate's.

If he called upon her on the morrow she would assure him so.

Nate stood at the edge of a group of men discussing the various issues before the Lords, but he was not attending. His gaze kept finding Eliza, even when he tried to distract himself from her presence.

He tried watching Lady Sibyl instead. At the moment she was fending off the flirtations of Lord Lymond.

Lord Jeffrey Everly, who Nate now knew was Eliza's brother-in-law, approached him.

Nate acknowledged him with a nod. 'Everly.'

The man leaned closer and inclined his head towards Lady Sibyl, laughing now at something Lymond said.

'What do you know of Lymond over there?' Everly asked.

'Only that he always attends these events.' Nate personally found the man to be unpleasant, not that he'd ever shared more than a few words with him.

Everly's expression turned serious. 'He is a notorious rake. A womaniser.'

'That does not surprise me.' Although it did surprise Nate that Everly seemed to be warning him about the man. 'Are you concerned for Lady Sibyl's sake?'

'Well, she is a woman and he is charming,' Everly said.

Did Everly expect Nate to warn Lady Sibyl about Lymond?

Nate responded, 'I dare say Lady Sibyl can handle Lymond.' She seemed an expert at handling the attentions of admiring gentleman, but then Lady Sibyl was at ease among everyone she met.

Everly's brows rose. 'I thought you should know.'

Why? Nate had no influence over Lady Sibyl. True, he spent a great deal of time in her company and in that of her father's, but Nate knew her father merely hoped to make him a political ally. Lady Sibyl, Nate suspected, used her charm and friendliness to help win Nate over to her father's side.

Did Everly think it was more than that?

Nate's gaze slid to Eliza, sitting quietly with her chatting sisters, but he caught himself. Everly was expecting a response.

'I thank you for your consideration,' Nate said.

Nate collected Lady Sibyl for the supper dance and escorted her to the supper room afterwards. Their table was filled with her friends and she occupied herself very well in conversation with them. It was a good thing because Nate was lost in his own thoughts.

Lady Sibyl briefly noticed. 'You are still woolgathering, sir,' she said in a cheerful voice.

He shook his head. 'I am not good company tonight, am I? Do forgive me.'

Lady Sibyl smiled. 'Do not fear. I will not complain of being neglected. Many gentlemen find these balls tedious.'

She did not ask him what troubled him, Nate noticed. Instead, she turned back to her friends.

After supper Nate stood alone, contemplating leaving the ball, when the wife of one of Lord Crafton's cronies bustled her way towards him.

'Hale.' She put her arm in his. 'I wish to speak with you.'

She led him to an even more secluded spot.

She gave him a stern look. 'I must speak, for Lady Sibyl's dear departed mother cannot—'

What the devil?

'I want to know what your intentions are towards that dear girl.'

'My intentions?'

'Are you betrothed to her or not?' she demanded.

'Betrothed?'

She gave him no chance to say more. 'You are exclusively in her company and she is exclusively in yours. It looks to all the world that you are betrothed. If you abandon that girl you will ruin her!'

Nate was annoyed. 'Why would that ruin her?'

Her eyes blazed. 'Because everyone would assume you cried off because of something she did or some flaw in her character and that would be so terribly unfair to her.'

He would not explain to this dragon of a lady that he had never given Lady Sibyl reason to believe he was courting her. Had he?

She ranted on. 'You have an obligation to Lady Sibyl for giving the impression that you were betrothed. Think of the Duke of Wellington—'

What did Wellington have to do with it?

'Wellington was in a similar situation and he did the right thing,' she went on to explain. 'The Duke married Kitty Pakenham solely because she'd presumed his earlier offer of marriage, years before, still held. It was his duty, you see. A point of honour.' She paused and looked away. 'Of course, the marriage is a dreadfully unhappy one, but that is neither here nor there. You have given the impression that you are betrothed to Lady Sibyl and now you must follow through. Or ruin her.'

This was ridiculous. 'I have given no such impression, ma'am.'

The dragon shook her finger at him. 'Oh, yes, you have. Everyone says so.'

She turned on her heel and marched off.

Because others assumed he would ask Lady Sibyl to marry him, he was honour bound to do so? If this was another of society's idiotic rules, he wanted nothing to do with it.

He glanced over at Eliza again. What if society knew he'd once spent the night with her?

The next morning, Nate walked around to Clarges Street and found the door with the Dionysus knocker. It was almost directly behind the town house he'd inherited from his uncle. Was that not irony, to be so close?

But ought they to be so close? He'd spent a sleepless night trying to sort it all out. Certainly their situations had changed. He was a different person, of that there was no doubt. He was the Marquess of Hale. According to some he was even obligated to another woman. He'd not been able to turn his head around that idea either. How was he to extricate himself from that mess? Lady Sibyl had been very helpful to him, introducing him to and explaining the various rules of society. He should have realised that even being in her company meant an obligation to her.

One thing he knew. Any moment he'd spent with Lady Sibyl had been nothing like one storm-filled night pairing two people both desperately needing comfort and connection.

How he wished he could approach this visit with Eliza with the surge of excitement he'd experienced at the ball. *Eliza!* He'd found *Eliza!* It had been as if time had not passed.

But time had passed. Seven years. Seven years in which their lives must be different. He knew he'd kept the memory of her in his mind and heart during that time, memories that had comforted him when life was bleak and helped him press on when death surrounded him. She'd been like a dream that night they'd spent together, a woman without a name, an ephemeral memory.

Although, that night with Eliza, had he not felt more like himself than he had since a child?

He forced his mind to be rational. Everything was different now. He was not off to war. She was not that distressed new wife with a husband who'd kept his true self secret. They had spent a profound time together that rainy night. They had shared each other's lives as well as making love. It made sense they would want to meet again to hear how the other had fared in the years since. Like finishing a book after you'd thought you'd lost the last volume. He wanted to know how those years had been for her.

Had her husband been good to her? Had she found happiness?

That was all this would be.

To expect more would be folly. Anyone who'd meant anything to him in his life had left him in one way or another. There was no reason to expect anything different from Eliza.

Nate stood before her door. He took a deep breath and attempted to quiet a sudden return of excitement rushing through him. He would see her again!

He sounded the knocker.

It was answered by a man a good ten years older than himself. The butler, no doubt.

'Lord Hale to see Lady Varden,' he told the man. 'She is expecting me.'

'Indeed, sir.' The butler stepped aside and Nate entered a small hall with a black and white marble floor and a mahogany bench along the wall. He gave the man his hat and gloves and waited while they were placed on a nearby table.

'Follow me, sir,' the butler said. 'I'll announce you.'

The stairs were directly facing the door. Nate followed the butler up the stairs to the drawing room on the first floor. From high above them on one of the top floors came a trill of laughter. A happy sound. For some reason, Nate found it unexpected.

The man knocked and opened the door. 'Lord Hale, m'lady.'

Nate did not see the furnishings, or the art on the walls or the decor on the mantelpiece. He only saw Eliza standing before him, her hands extended. She looked radiant. Eyes sparkling. Cheeks flushed. Lips parted.

'Nate. You came.' Her voice conveyed surprise.

He knew then he could not have stayed away.

He stepped forward and clasped her hands. 'Of course I came, Eliza.'

The butler backed out of the room and closed the door.

Nate stood with Eliza's hands in his, looking down at her joy-filled face and glittering eyes, the pale grey he remembered so well, like eyes that had once seen the storm. His heart leapt in an answering jubilance that jarred him. This was Eliza whom he expected never to see again!

Without another thought, he released her hands and wrapped his arms around her.

She was here! In his arms again! As he'd dreamed so often in the cold and lonely and dangerous nights of the war.

She pressed herself against him, hugging him in return. 'Nate. I have missed you so.'

When he inherited the title, he'd dared hope he might encounter her somewhere. She'd be married, though, he'd believed.

But she was no longer married. She was out of mourning. And his spirit immediately flew back to that cabin, that night of rain and lovemaking.

His body flared with desire at the feel of her in his arms. The scent of her came back from vivid memory. Lavender and roses. He also remembered the feel of his skin against hers, her eager response when he'd coupled with her. She lifted her face to his, bringing those lips tantalisingly close. He remembered well the taste of those lips, the soft joining of his mouth on hers, sealing the connection they'd already made by sharing their stories. Their emotions.

Oh, to taste her lips again! To plunge his tongue inside her mouth as she pressed against him.

By god, he wanted her again! Completely. Right here. Right now.

He lurched away, aghast by the intensity of his reaction, of what his body demanded.

His breath came hard, as if he'd run a great distance. She stared back at him, eyes puzzled, brows knitted.

What had he almost done, acting like the basest soldier lusting after a tavern maid?

He couldn't even speak.

* * *

Eliza was shaken, shocked at sensations within her she'd merely aroused in fantasy over the years. Thinking of him. No, not of *him*. Of Nate. Her captain. This man looked like him. Sounded like him. Even seemed to be him, enough to propel her right back to that rainy night.

But now he looked appalled at having embraced her and that tiny glimmer of hope inside her for the return of her captain grew dark, like a candle's dying flame. She'd thought for a moment he would kiss her and her body had flared with desire.

But, then, he thrust her away.

Like Henry had done all those years ago. Not at all like the Nate of that rainy night, not like the Nate of her fantasy.

She straightened her clothes and told herself to simply pretend that passionate embrace never happened.

She took a breath. 'I—I am so glad you called, Nate. I—I wanted to thank you again for that night.'

For making love to me. For giving me my daughter. For teaching me to face what life throws at me.

'You helped me in so many ways. You made it possible for me to go back to my husband and build a life.'

His brow furrowed. 'Was it a good life?'

She smiled wanly. 'Good enough. Henry and I were able to remain on good terms and I was able to accept him as he was.' Both good things, but there was also the emptiness and loneliness that was her marriage. She would not bother to tell him of that, though. 'He was a good man. He loved me as best he could.'

And he adored your daughter.

He glanced around the room. 'Are you as secure as you seem? Do you have sufficient funds? I am in a position to help you, if you require it.'

Still the rescuer, she thought. Still a little like her captain. 'Henry left me with plenty. I am in that enviable position, you know. A wealthy widow. An independent woman.'

His features softened. 'I am glad of it—that you are secure, that is.'

She tried to act as if this was a normal conversation. She'd said what she'd intended to say to him, even with that unexpected burst of passion—and his rejection. 'It— it has been a strange game of cards, you might say. But I did as you told me to. I faced it. I faced everything.' And she would face this disappointment, as well.

'I often wondered if I'd given you good advice,' he responded, sounding more and more as he had that wonderful night when they'd talked of real things. 'I was unsure of the character of your husband. If he might resent you or be unkind—'

If he seemed like two people, she felt the same about herself. There was the rational one of her who talked as if they were only filling in the seven-year blanks in their lives. And the other Eliza whose body still called out to him like a lover, saying *I want you. I want a repeat of that night.*

'Henry was good to me,' the rational part of her went on, but she couldn't bear talking more about herself, well aware she was avoiding the most important information.

About their daughter.

'But what of you?' she asked.

He attempted a smile. 'How did I, a proper nobody, inherit the title of Marquess, do you mean?'

She'd not meant that. She'd meant how had he survived the war? Had he endured hardship? Injury? Had he lost more friends?

He averted his gaze. 'My uncle died over a year ago. His sons went before him, leaving no heirs. I knew nothing of their deaths. I never knew them, really. My uncle made certain of that. So I could only grieve a loss I never really had. I learned all this right before Waterloo. A missive came to me, but by then I could not leave the regiment.' He shook his head. 'I never expected to inherit. I am certain my uncle is turning over in his grave at the thought of it.'

So he would not talk of war.

They still stood apart from each other, further than an arm's reach. It had not occurred to her to ask him to sit.

She made herself return his smile. 'But you faced the challenge, did you not?'

He nodded. 'I have tried.' He met her gaze again, his expression sober. 'I looked for you when I first attended these *ton* events. I thought it possible you were part of the aristocracy. I thought I might see you.'

He'd looked for her? 'I—I was in mourning. I had no real intention to come to town even now, but business compelled me. I only accepted last night's invitation because my sisters insisted.'

Now. Now was the time to tell him about Natalie.

'I am glad you accepted,' he admitted, his voice rough. 'I am glad to see you well.' His expression stiffened. 'But I must tell you something—'

Oh, yes. She'd nearly forgotten. She had a good excuse not to tell him about Natalie. At least not now.

She lifted a hand to stop him. 'I already know. You are to be betrothed to Lady Sibyl.'

He looked surprised. 'You heard this?'

The air suddenly felt heavy to her. 'My sisters spoke of it.'

He frowned. 'It is more widely spoken of than I'd thought.'

She crossed the room so she could rest her hand against the back of a chair.

For support.

She gripped the chair. 'She seems a lovely girl.' That was the polite thing to say. 'My sisters think well of her.'

'She is admirable.' His voice was flat.

She'd heard more emotion from Henry over purchasing a new horse. Was her captain intending a marriage of convenience? One without love? His attachment to Lady Sibyl sounded so dispassionate. Again he disappointed her.

Still, she must assume such a marriage was what he wanted. 'I want to assure you there is no reason for anyone to know our—our connection with each other.'

Especially that she'd begged him to bed her all those years ago and came within a hair's breadth of again doing so now.

She might be gifting him with permission to avoid her, but at the same time she could not bear it. She dreamed of seeing her captain again and again. She'd dreamed of making love with him again. She was that wanton.

But had he changed? Had inheriting wealth and status altered him? It certainly seemed so.

He cleared his throat. 'I will not lie, however. If someone asks if we met before, we must say yes, must we not? Because the truth will never trip us up like a falsehood might.'

But falsehoods were more convenient, were they not? Eliza's parents would completely agree with that. As was omitting the truth. Omitting the truth avoided the drama of telling the truth, the way she was avoiding telling him about Natalie.

He went on. 'If someone enquires, we say we met once. On the road. Briefly. Which is the truth.'

Oh, she well knew that trick. Her parents were masters of concealing the essential information in a partial truth. 'Very well. But only if someone asks.'

No one would ask. Why would they? Any more than he would ask, *By the way, did we create a child that night?*

He took a step towards her but stopped. 'I should take my leave.' He started for the door but stopped again and turned to her. 'We shall see each other, I expect, at the society entertainments.'

She looked up at him, consumed by sadness. 'I do not plan to attend society entertainments. I am really only in town for business.' And to show Natalie some of the sights and take her shopping at some fine toy shops, not places she would likely encounter him.

His brows drew together. 'You are not re-joining society?'

She gripped the back of the chair again. 'No. So I expect we will not see each other.' Her heart wept. Part of her wanted to see him again, even if he was not the captain of her fantasies. Even if he married Lady Sibyl.

His mouth became a grim line. 'I see.'

Then he started for the door again, but changed course and walked up to her, extending his hand.

Hers shook as she placed her hand in his. His touch was igniting that fire again. She begged her body not to betray her again, not to throw herself into his arms again.

He made no further move, nor did she. He looked directly into her eyes. 'Please know, Eliza. If you need me—for any reason—if you need help for any reason, send for me. I will come.'

She nodded.

The marquess released her and left, taking her captain with him.

Chapter Seven

It was all Nate could do to walk sedately down the stairs and collect his hat and gloves from the waiting butler. His emotions were in turmoil. He might not see her again? Intolerable! Once out the door, he walked quickly down the street, aimlessly turning on Piccadilly in the direction of his town house on Half Moon Street. He stopped, mid-stride.

He could not bear returning to his town house. Although his servants included men who'd once been in his company during the war, it was a lonely place. One was expected to make calls on Sunday afternoons, Lady Sibyl had instructed him. But it was still morning and there was no friend or acquaintance he could think of who might make him feel less alone.

He headed to Hyde Park, entering at Hyde Park Corner and following one of the footpaths until he came to a bench in a wooded area.

He collapsed on to the bench and put his head in his hands and finally let himself think about Eliza.

He'd behaved so badly with her. He'd always prided himself on his self-control. Even in battle he'd never lost his wits or had gone mad with bloodlust like many men did. He'd learned to control his emotions when a boy, right after his parents' deaths. At school the ploy fared well. Other boys could not make him cry. Tutors could not humiliate him. In the army no one could intimidate him. Not the enemy. Not his superior officers. Not his men. Because he never lost control.

Except that rainy night when his own despair led him to need Eliza as much as she'd needed him. But even that night he'd controlled himself, had he not? He'd done no more than comfort her.

Until she'd asked for more.

All those emotions from that night came pouring back when seeing her again, when holding her again in his arms. He was that lonely, unloved soldier again, that orphaned little boy again, so hungry for a connection with someone again, he'd almost carried her off to bed right there and then.

Had he mistaken it? She'd responded to his embrace with passion as well, had she not? What would have been the harm if they'd given in to it? She was a widow. He was free.

No. It was too soon. It would have been taking advantage of her. She did not know him. War had changed him. Inheriting the title had changed him. He hardly knew himself sometimes. She knew the man he'd been seven years ago. He ought to have given her time to know him as he was now. Instead he'd lost control.

He could not despise himself more for it.

How he wished to be at war again. The rules of a soldier were so much simpler. Obey. Fight. Survive. He'd been skilled at all of those, but was he ready for polite society?

He often did not think so. So many of society's rules seemed ridiculous to him; he could not help but disdain them.

In any event it had not been society dictating gentlemanly behaviour towards Eliza. Nate had broken his own standards.

What had that meant? Surely it was not loving behaviour. He could not call it love when he'd not spent even twenty-four hours in her presence. Was it a mere lustful urge, then, because he'd not embraced another woman like that in over a year? Why should it be? She was lovely, very pleasing to his eye, but so were many women. Lady Sibyl, for instance, and he'd never had a single impulse to embrace her like that, let alone ravish her.

Yet he could not keep his hands off Eliza.

He closed his eyes and tried to conjure up an image of Lady Sibyl, like he'd once conjured up Eliza on lonely nights between battles. Remembering her used to warm him, comfort him, give him something to live for.

Lady Sibyl's image did nothing to crack the walls around his emotions, did nothing to fill the emptiness inside him.

And yet he was expected to marry her?

He stood and walked on, passing workmen who were using the park as a short cut. Couples strolling arm in arm. Nannies with their small charges. People looking ordinary enough. Why was he not feeling like one of them?

He stopped and retraced his steps. Had he not instructed Eliza that facing what one did not wish to face was the better choice than running?

He would heed his own advice.

He would call upon Lady Sybil without delay. In the morning. Society's rules be damned.

Eliza stood staring at the door after Nate left.

At the end, at the goodbye, he almost seemed like her captain again. The Rescuer. And he'd touched her, more than a mere shake of her hand.

She had not been mistaken, though, had she? As soon as she'd embraced him and her body flared with need and her lips begged to be kissed, he'd pushed her away.

She must have misread something, but what was it? Had he not felt the completeness of being together again? Or had he been appalled at her wantonness?

She had, of course, openly embraced a man she knew to be bound to another woman, even though he'd been as unemotional as possible about Lady Sibyl. He certainly had not been unemotional embracing her. Spurning her.

The pain of it jabbed at her heart again.

Was that why she had not told him of Natalie? Because he'd wounded her? Was that her little revenge?

No. That was not like her. At least she hoped it wasn't. She'd not told him about Natalie because Natalie was so fragile at this time and Eliza was no longer sure of Nate's character. Nate had confused her. Could she trust him to know of Natalie? What if he insisted upon meeting her? Insisted upon telling Natalie that he was her father? Natalie could not take such a new upset in her short little life.

Eliza wished she could trust that the Nate she knew in the cabin was the same man who'd just left the room. Had he changed? Or was it that she'd merely invented that Nate in her mind to suit her needs, her captain who comforted her bleakest of days?

Perhaps he concealed his true character as Henry had done? Perhaps everyone was duplicitous. Even her beloved captain.

She took a breath and slumped into a chair.

What difference did it make, really? He would marry Lady Sibyl and she would return to the country where she intended to live a quiet life, away from society. He might never learn of Natalie.

Secrets too often had a way of becoming known, though. He would hear of Natalie somehow and guess. By her name. Her age. An offhand comment from one of her sisters. Or her brothers-in-law whom he often saw in Parliament. Or, heaven forbid, meeting Natalie when she was grown and entering society.

Besides, he had a right to know.

She must tell him.

He'd taught her to face life's difficulties head on and this she was determined to do. It would mean seeing him again.

She clutched her head with her hands. How quickly misery followed joy.

But what was the use of sitting here in her misery? She needed to face this. Call upon him. Tell him.

She left the room and went to her bedchamber where Lacy, her lady's maid, was folding and putting away her freshly laundered underclothes and nightdress.

Lacy curtsied at her entrance.

Lacy had been with her since before her marriage and was only two years older. She'd come with her from her father's estate to be her lady's maid and was as dear to Eliza as a sister. She confided in Lacy about all sorts of things, except, of course, the most important matters. Like about Henry. Or Natalie's conception.

'Do you have need of me, ma'am?' Lacy asked.

Eliza nodded. 'Would you help me into a walking dress? I—I wish to go out.' She could not say where. Eliza began shedding the more casual morning dress she wore for Nate.

Lacy closed the drawer in the wardrobe. 'Any particular one?'

Goodness. Should she wear her best, her most flattering? Or should she not care as much about her appearance as she had earlier, dressing for his visit?

'Your choice,' Eliza finally replied.

The walking dress Lacy brought was perfectly fine. One made right before Henry's death and one she'd hardly worn. It was not the very latest in London fashion, but Eliza did not care about that.

Lacy helped her dress and tidied her hair. As she left the bedchamber and descended the stairs, Natalie and her governess, Miss Gibbons, were in the hall about to go outside.

Natalie spied her. 'Mama! Miss Gibbons and I are going to the park. Will you come with us?'

'Well, I—' she started to say.

'Please, Mama! Please come with us,' the child entreated.

'Miss Natalie,' Gibbons said. 'Your mother might have somewhere she needs to go.'

Eliza gazed down at her daughter's pleading face, so very, very dear to her. The little girl had been through so much since Henry died. How could Eliza refuse?

'As a matter of fact,' she said, 'a walk in the park with you is just what I wish most to do.'

She could put off her visit to Nate's a little.

Actually, a walk in the park felt like a reprieve.

The closer Nate came to Lord Crafton's town house on Dover Street, the more certain he was in his decision. He only hoped he would find Lady Sibyl alone.

Although Lord Crafton had been very helpful to him in learning the ropes in the Lords, Nate found him too strict a Tory for Nate's taste. Nate joined the Lords as a Tory, but the more he learned and listened, the more Whigs appealed to him. Men like Everly, Eliza's brother-in-law, and his father, Lord Locksworth, had also been quite cordial to him of late and Nate's political tastes seemed more akin to theirs. Nate was finding his own footing and was gaining confidence that he could manage independent of Lord Crafton.

Chances were good that Lady Sibyl would be alone. Nate doubted there would be other callers so early and she did not usually attend Sunday church services. But Nate did not make unexpected calls to Lady Sibyl or her father. He appeared only by invitation. There had been several invitations.

Perhaps he ought to have refused many of them.

He wished he had.

As he reached for the knocker, the more typical brass

lion head, he felt none of the pent-up excitement he'd experienced at Eliza's door. He felt only a sorrow that he might have inadvertently done an injury to Lady Sibyl.

He knocked and the door was opened almost immediately by the Crafton butler.

'Lord Hale. Good day to you.' The man bowed.

'Is Lady Sibyl at home?' Nate asked. 'And able to speak with me?'

'I shall see directly, sir.' The butler reached for Nate's hat and gloves. 'Perhaps you would like to wait in the drawing room.'

Nate followed him to the drawing room, a room he'd been in several times. The butler gestured for him to sit, but Nate remained standing. The butler left, presumably to ask Lady Sibyl if she were at home.

Waiting, Nate surveyed the room, decorated in the latest and finest taste. A tented ceiling. Striped wallpaper. Furniture which looked to be plucked from Cleopatra's palace. Obviously the decor was Lady Sibyl's doing. Her mother had died when Lady Sibyl was a child, Nate knew, and Lady Sibyl had acted as the lady of the house ever since her first Season at age eighteen.

She was now twenty, a bit old for a society miss, but Nate had never asked her why she'd not married earlier. He'd not been curious enough.

He looked around again. Even the vases on the mantel and the lamps looked Egyptian. Lady Sibyl had certainly embraced that style.

The town house Nate inherited from his uncle had nothing like that. It probably had not been refurbished in half a century. He still felt uncomfortable in the formal rooms with their elegant pale walls and brightly coloured plasterwork, perhaps because the decor reminded him of his uncle. He rarely sat in the drawing room and never ate in the dining room.

Nate tried to recall the decor of Eliza's drawing room. He laughed to himself. He could only remember her.

He walked over to the windows and looked out on the street below. Like his street and Eliza's, Dover was losing its status as a fashionable address. This mattered little to Nate but matters of that sort seemed to rankle most of the *ton*. He'd never heard Lady Sibyl complain, though. She never complained.

That pang of guilt struck him again. If all of society thought he and Lady Sibyl all but betrothed, what did she think? Was he about to wound her? She'd been welcoming to him, pleasant and very willing to help him negotiate the intricacies of society life. Had she also been counting on an offer of marriage from him?

She entered the room, a vision in white muslin and lace, her blonde hair partially covered by an elegant cap that looked more decorative than useful.

'Hale! What a lovely surprise!' She extended her hands to him much like Eliza had.

He clasped them for just a moment. 'I wanted to speak with you.'

Her brown eyes sparkled. 'Did you? Shall we sit, then. I will ring for tea.'

'No need for tea,' he said.

She sat on the *chaise longue* with its eagle claw feet and gold gilt trim. He chose an adjacent backless chair.

'It has come to my attention that you and I are a topic of interest to many,' he said.

'Are we?' Her smile widened and she leaned forward, her expression eager.

Good God. She did expect a proposal.

Nothing to do but get straight to the point.

He sat back. 'Lady Sibyl.' He lowered his voice as if that would ease her disappointment. 'I am not going to marry you.'

She straightened, eyes flashing. 'What?'

'I am very regretful if I gave the impression that I was intending to propose—'

'You certainly did!' she cried. 'Courting me exclusively!'

He needed to be honest with her. And with himself. 'I admit I have enjoyed your company and appreciated your kindness in helping me through these society events—'

'But?' Her voice was scathing. And totally unlike her.

He tried again. 'You would make an excellent marchioness, I admit, but I am not prepared to marry. I need more time—'

Her expression softened and her smile returned. 'Oh, if it is merely time you require, I am in no hurry.'

He stood, unsure of how to proceed. Unsure, because he did not know himself or what he wanted. He knew what was expected of him and he knew what he did not want, but the rest was a muddle.

A muddle with Eliza in the centre.

He made another attempt to explain. 'I had no idea that simply accepting yours and your father's hospitality would give the impression that I was courting you or that a proposal of marriage was imminent. I think it best we figure out a way to disavow this impression, one that will not adversely affect you.'

She stood as well, her face twisted in anger. 'But it will adversely affect me! *You* left the impression that you would make me an offer. Now you have to fulfil that obligation. What will people think of me?'

He faced her. 'You tell me what we can do to make certain no one thinks ill of you.'

She lifted her chin. 'There is nothing to do but to marry me.'

He met her eye. 'That is what I will not do. I admire

you, Lady Sibyl, but I do not feel those emotions one ought to feel to become betrothed.'

'What emotions!' She put her hands on her hips. 'Love, do you mean? Do not be such a bumpkin, Hale. What has love to do with marriage? I get to be a marchioness. You get a society hostess. We produce an heir and then go our separate ways. What could be better?'

Nate felt himself go cold inside. What she described sounded bleak. No real connection. A nightmare.

And too much like his relationship with his uncle. Family who were no family at all.

'I am not going to marry you,' he repeated, this time straining to keep his voice even.

'Oh, yes, you will!' Lady Sibyl spat out the words like venom and paced in front of him. 'I demand it. You've been leading me on all this time. Making me think I would be a marchioness! You cannot take that away from me! I forbid it.'

Nate had never seen her like this. Raving.

She swivelled back to him. 'Wait until my father hears this! He expects you to marry me.'

Realisation dawned. Lady Sibyl and her father had manipulated him with their overtures of friendship, of wanting to be of assistance. They merely wanted her to marry a marquess.

He stepped towards her and looked her directly in the eye. 'We can either discuss how to make certain your reputation is not damaged or I can take my leave. But I will not marry you.'

She shrieked, picked up one of those Egyptian decorations and smashed it against the wall. Nate turned away and strode out of the room, the sound of another vase shattering on the door that closed behind him.

Chapter Eight

Nate made his way down Dover Street to Piccadilly and past Devonshire House. Though a part of him was still reeling from the unexpected change in Lady Sibyl, mostly he felt as if he'd dodged a cannonball.

He'd thought he was availing himself of the political and societal expertise of Lord Crafton and Lady Sibyl; instead, their designs on him were completely self-serving. Lady Sibyl had not been merely kind. She'd been calculating, intent upon marrying a marquess, of gaining the title of marchioness, not of finding a husband and creating a family.

How he despised this world he was now a part of where titles mattered more than people and appearances mattered more than genuine emotion. He wished he could leave it, return to the simple world of the army, but the army no longer needed him, and countless people depended upon the Marquess of Hale for their very survival.

At least his eyes were opened now.

Seeing Eliza again had woken him up, he thought. They had shared something real all those years ago. He needed to believe that. He did not know what could exist between them now—maybe nothing—but now they had time to find out. That embrace they shared meant something. That embrace, that near kiss, wrong as it was, felt more real to him than the months he'd spent as the Marquess of Hale.

They'd parted awkwardly that morning. Nate was keen to undo that, to let Eliza know he was Nate again, not the Marquess of Hale. He was not sure he'd made it clear he was not betrothed to Lady Sibyl. He needed to let her know he never intended to be.

He continued to Clarges Street. As he turned the corner there was Eliza only a few steps away. A little girl and her governess were ahead of her.

'Mama! Watch me run!' the little girl cried.

'Be careful, Natalie,' Eliza called out to her.

A sound escaped his throat and Nate froze.

Eliza looked back, saw him and her expression turned to alarm.

Eliza felt the blood drain from her face. Nate. So close she could touch him. He'd seen Natalie. Heard Natalie call her mama.

'Nate,' she managed to say, unable to move.

'Lady Varden?' The governess sounded uncertain.

Uncertain could not begin to explain how Eliza felt.

Eliza turned back to her. 'Take Natalie inside, Miss Gibbons,' she told her. 'I will be in directly.'

Nate merely stared, saying nothing, but looking like thunder. Glaring at her.

Her heart pounded. Luckily there was no one else on the street at the moment.

'She is yours,' she said quietly.

'Mine,' he repeated.

'From our night together,' she explained. 'I—I meant to tell you—'

'But it slipped your mind?' he cut in cynically.

'I—I intended to. Really,' she stammered.

'But you did not,' he stated. 'How was that, Eliza? How was it you neglected to tell me about the child?'

She could try to explain that their encounter earlier had shaken her resolve, made her keep silent. Or was that merely her excuse?

'Did you mean to keep it secret from me?' he pressed.

Had she? She'd seemed to seize on any excuse not to tell him.

'That was not well done of you, Eliza,' he continued.

He'd already disappointed her in pushing away from their embrace. Now this haughty, angry man further disheartened her.

Even if she deserved his anger.

She straightened. 'Come now, Nate. I have seen you only twice and very briefly. Do I not have the right as a mother to be certain of you before disclosing such information about my child?'

'As the child's *father*,' he said scathingly, 'do you have the right to keep the fact of her existence from me?'

'I do!' she insisted. 'Natalie is my responsibility. I must be certain nothing can harm her.'

He leaned towards her, dropping his sarcasm for more open anger. 'You thought I would harm her?'

No. She did not think that. Did she?

She'd only known that he'd hurt her when he pushed her away. And confused her. And he was going to be married. And she was not sure she could trust him not to upend Natalie's life.

Even so, she'd meant to go after him and tell him about Natalie, hadn't she?

'Yes, she is yours. But I ask nothing of you about her. Henry acknowledged her. He adored her. Loved her better than he ever loved me. His death shattered her. I will not allow anything else to hurt her in that way—'

'Like me?' he cut in. 'What did you think I would do?'

'I don't know!' she cried. 'Do you not see? I do not know you. People hide their true natures all the time!'

He glanced away. 'That is certainly true.'

Did he mean her? Perhaps she did hide herself from him. She certainly hid how dearly she'd longed for him over the years, how that one night with him had changed her. Saved her, perhaps. But she hadn't hid her desire for him that morning, had she? And see how he'd responded.

He faced her again, looking as if a new thought had come to his mind. 'You said you were leaving London. Did you intend to leave without telling me about her?'

'No,' she protested, but in a weak voice. 'I planned to tell you.'

He rubbed his face. 'I am not certain I can believe anything you say now.'

That particularly wounded her. He'd been the one person in her life to whom she'd been able to speak freely.

Well. Almost freely.

She changed course. 'Nate. Think of this. I knew you were to marry Lady Sibyl. I thought perhaps knowledge of Natalie would—would interfere. Spoil your happiness, perhaps.'

'Marry Lady Sibyl.' He scoffed, then glared at her again. 'Oh, come now, Eliza. There is no need to flummox me. What did that have to do with telling me the truth?'

He was right. It was a mere excuse.

But her hesitation had been human, after all. Perhaps not the best of her, but understandable, was it not?

Why did he not understand?

The Nate of that one fateful night would have understood. The Nate of her fantasies would have believed her.

She collected herself and looked directly into his eyes. 'Enough, Nate. Whether you agree or not, I had reasons not to tell you about Natalie right away. You may believe me or not that I intended to tell you once I was more certain of you. But I am not going to argue with you on the street, not another minute.'

She turned around and walked away from him. She did not look back but heard no footsteps behind her. She reached her door and entered her town house.

And wondered what would happen next.

Nate watched Eliza walk away from him. He watched until she entered her town house and closed the door.

She'd deliberately intended to keep him away from his daughter, he was convinced.

His daughter. Connected to him by blood, the blood of family.

When his uncle and cousins were alive, Nate could at least tell himself he was connected by blood to them, if not by any familial affection. Perhaps he had other, more distant relations, but, if so, he did not know them, not even their names. Any blood he shared with them would be very thin, indeed.

But he had a daughter! There could be no closer connection than that!

His daughter. Natalie. His *namesake*. His *family*. He was not about to give up on knowing her.

Eliza had not heard the last of him.

Natalie waited for Eliza in the hall.

'Who was that man, Mama?' Natalie asked as soon as Eliza entered. Her little face was pinched with worry.

Eliza forced herself to appear calm. She crouched down to Natalie's level and brushed the hair from her child's face.

'A friend,' she said mildly. 'Someone I have not seen in a long time.'

'He was angry at you!' Natalie said.

Yes. Very angry.

'Oh, no,' Eliza said instead. 'He was simply worried about something. It is all sorted now. Nothing for you to fret over.'

She glimpsed Miss Gibbons standing nearby. The governess looked sceptical, but immediately composed her expression.

'Natalie,' Miss Gibbons said brightly. 'Shall we go to the kitchen and see if Cook has some nice refreshment for us?'

Natalie turned to Eliza. 'Mama, will you come with us?'

Had that little encounter with Nate chipped away at Natalie's sense of well-being? Natalie had clung to Eliza after Henry died and when they'd had to move. The child's insecurity was one of the reasons Eliza had brought her to London, so Natalie would not have to endure a long separation from her. Eliza thought Natalie was getting stronger. How little it took to shake her.

Eliza touched Natalie's hair again. 'I could do with some refreshment. We walked a great deal, did we not?'

Natalie happily chattered on about what they had seen in the park, especially about the swans they'd spotted on the Serpentine.

Natalie was still chattering on about the swans when they entered the kitchen and sat down for Cook to find some milk and biscuits for Natalie and tea for Eliza and Miss Gibbons.

'Have you ever seen the swans, Cook?' Natalie asked.

'Oh, yes, miss,' Cook responded, pouring some milk into a glass. 'In fact, I remember when I was a girl and worked in the kitchen of the old Earl, we served swan every Christmas day.'

Natalie's eyes grew wide. 'You *ate* the swans?' Her lip trembled.

Cook turned red and glanced apologetically at Eliza. 'Well, miss—um—that was in the old days. It is not done now. No. Not done now at all.'

At least not very often and certainly not in this house. They were not so grand.

'And I think the swans in the Serpentine are under the protection of the King so no one will eat them,' added Miss Gibbons.

Natalie looked only a little mollified.

There was no dispute. Natalie was a very sensitive child and Henry's death had affected her deeply. Eliza had been right to be protective of her, hadn't she?

Even from Nate.

For the next two days, Nate busied himself with the business of the Lords, which seemed mostly to be filled with fears of insurrection and revolution. Lord Sidmouth, the Home Secretary, fuelled these fears, but never was there much discussion about the high prices for bread or the vast unemployment created by the end of the war.

Nate had hired as many of his former soldiers as he could, to work both on his estates and in his houses and stables, but that was not even a dent in the problem.

Today was Wednesday and there would be no session in the Lords. Nate was at loose ends. He'd risen early and had taken Pegasus for a nice gallop on Rotten Row, enough to satisfy the horse, but not nearly enough to quiet the storm inside him.

As expected, he'd been given the cut direct by Lord Crafton, whose coterie also gave him a wide berth. Nate did not mind so much that those men were not talking to him. And to be free of Crafton and Lady Sibyl was frankly a relief.

What consumed his mind was his daughter. His *family*. What was he to do about her? Now that he knew of her, had seen her, being separated from her was excruciating. Why did Eliza want to keep her from him? He would never harm either of them.

Or—like with his uncle—did his very existence upset them?

But Eliza had been glad to see him. Overjoyed, like he'd been, he was certain of it. That did not fit with her desire to keep his daughter secret from him.

After returning Pegasus to his stable, Nate had walked over to Angelo's *L'Ecole des Armes* on Bond Street, a fencing salon where he could refresh his fencing skills. Attending the salon was one of the advantages of wealth. Nate could afford a session with the third generation of Angelos to run the place. Although this Henri Angelo's version of a fencing match was a lot more civilised than swordplay in battle, it had been satisfyingly exhausting.

But on the walk back to his town house, Nate's restlessness returned, especially when passing Eliza's street. He decided to return to Hyde Park, which lately seemed to be his preferred place of solace.

He entered the park and walked briskly down the path, heading towards the Serpentine. The sun shone high in the sky and the area was filled with children and their nannies and governesses, playing at the water's edge, feeding pieces of bread to the swans and ducks.

He turned away. He was trying not to think of his daughter. Frolicking children were like salt in a wound right now. He followed another path and found a bench set back from the path. It offered more solitude, although he could hear the children's laughter in the distance.

As he settled on the bench, he realised he'd run away from the sight of children. Or, rather, he'd tried to run away from the yearnings evoked at the sight of them, that raw need to belong to someone and have someone belong to him.

When had he started to run away from what was difficult? That was not his character. He confronted hardship and pain and difficulties the way he'd confronted Lady Sibyl, the way he would confront Lord Crafton if the man ever spoke to him again.

The way he would confront Eliza.

He refused to allow this to be the end of the matter of his daughter. He must speak to Eliza again. Come to some better solution, some way for him to be connected to his daughter's life. To know her. To help her.

Nate heard the approach of a child, singing and skipping towards him. And, like a miracle, his daughter appeared.

She stopped when she saw him but walked closer. 'You are my mama's friend, are you not?'

'I am,' he replied. 'You remember seeing me talk with her?'

She nodded. 'I remember things.' Up close she was even more precious than he could have imagined. Large eyes as blue as a summer sky. Hair as dark as his own. Skin as fair as her mother's. 'What is your name?'

He stood and bowed. 'I am called Lord Hale.'

She giggled and curtsied. 'I am Miss Natalie Varden.'

Nate sat again, mostly so he could be more at her level.

'Where is your governess, Miss Natalie?' he asked. She should not be in the park alone.

She giggled again. 'Looking for me, I expect. I ran ahead of her.'

He thought of all the dangers that might befall a little girl alone in the park. The desire to protect her surged through him as if she were truly threatened. 'You had better stay right here until your governess finds you. You should not have run from her.'

Little Natalie frowned and her eyes glistened.

Good God! Was she about to cry?

'You are angry at me like you were angry at Mama,' she accused.

Nate immediately composed his features into something more friendly. 'I am not angry with you. I was worried, is all.'

'Oh.' She looked as if she was considering this possibility. 'Mama said you were not angry at her either. But you looked angry.'

He had been angry. Angry that he'd not learned of this enchanting little creature right away.

'I like to run.' She grinned and two endearing dimples appeared on her cheeks. 'Miss Gibbons does not. At home, though, I used to be able to run wherever I wanted to. We had a very big garden and my papa said I could run all the way through it whenever I wanted to.' Her expression turned sad and her eyes glistened again. 'But then my papa died and now we live in a little house with a little garden and it is no fun to run in at all!'

Nate had no idea what to say to the child about that. About anything.

But he was saved from the need to.

'Miss Natalie!' Her governess appeared, out of breath, face filled with worry. She came directly to the child's side. 'Do not ever run from me again!'

Natalie bowed her head.

The governess noticed Nate, then. 'Oh, sir. I did not see you.'

He stood and greeted her with a nod. 'Miss.'

She put a protective arm around Natalie. Had she been told to be wary of him?

'Miss,' he said again. 'I assure you I told her the same thing. That she should not have run from you.'

She still looked at him suspiciously. 'Why are you here,

sir?' she asked boldly, then seemed to lose her nerve. 'If you do not mind me asking.'

Did she think he designed this encounter? He might have done, had he thought of it.

'I was seated on the bench when she appeared,' he responded. 'I thought it better to keep her here so you could more easily find her. A child should not be left alone in this park.'

'I know!' the governess cried. 'She made me frantic!'

'I suspected so,' he said.

'We must be gone,' she urged Natalie away from him, taking her hand and hurrying down the path the way they'd come.

Before they were out of sight, the little girl turned and waved to him. 'Goodbye, Lord Hale.'

Nate sat on the bench again, savouring the moment that had just passed, the dear look on her face as she waved goodbye. Oh, yes. He would be a part of this little girl's life. His *daughter's* life. He would see to it.

Chapter Nine

Eliza was in her library, answering a letter from her mother who'd entreated her to invite her and her father to stay with her in London. London was filled with way too many temptations for her parents. Without Henry's help, Eliza feared she would not be able to keep them out of trouble, whether it be romantic trouble or financial. Or both. Henry had been excellent at putting limits on her parents. He had firm control of their purse strings and had used that power to keep them in line. Eliza had the control now, but they did not heed her nearly as well.

So, no. They could not come to London and stay in her house. She would be returning soon and closing up the house until the next time she needed to be in town. They, of course, would threaten to come and stay with one of her sisters, but years ago Henry had warned her brothers-in-law about her parents. Jeffrey and Francis were even more controlling than Henry had been, so no fears that they would descend upon Susan or Joanna.

Natalie came skipping in. 'Mama! Mama! Guess what?'

Eliza put her pen down and opened her arms to embrace her daughter. 'You are back from the park, then? Did you have a good time?'

'A very good time,' Natalie responded in an annoyed tone. 'But guess what? You never will guess.'

Eliza released her and smiled. 'If I never will guess, you must tell me.'

Natalie had a look of triumph on her face. 'I saw your friend in the park.'

'What friend?'

'Your *friend*,' Natalie repeated as if she were a dolt. 'You know. Lord Hale.'

For one second Eliza did not know who Natalie meant— Then she remembered. Nate. Nate was Lord Hale.

Nate had been in the park? What was he doing? Spying on Natalie?

'You saw him in the park?'

Natalie nodded. 'And I talked to him, too. He told me his name and he said I must stay with him until Miss Gibbons comes, because Miss Gibbons was not there.'

'She wasn't there?' Eliza's anxiety rose. What had happened?

Miss Gibbons entered the room at that moment. 'Ma'am, Miss Natalie ran ahead of me. When I caught up to her she was talking to—to Lord Hale.'

He'd obviously introduced himself.

Natalie's eyes widened as if she suddenly realised she might be in trouble. 'Do not be cross with me, Mama! I only wanted to run.' She stamped her foot and wrapped her arms around herself. 'I wish I could run like in our garden. I miss our garden! I wish I was back there! Papa said I could run all I wanted to there. Papa would have let me run!'

Eliza rose and went to her sobbing daughter, enfolding her in her arms. 'There now, Natalie,' she soothed. 'I miss Papa and our garden, too. But we must go on, mustn't we? We have to be strong.'

'I don't want to be strong!' Natalie wailed.

Eliza picked her up and carried her to an armchair near

the window. She held her on her lap and rocked her. 'We'll get through this. Never fear. We'll think of all the nice things we have and all the people who do care about us and we'll even be happy again some day.'

Although happiness seemed an unattainable goal. Eliza had been unhappy for as long as she could remember—except for that brief time with Nate. She'd aspired to contentment instead.

Finally Natalie's little body relaxed in her arms, her head resting against Eliza's heart. Her sobs ended in a long sigh.

Eliza looked up at Miss Gibbons who regarded them both with a sympathetic expression. The grieving child and her grieving mother.

Eliza did grieve, but not only the loss of Henry, her dear friend, but also the loss of what marriage might have been. The loss of that girlhood dream she'd so briefly possessed when her best friend married her. Before she discovered what he'd hidden from her.

Natalie took a deep breath and murmured, 'He's not angry at me, he said. And he's not angry at you.'

'Who?' Eliza asked. 'Papa?'

'No,' she answered in that impatient tone only a child can use. '*Lord Hale*. But he does look fearsome when he scolds.'

Miss Gibbons spoke up, her voice anxious. 'Ma'am, Miss Natalie was only out of my sight for a few minutes. I had the impression Lord Hale engaged her in conversation so that she would stay until I found her. But it was minutes, truly.'

Eliza was certain Miss Gibbons had not been neglectful. She was such a dear person, so kind and patient with Natalie. She'd grown up not unlike Eliza, in a good aristocratic family. But Miss Gibbons's father had shot himself after losing the family fortune and Miss Gibbons had been forced to seek employment. Eliza paid her well, knowing

Miss Gibbons sent money to help her mother and younger siblings.

In other words, Miss Gibbons was who Eliza might have been had it not been for Henry.

And Nate, who'd helped her stay with Henry.

Why did everything lead back to Nate?

Eliza looked up at the governess. 'I know how she can be, Miss Gibbons. Running off before you can think. You must have been quite alarmed.'

'Oh, ma'am!' Miss Gibbons replied. 'I was in a fair panic!'

But Nate conveniently was there, right at the moment Natalie ran off. Had he been watching her?

'Did—did Lord Hale say why he was in the park?' she asked the governess.

Miss Gibbons seemed to take this as an odd question. 'No, ma'am. He was just there.'

Natalie squirmed on Eliza's lap and she helped her climb down. 'Have you had some refreshment since your visit to the park?'

Miss Gibbons replied, 'No. Miss Natalie came looking for you straight away.'

Natalie pulled Eliza's hand. 'Will you come to the kitchen with us, Mama?'

'No, dear.' Eliza rose. 'Not today. I must dress and go out. I—I have an errand.' She combed her child's hair with her fingers. 'But I will look in on you when I return, I promise.'

Natalie needed that reassurance. That her mother would return. Because her papa had not.

'Very well, Mama!' Natalie said, at least trying to sound strong.

After they left, Eliza rang for Lacy. She'd dress as quickly as she could and make a call upon Lord Hale. She'd make it very clear he was not to attempt to see Natalie, under any circumstances.

* * *

Nate sat at his desk in the library, reading the latest missive from his estate manager detailing several issues needing his attention on his principal estate, all matters requiring the expenditure of what seemed to Nate like large sums of money. He really had no idea whether the expenditures were justified or not. He'd never lived on an estate, never farmed or raised livestock. He had no choice but to trust the manager.

He'd trust that the former soldiers he employed would let him know if they saw anything suspicious. Of course, only one or two of them could write.

Hawkins appeared at the door. Hawkins was one of the men from Nate's company. He'd been in service before the army and so became Nate's rather unorthodox butler. Nate's uncle's London butler, even more ancient than his uncle, had received a very nice pension, as did most of the old servants.

Hawkins looked like a cat who'd eaten a canary.

'What is it, Hawkins?' Nate asked.

The butler's brows rose. 'A lady to see you, Major.' He sometimes forgot to call Nate *m'lord*, using his latest rank instead. Nate actually appreciated it.

'A lady?' His spirits plummeted. Do not say it was Lady Sibyl. 'Who?'

He smirked. 'Lady Varden, she says.'

Lady Varden?

Eliza!

'Have her come in, by all means.' He hurriedly tidied his desk and donned the coat he'd hung off the back of his chair.

Footsteps approached. He ought to have told Hawkins to show her to the drawing room, a much nicer room than this. And the more proper place to see a lady guest.

Too late.

Hawkins appeared again. 'Lady Varden, Major.'

She breezed in, but more like a charging cuirassier than—than—what had he been hoping? Than a lover? Someone who cared about him?

Hawkins closed the door.

'Eliza?' Nate said.

Her eyes flashed. 'Do you realise your house is directly behind mine?'

'I did after calling upon you,' he responded.

She waved a hand. 'Never mind that. I came to tell you not to seek out Natalie. Not to speak to her!'

He bristled. 'I did not seek her out, Eliza.'

'You did,' she insisted. 'You talked to her in the park.'

Why this anger? Because he had spoken to his own daughter? 'I did speak to her, but because she came by where I was sitting.'

'You met her by chance?' she scoffed. 'Do you expect me to believe that?'

Now his ire was piqued. 'I do not lie, Eliza.'

She blinked. 'Well, you should not have spoken to her.'

What had been said to her that she should accuse him so? 'She spoke to me, Eliza. She recognised me. What would you have had me do? She was there in the park alone, without her governess. Should I have sent her on her way?'

'No. Of course not.' She seemed flustered for a moment. 'But I—I don't want you to speak to her. I don't want you to see her.'

Her words wounded. He strode closer to her, glaring into her face. 'She is mine, Eliza. My daughter. You told me so.'

Her eyes filled with pain. 'Do you not see? She knows only Henry as her father. It is difficult enough for her to adjust to losing him, to losing her home and everything that felt secure to her. You cannot come in to disrupt her life. You just cannot.'

It took all his effort to temper his anger. 'What do you

take me for, Eliza? She spoke to me. I spoke to her as I would any child in that situation. I have done nothing to deserve such an accusation from you.'

If they had been in that cabin on that rain-filled night—and if he were not so damned angry—he might have explained to her that Natalie was the only family he possessed and he desperately wanted to know her. That the chance meeting with her had been precious to him.

Her shoulders slumped. 'Oh, Nate. Forgive me.' She looked at him again, more anguished than angry. 'It is only that I am so worried about her. It takes nothing to set off her weeping. Henry doted on her, you see. His death was terrible for her. But, as if that were not enough, we had to leave the only home she ever knew and almost all the servants she loved. Everything changed for her.'

The tide of fury inside him washed away. He went to her, intending to fold her in his arms.

She stepped away.

That hurt.

His voice lowered. 'Do you not think I, of all people, should know how she feels?'

Her gaze met his. She understood.

That feeling of connection returned, the feeling that they could tell each other anything, that he could tell her, only her, how painful and difficult the loss of his parents had been. But her eyes shuttered again and the moment was gone.

She folded her arms across her chest. 'I—I am leaving London soon. May I ask that you not try to see Natalie again? She is too easily upset. I think it best to take her home. We live near Henry's estate…near the village she's grown up around. I thought a change of scenery would do her good, but now I think I was wrong. I need to take her home.'

He felt the wound of her words again. She meant she

needed to make certain his daughter did not see him again.

'Because you fear I will see her again?'

'No. I—' She shook her head as if confused. 'I just need to take her home.'

He walked away from her, returning to fuss with papers on his desk. 'Very well, Eliza. Your message is clear.' He looked up at her. 'Is there anything else?'

'Nate.' Her voice turned low and she did not move. Finally she nodded. 'Good day, Nate.' She spun around and rushed out the door.

Nate dropped into his chair and lowered his head into his hands.

Lady Sibyl crossed on to Half Moon Street, pausing to stare at Lord Hale's door. Certainly it was bold of her to call upon him, but he would not refuse to see her, would he?

She trusted he was home. Where else would he be on a day that the Lords was not in session? He rarely made morning calls. Another oddity of his, in addition, of course, to his failure to succumb to her charms, as she'd intended. He simply did not understand how these matters ought to proceed.

She ought not to have lost her temper with him, though. How humiliating that she must *beg* for *his* forgiveness when it was he who was at fault for not coming up to snuff.

She took a step towards his door but stopped when she saw it open. A lady walked out and briskly strode away.

Lady Varden?

Sibyl had barely taken any notice of Lady Varden at the ball last Saturday, except when Hale had danced with her. She'd asked Hale about it. He'd merely said he'd felt obligated.

Obligated, indeed.

Oh, Sibyl did not care if Hale was having a tryst with

the widow, but not if an infatuation with Lady Varden was the cause of his abrupt alteration towards her.

Sibyl turned and walked in the opposite direction. This complicated matters, though. Sibyl must carefully decide how to proceed.

One thing was certain. She would not give him up.

How many marquesses came on the marriage mart, after all?

That night Sibyl became too bored at Almack's to remain another minute. She'd convinced Lymond to leave with her. Of course Sibyl knew Lymond would not take her directly home. Instead he spirited her into his apartment at Albany where several single gentlemen had rooms, including, at one time, the scandalous Lord Byron.

As Sibyl had hoped, Lymond took her to his bed and relieved her of the agitation of this day. Lymond had been her lover on and off over the past two years, after she'd first succumbed to his seduction, something she did not regret. She only regretted that he was a mere baron and a near penniless one at that. But at least he could always be counted on to be generous with his lovemaking whenever she wished.

Afterwards when he poured them each a glass of claret which they drank still in their *dishabille*, she told him the whole story of Hale's calling upon her and pointedly stating he would not marry her.

He finished his glass of claret and poured a third. 'Come now. You can still use your charms on him. Or entrap him in some compromising way.'

She sighed. 'I doubt entrapping him would do any good. He doesn't care what is expected of a gentleman and it seems I have a rival.'

His brows rose. 'A rival?'

'The worst sort of rival,' she moaned. 'A widow, who can entice in ways that I am not at liberty to.'

He smiled. 'Tell me, who is this enticing widow?'

'Lady Varden.' She spat out the name. 'Why did *she* have to come to town this Season of all Seasons?'

He sat up. 'Varden? Oho, I have some great gossip about Varden. Her late husband, that is.'

She rolled her eyes, not much interested in tales about a dead man. 'Tell if you must.'

He rose and donned his banyan. 'I went to school with Lady Varden's husband, the late Lord Varden. Knew him for years. Even at Oxford. All that time, you know, he had a great friend. Ryland. Do you know Ryland?'

'I was introduced once,' she responded.

He smirked. 'Ryland's great attachment was to Lord Varden. As Varden was to him. They were lovers, do you see?'

She sat up, then. 'Lovers? Varden and Ryland?' She burst out in laughter. 'Oh, that is rich! Why is this not widely known?'

He handed her her shift. 'Varden and Ryland were very discreet. No one ever caught them.'

'Then how can you say it is so?' she asked, climbing off the bed and donning her shift.

'I saw enough to convince me.' He helped her with her corset.

She stepped into her dress. 'But Varden is dead. Does not that make it merely old gossip?'

He tied her dress's laces and put on his coat. 'Varden is beyond scandal, but his widow is not.' Lymond's smile turned malicious. 'Suppose it became known that Varden had been a man of *unnatural propensities*—would that not create quite a scandal for his poor widow?'

'Scandal.' It was Sibyl's turn to smile. 'Yes. It certainly would.' She kissed him on the cheek. 'I knew I could depend upon you.'

'Always, Sibyl, dear.' He lifted a finger. 'But you never heard this from me.'

Just like Lymond to keep his own nose clean.

She kissed him again. 'Never.'

The next morning Sibyl waited until she heard her father rise and descend the stairway to the breakfast room before summoning her maid. She dressed hurriedly, breezing into the breakfast room where her father sat reading the *Morning Post*.

'Good morning, Papa.' She kissed him on his cap and took the seat across from him.

'Morning, Sibyl, my dear.' He put his paper down. 'How was Almack's?'

She signalled the footman first. 'Some tea, please. And fix me a plate of buttered toast and jam. Not too much butter, though. I detest too much butter.' She turned to her father and sighed. 'Almack's was dreadfully dull.'

The footman placed the plate in front of her and stepped back. Crafton gestured for him to leave the room.

He leaned towards Sibyl. 'Did you expect to meet another marquess? I told you Hale was your best prospect and you let him slip through your fingers.'

She glared at him. 'I did not let him slip through my fingers. It turns out Hale has…say…another *interest*.'

Her father's brows rose. 'Another interest?'

She nodded. 'Lady Varden.'

'Lady Varden!' he cried.

'I saw her leaving his house yesterday. Alone. All flustered.' She cocked her head. 'Some sort of tryst, obviously.'

He frowned. 'Lady Varden. Of all people.'

'Oh, Papa,' she pleaded now, blinking over at him as she'd done since a little girl when she wanted something from him. 'Will you help me? I can do nothing without your help.'

She watched his expression melt.

He reached over and patted her hand. 'You know I will help in any way I am able.'

She turned calculating. 'I heard some gossip about Lady Varden. Perhaps you could do something with it?'

She relayed all Lymond told her.

Her father peered at her. 'You are sure of this?'

'Very sure.'

'Well, well.' He seemed lost in thought for a moment. 'We can do something with this, indeed.' He rose from the table. 'Do not fear, my dear. We'll contrive a way to use this to get Hale back for you. I am sure of it.'

Sibyl leaned back in her chair and nibbled on her toast. Her father was nothing if not cunning. And conniving.

Lord Hale did not stand a chance.

Chapter Ten

Nate defied Eliza's directive. He'd been brooding about it for three days. Her way simply would not do.

He walked to the park that morning, around the same time he'd been there two days before, guessing Natalie and her governess would go to the Serpentine to feed the ducks and swans.

As soon as the water came into view he saw them, but he chose not to come close. He leaned against a tree and watched little Natalie gingerly hand a duck a piece of bread, then draw her hand back quickly when the duck grabbed it with its beak. He watched her laugh. Watched her play with some other children there, her governess chatting with her counterparts.

Enchanted. That was the word to describe the feeling of witnessing his daughter twirl, smile, giggle, cry out. Enchanted.

Finally the governess seemed to be saying goodbye to the others and calling to Natalie to come to her. They started walking in his direction, leaving the park, apparently.

He turned and strode away. He'd wanted to see Natalie, but he knew he must not have her see him or speak to him again. If her sensibilities were so fragile, as Eliza said, he did not want to upset her, although he suspected it was not Natalie who feared knowing him. It was Eliza.

Her manner towards him had changed. Was it merely because of their daughter?

He left the park and returned to his town house. Sat in one of the high-backed upholstered chairs in his library and stared into the fireplace where a few lumps of coal burned.

He could not let them go. Both Eliza and Natalie. He could not lose them. This was not death, something so final one never came back. They could be together.

A vision of his mother on her deathbed flashed through his mind, followed by his father's death, his friend in the West Indies, countless officers and soldiers, all alive one day, gone for ever the next.

Yes, it was death that was final, but Eliza and Natalie were alive. He could not let them go.

He rose from the chair.

She might not wish to see him, but Nate would call upon Eliza again. Make her see reason.

Eliza had just walked into her town house from her visit to Henry's man of business who was managing several of her affairs and who was the reason she'd come to London in the first place. At her insistence, she'd demanded he cover everything over which she needed to make decisions and give her everything she needed to sign by the following Monday. She wanted her business concluded.

Begrudgingly he'd agreed. She'd be free then. No reason to stay in London. Of course, she'd not yet let Natalie visit all the toy shops Eliza meant for her to, and she'd not taken Natalie to see the curiosities at the Egyptian Hall or the equestrian displays at Astley's, or the beasts at the Tower.

But she could not have Nate disrupting Natalie's fragile sensibilities, not when she'd seen how easily Natalie broke down merely because Eliza questioned her about

Nate. She'd thought Natalie needed novelty, but the child, Eliza was now convinced, needed stability, the stability of their home outside the village.

And who was she fooling? Eliza also needed to keep Nate from disrupting her own fragile sensibilities. She still wanted what they'd shared that night in the cabin, but he was different now. He was the Marquess of Hale and willing to contract a loveless marriage. And, preferring such a marriage, he'd pushed her away.

Eliza removed her hat and gloves. The knocker sounded and Barlow, her butler, opened the door.

Nate stepped in, removing his hat as he did so. Involuntarily Eliza's heart leapt at the sight of him. So tall and handsome. So comfortingly familiar.

'May I see Lady—?' He spoke to Barlow but stopped when he saw her. 'Lady Varden, I wonder if I might have a word with you.'

Her heart was racing because she did not want to see him—was that not right? Except her heart leapt that very way it had when she'd first spied him at the ball.

'Lord Hale. I—' She ought to say she was needed elsewhere, but could not form the words. Probably because he'd know it was a lie. She put her hand on the banister. 'Yes. Come to the drawing room.'

Nate handed his hat and gloves to Barlow who asked her, 'Shall I send for tea?'

Eliza shook her head. 'No, that will not be necessary.'

She started up the stairs, very aware Nate was right behind her. He stepped ahead of her to open the door for her and she had to pass him as she entered the room. His familiar scent filled her nostrils and it brought her back to when his bare skin touched hers and the glorious pleasure his lovemaking created. Her body remembered, too. All her senses heightened.

She moved away from him as quickly as she could, then

turned to face him. 'What is it, Nate? I thought we had said everything to each other already.'

'I have not said everything.' His voice was deep, earnest. 'I want you to give me a chance, Eliza.'

She stepped back, shaking her head.

'Listen to me,' he said more forcefully. 'We shared something profound together. Our daughter was the result. I know much has happened since, but I want the chance to see if we could—could find some way to be a family, some way for me to be in Natalie's life.'

She laughed. 'How can that be if you are to marry Lady Sibyl?'

He stepped closer. 'I am not going to marry Lady Sibyl.'

She backed away. 'You told me you were going to marry her. In this very room.' After he pushed her away.

'No. I never said I would marry her,' he insisted. 'You assumed, like everyone else apparently assumed I would marry her, but I never offered for her. I never even courted her. After we spoke, I called upon Lady Sibyl and made it clear to her that I never intended to marry her.'

Eliza did not know what to believe. 'You never intended to marry her?'

He held her gaze. 'Never.'

Was he telling her the truth? She herself had seen him be attentive to Lady Sibyl. 'Then why did everyone say you were going to propose to her?'

He shook his head, looking genuinely baffled. 'I do not know why. I was never alone in her company. Her father was always present.'

She lifted her chin. 'Everyone seemed certain you were courting her.'

He countered, 'How could they be certain? Why did they not merely assume I was in Lord Crafton's company, and, therefore, in Lady Sibyl's, as well?'

Eliza's heart was pounding.

He went on. 'I know it is too soon to court you openly, Eliza. But we have a daughter together. I want us all to be together.'

To be with Nate every day? Every night?

No. No. No. He'd pushed her away. Why had he pushed her away if he was not intending to marry Lady Sibyl? His tune only changed when he learned of Natalie.

She'd once fancied that Nate was the only person she could trust, but at this moment it seemed safer not to trust him, not to believe him. She did better by not trusting anyone, not really. Like her parents before him, Henry had taught her that everyone lied, misled and manipulated to get what they wanted.

Perhaps even Nate. Perhaps even her captain.

She bordered on irrational. 'You would tell Natalie you are her father! I cannot have that. Not now. She loved Henry so.' It would undo Natalie. She was certain of it.

His eyes burned into her. 'I did not say I would tell her who I am to her.'

He stated that now, but could she trust him not to tell Natalie later?

'You only want to marry me because of Natalie!' she cried.

He moved even closer and put his hands on her shoulders. 'Eliza. Do we not belong together as a family? Can you not see that? I had no prospects as a soldier, but now I have wealth and I'm told I have influence, that I'm important.' He averted his gaze. 'Or at least the Marquess of Hale is important.'

His hands touching her made her knees weaken. If he only knew how difficult it was for her to not simply melt into his arms and agree to anything as long as he held her.

And loved her.

And did not push her away.

His hand slipped up her neck to gently touch her cheek.

She felt his breath quicken. She even fancied she felt his body flare with heat. Did he know? Did he know how powerful his touch could be? How dangerous?

Oh, yes, he touched her now when he wanted something from her. Like Henry who was at his sweetest when he told her he and Ryland were going away somewhere. *Hunting*, he'd say.

But days ago Nate had thrust her away, just as she was melting into him.

This time she pushed him away.

'No, Nate, you cannot convince me that way.' She took a breath. 'This time I can make the choice. You are not my father forcing me to marry one of his creditors. You are not Henry, marrying me to cover his secret. This time I can decide. I have money. Independence. I do not need to marry anyone.'

'Eliza. I am not forcing you.' His whole body tensed.

It felt like years of emotion burst from her. 'But you are manipulating me! Using Natalie. Using—using what happened between us once. To do what *you* want.' She paced away and then whirled on him again. 'First I must do what my father wants or my whole family is ruined. Then I must do what Henry wants or my whole family is ruined. Well, they are all safe now. Now I do not have to do anything but what I wish to do. What pleases me. I do not have to marry you because you want to be with our daughter. I can do what I want, what I think is best for me. And for her.'

She could not stop herself, even though she despised herself for it. She well knew why he wanted a family.

She remembered.

But she still went on. 'All I want is a quiet place in the country to keep my little girl safe and happy. That is all I want.'

He looked as if she'd thrust him through with a sword. Oh, yes, she hated herself at this moment.

'I am leaving London next week, Nate, so this is all moot.' She was running away. 'Go now. There surely can be nothing else to say.'

'Eliza,' he rasped. Then he straightened and she felt the force of his suppressed anger—and his pain—and felt miserable.

He walked out and she collapsed on the sofa, too unsettled to even cry.

Nate attended the Lords that Monday, but barely heard any of the loud words tossed back and forth. His mind was elsewhere.

On Eliza.

He'd been so certain they belonged together as a family, he, Natalie and Eliza. Now he was not so certain. Eliza could not have been clearer about rejecting him. She did not need him. She did not *want* him.

How many times in his life had he felt that particular sting?

But she could not keep him from Natalie, could she?

Truth was, she could. He had no legal way to claim Natalie as his daughter. Eliza's husband had claimed her and nothing legal could change that. Once again Nate was on the outside looking in, yearning for a family lost to him.

Perhaps he was meant to be alone. Perhaps he would not even make a decent father. His memories of his own father were fleeting. His father's smile. His laugh. The rasping sound of his voice when very sick telling Nate to be strong...

This was all too painful to think about. He must focus. Or think about anything else.

Suddenly the Lords were talking among themselves. The debate was over and he'd not paid attention enough to know what had been discussed or settled. Whatever it was, Lord Crafton was very animatedly talking to some of his more conservative Tory friends. There were lots of head nods and slaps on the shoulder. No doubt that topic would not interest Nate. The longer Nate sat in this august body, the more he realised that his sympathies were more with the common folk in the streets than with men like Crafton. Nate's sentiments were more akin to the Whigs, but most of those men were more protective of their own status than for what the common folk needed.

He glanced at Crafton again.

The man had clearly avoided him. Nate discovered he did not care a whit that Crafton chose to cut him. It seemed as much of a relief to end his association with Crafton as it had been to end things with his daughter.

How long before it became known in society that he'd broken off with Lady Sibyl? Or rather, that he'd never made a commitment to her in the first place? He would not be surprised if Crafton had already spoken about it. Any damage to Lady Sibyl's reputation, as she and the dragon lady insisted there would be, mattered less to him than it had at first. Of course, knowing Lady Sibyl merely wanted his title and that she and her father were willing to manipulate him so she could get it helped a great deal.

When he'd confronted Lady Sibyl, he'd done so not knowing precisely what he wanted—only what he did not want. Now he knew he wanted to be a part of his daughter's life.

And he wanted the Eliza he'd known in the cabin, the Eliza who'd needed him, but she was gone, as was that captain who had shared that cabin with her.

Too bad she was running away to the country. Perhaps if they had time to learn about each other again, time to discover if they could trust one another with their most vulnerable secrets again, they might forge some new sort of relationship.

Of course, he knew precisely where that cabin they

shared was located. Her house could not be far from there. It should be quite easy to discover where she lived. He could travel there and try again.

If only he knew for certain Eliza would not despise him for trying.

To think about this endlessly was useless. Eliza would be gone in a few days, gone with Natalie to live her life without him.

Chapter Eleven

The business that had brought Eliza to London concluded the previous day, so Eliza set the household to packing with plans to leave on the morrow. This Tuesday morning she and Miss Gibbons took Natalie on a last minute excursion to Noah's Ark, a toy store on High Holborn Street.

The store was a child's dream. Dolls of all sorts. Toy soldiers. As befitting the store's name, a variety of Noah's Ark sets with pairs of all kinds of animals. Balls and hoops and skipping ropes. Natalie was silent at first, merely taking in all the wondrous objects created only for the enjoyment or education of children.

'You may select whatever you like,' Eliza told her, taking advantage of a rare opportunity to indulge her daughter.

Like Henry had so often done.

Natalie fixed upon a wall displaying all sorts of beautiful dolls, some made of wood, some of wax, most dressed in the fashions of the day, of the same fine fabrics purchased in the best drapery shops.

Almost immediately Natalie pointed her finger. 'I want that one.'

The doll she selected was not one of the beautiful lady dolls, but a lone gentleman made of wood and dressed in buckskin breeches, a striped waistcoat and black topcoat, complete with an intricately tied, snowy white neckcloth and Hessian boots. He appeared to have real human hair. Blond and curly like Henry's. Painted on blue eyes.

Eliza's heart broke for her. The doll could have been created from Henry's image.

The shop clerk took the doll down from the shelf and handed it to Natalie. She grasped it to her chest.

'Perhaps the child would like one of the lovely lady dolls to match?' he asked.

'No,' Natalie answered firmly. 'Just this one.'

She continued to clutch the doll while Eliza, the clerk and Miss Gibbons all encouraged her to pick out more toys. She was finally persuaded to accept one of the beautifully carved and painted Noah's Ark sets, a ball, a skipping rope, a set of knucklebones and three wooden puzzles, one of which was of the latest boundaries of the Continent.

And the gentleman doll who looked like Henry.

She did not want it to be wrapped and delivered to the house that afternoon, like the other toys. Natalie carried it against her chest while they stopped in to Arpthorpe's Stay and Corset Shop and took some coaxing to put it down long enough to be measured for some children's stays. She, Miss Gibbons and Eliza all were fitted for new undergarments, as well as for new shoes when they visited Wood's shoe shop next.

When the hackney coach returned them to Eliza's town house and Barlow opened the door, Natalie greeted him with, 'Look, Barlow! Look at my new doll!'

'What a lovely doll, Miss Natalie,' the old butler managed to say, but he looked distracted. He closed the door. 'Lady Varden, I must speak with you.'

Eliza removed her hat. 'What is it, Barlow?'

He inclined his head to the stairway. 'We have visitors, ma'am.'

Nate? Her heart leapt. 'Who is it, Barlow?'

His expression turned grave. 'I am afraid it is Sir John and Lady Wolfdon.'

Her father and mother.

Eliza felt her face heat. What were they doing here?

'Grandmama and Grandpapa?' Natalie cried excitedly. She turned to her mother. 'May I show them my doll?'

'Yes. Yes,' she said. 'Tell them I will be up directly.'

Miss Gibbons gave Eliza a concerned look. 'May I help in any way, ma'am?' The governess knew some of the difficulties her parents could create.

'Oh, Miss Gibbons!' She sighed. 'I have no idea. I suppose just amuse Natalie. It should not be long before my mother or father send her away.' Eliza closed her eyes and took a deep breath. She turned to Barlow. 'Are they staying?' she asked, her voice squeaking.

'I gather so,' he responded. 'They've come with luggage. And their valet and lady's maid. I've had the maids ready rooms for them all, just in case.'

'Oh, the poor maids. What a day for them,' Eliza said. 'First all the packing, now *this*…' And now they would need to unpack as well.

There was no way she would leave her parents on their own in London and she had no hope she could persuade them to return to the country after travelling this far. 'Barlow, I am so sorry, but could you get messages to Arpthorpe's Shop and Wood's and have them deliver our purchases here instead of shipping them to the house in Sandleigh?'

He bowed. 'Very good, m'lady.'

So much extra work for everyone. 'Thank you, Barlow.'

Miss Gibbons had already started up the stairs. Eliza followed her. The governess stood aside so that Eliza entered the drawing room first.

Natalie sat on the sofa with her grandmother, showing

her gentleman doll. She'd taken the doll's coat off and the two of them were examining its construction.

'The coat is very well made, is it not?' Eliza's mother examined it as if she were inspecting the work of a tailor at Weston's. She turned to Eliza's father. 'Do you not think that is amazing, John, dear, that the doll's coat is stitched so fine?'

Her father folded the newspaper he was reading down and glanced fondly at Natalie. 'Indeed. He is quite a fine doll, Natty.'

Her parents might be many things Eliza could not admire, but they were doting grandparents who were generous with their affection towards Natalie. Until they tired of her, that was.

Eliza finally spoke. 'Hello, Mama. Papa.'

They immediately turned to her with huge smiles. Her father rose from his chair and her mother extended her hands for Eliza to grasp.

'Oh, Lizzie,' her mother exclaimed. 'How good to see you! We have missed you excessively.' She turned to Natalie and gave her a kiss on the top of her head. 'And this dear child as well.'

Eliza needed to keep her anger in check. For Natalie's sake. 'Why are you here?'

Her mother gave Natalie a hug. 'Why, you should know why we are here, Lizzie. It was all in the letter.'

'I did not receive a letter.' And she doubted one had been written.

Her father spoke. 'Needed to come to town. Important matters being discussed here and I must say my piece about them. Have to help, you know.'

'Say your piece where?' Eliza asked. Her father was a baronet. He did not sit in the Lords and he certainly had not been elected to the Commons.

'Well. To the others,' her father responded. 'You know.'

He started for the door. 'In fact, I fear I must take my leave. Burnie is expecting me. Must tell him I've arrived.'

Burnie was Lord Blackburn, one of her father's gambling friends.

'Papa!' Eliza cried. 'No gaming. Remember? You gave your word.'

His good humour disappeared. 'What do you take me for, Daughter?'

'Do not forget to have the announcement of our arrival put in the papers,' her mother chirped.

'I will indeed, my dear.' He stopped to give Natalie a pinch on her cheek and hurried out, nodding to Miss Gibbons as he passed her.

After he left her mother grumbled. 'I would wager he is not calling upon Blackburn at all, but that detestable Gwendolyn Holback.'

Lady Holback was a widow with an uncertain reputation who was one of the many of Eliza's father's past paramours.

'Mama, I was about to return to Sandleigh—'

Her mother interrupted. 'Oh, that is very well, Lizzie. Your father and I do not need you here.'

Oh, but they did need her. Who knew what mischief they would be into without some supervision? Eliza already feared her father would start gambling and she'd no doubt her mother had plans of her own in town.

There was no use in suggesting her parents stay with one of her sisters. Her sisters' husbands had forbidden that long ago. Besides, why disrupt her sisters' happiness? They both so enjoyed the Season in London.

'We will stay a little longer, then,' Eliza said.

Her mother leaned down to Natalie. 'Grandmama must freshen up, my love. I have many things to do, but I will look in on you later.'

'Very well, Grandmama,' Natalie said happily, redressing her treasured doll.

'You enjoy your lovely new doll.' Her mother smiled. 'We must find someone to make him more clothes. A whole proper wardrobe.'

Natalie hugged her. 'Thank you, Grandmama.' She jumped down from the sofa and left the room with Miss Gibbons.

Eliza turned to her mother again. 'Mama, you and Papa must behave yourselves if you are to stay here. I cannot afford to pay off any debts you make and I'll not have Natalie upset by any antics.'

Her mother smoothed her skirts. 'I have no idea what you are talking about, Lizzie dear. To think your father and I would ever do anything to upset that child. He, of course, will try *my* patience, but I will bear it as I always do.'

Which was to find petty ways to seek revenge or engage in screaming fits with him.

She started for the door but stopped to pat Eliza's hand. 'We should call upon Susan and Joanna today, dear. I will be ready in half an hour.'

Nate sat in the coffee room at White's, reading the *Morning Chronicle*, the newspaper with a decided Whig bent. Most of the members of White's were confirmed Tories, so he supposed he caused a few lifted brows, but then, he'd always caused lifted brows ever since he assumed his title. There were others in the room, seated at a few other tables, but the room was not at all busy.

Most, like Nate, would be off to Parliament later that day. Nate supposed they were discussing the issues at hand, issues which he was attempting to learn more about, issues about which he was changing his mind.

He'd often met Crafton here for a midday repast before this, but now he sat alone. It was better than isolating himself. Occasionally some of the gentlemen stopped by to converse with him.

He lowered the paper and took a sip of tea.

Of all people, Lord Crafton entered and surveyed the room. Nate lifted his paper again but needed to lower it when the man approached his table.

'Hale. Good day to you.'

It was a more cordial greeting than Nate anticipated, especially after being cut by the gentleman in recent days. Nate decided to be civil. He certainly wanted no unpleasantness in this august place.

He nodded. 'Crafton.'

The older gentleman smiled. 'Mind if I join you?'

The last thing Nate wanted, but he gestured to the chair across from him. 'By all means.'

Crafton settled in the chair and summoned the servant to bring him a glass of port.

When the servant left, Crafton placed his hands on the table. 'Have something to talk with you about.'

Nate did not expect anything good. He simply waited.

'This is something I am certain you will support.' He leaned forward. 'I am resurrecting the Society for the Reformation of Manners.'

'And that is?' Nate hadn't a clue.

'It was active several years ago, to rid the city—nay, the country of vice.' He looked smug. 'First, I will start with the Society of Original Gentlemen, you know, members of Parliament, but also lawyers, judges and the like. Then we'll organise the Second Society, tradesmen and those who can produce a blacklist of offenders, and, of course, the Association of Constables and Moral Guardians—'

'Stop. Moral Guardians? What the devil is this society all about?'

'Why, to rid the city of vice. To protect our citizens from the moral corruption of men who would perform unnatural acts on other men…' The man pontificated as though he stood on a pulpit.

Nate raised his paper again. 'I'll not support that.'

Crafton rustled in his seat. 'What? Why ever not?'

He lowered the paper again. 'The country suffers from unrest, hunger, unemployment. Those are more important matters to address.'

Crafton's expression turned indignant. 'What could be more important than ridding the country of vice? I was certain you would embrace this cause.'

Nate levelled his gaze at the man. 'I've never known any men who engaged in such acts unless it was with someone of the same nature. Let them be. I certainly want no part in seeing such men hang or pilloried for what seems natural to them.'

Crafton stood, just as the servant brought his drink. 'Natural? I am appalled, sir!' He raised his voice. 'First you thrust away my daughter, now this. You, sir, are not a gentleman.'

'I made no offer to your daughter, sir. Never. Not even once.' Nate spoke loud enough for at least some in the room to hear him. 'I regret that others misinterpreted that fact.'

'I expect they all hold you in the contempt that I do!' Crafton turned and strode past the servant who carried his drink on a tray.

'Place it on my account,' Nate told the servant, then lowered his voice. 'And enjoy it for yourself.'

After Crafton noisily left the room, two gentlemen rose from their chairs and walked over to Nate.

Lord Jeffrey Everly and Mr Bentham.

Eliza's brothers-in-law.

He half expected them to demand he leave the club, but instead they sat down and seemed to be suppressing smiles.

'I take it you did not agree to join the new society Crafton is organising,' Bentham said.

Nate remained on his guard. 'I did not. It seems a distraction from the work we should be engaged in.'

'Certainly a distraction!' Everly agreed. 'But it makes him important, does it not? That is the whole object of this, my father says.' His father, the Marquess of Locksworth.

Both Locksworth and Bentham's father, Viscount Winbray, sat in the Lords with Nate. And Crafton.

'Pay no attention to Crafton,' Bentham insisted. He lowered his brows. 'But if you do not mind, what can you tell us of this break with Lady Sibyl? We heard what you said to Crafton. I suspect his version of events is quite different from your own.'

Everly added, 'Crafton's version is out there, Hale, saying you are in breach of promise to her. Our wives may undoubtedly be depended upon to present your side of this, if you so desire. Let gossip work for you, so to speak.'

Nate had not expected such offers of support.

'I can tell you little more than what I just said to Lord Crafton,' he responded. 'I never spoke of marriage to Lady Sibyl. I never proposed. In fact, I was never alone in her company.' But perhaps these men, too, would say he used Lady Sibyl ill. 'If by spending so much time with Crafton, I left the impression that I would propose to his daughter, then I am sorry for it. But I cannot control what others assume.'

Everly gave a dry laugh. 'That is what gossips do, I'm afraid. Assume whatever they wish.'

'We'll have our wives repeat what you've said here,' Bentham added. 'It might help.'

'Perhaps they will not wish to become involved,' Nate said.

Everly laughed. 'Oh, they'll be delighted to be involved.'

At that moment two older gentlemen emerged from the back dining room, a little unsteady on their feet.

One of them loudly said, 'Shall we see if anyone is in the card room?'

'Absolutely,' the other responded. 'Excellent idea.'

'Good God,' Bentham said. 'He is in town? How can that be?'

'My wife knew nothing of this, I am certain,' Everly responded.

'Who is that?' Nate asked.

'Sir John Wolfdon. Our father-in-law,' Everly responded. 'Where the devil is he staying? At Lizzie's, do you think?'

'Must be,' Bentham replied.

Everly shook his head. 'I cannot see her agreeing to that.'

'She probably did not agree. You know how they are.' Bentham turned to Nate. 'So sorry, Hale. We must take our leave. Sir John has a bit of a gambling problem. We cannot allow him to sit down to cards.'

'Let us get him out of there.' Bentham sighed.

Apparently Eliza's father had descended upon her uninvited? Nate's first thought was to help. How odd a thought, since Eliza did not wish to have anything to do with him.

He could watch out for Sir John on his own, though.

Eliza need not know.

Eliza and her mother called upon Susan first. Eliza was certain her mother hoped Susan's mother-in-law, Lady Locksworth, would be at home. Her mother liked pretending that Lady Locksworth and she were great friends, although Eliza suspected the Marchioness merely acted friendly because her son was married to Susan.

The butler announced them. 'Elizabeth, Lady Varden, and Lady Wolfdon.'

'Mama!' two voices cried as they entered.

What luck, Eliza thought, Joanna was visiting Susan as well. They would need to make only one call.

'What are you doing here?' Susan demanded, barely making her voice sound welcoming.

It did not matter. Their mother was oblivious.

'Well, your father and I just arrived in town and I could not wait another minute before seeing my girls.' She clasped their hands and air-kissed their cheeks and glanced around the room.

There were no other callers at the moment.

'Where is Lady Locksworth? I was so hoping to see her again,' their mother asked.

'My mother-in-law has the headache,' Susan responded. 'And you just missed Lady Ferndale and her daughter. They called a few minutes ago.'

'What a shame.' Their mother sat in one of the brocade-upholstered chairs.

This drawing room had been opened up to the room adjoining it to make the ballroom that night of the Locksworth ball—that night she found Nate again. Danced with him—this day the connecting doors were closed and the furniture arranged for friendly seating. On the table in front of them was a pot of tea and cups and a tray of biscuits decorated in pink and yellow icing.

'Tea, Mama?' Susan asked.

Their mother nodded.

Joanna turned to Eliza. 'Lizzie! We have not even greeted you! How lovely to see you. You did not tell us Mama would be in town.'

That last was said with a slight chiding tone.

'I did not know,' Eliza responded, sitting on the sofa. 'Mama and Papa surprised me.'

'Now I did send you a letter,' her mother added defensively.

'A letter I never received,' Eliza said under her breath.

Joanna nodded knowingly.

'Your father is to put an announcement in the newspapers that we are in town, so I expect to receive invitations soon. But tell me how you both are. What is happening in town? I am eager to hear it all.'

Susan and Joanna told her all about the balls they had attended and who was in town and what the latest fashions were showing.

Susan turned towards Eliza. 'Oh, Lizzie! Have you heard the latest about Lord Hale?'

'Lord Hale?' her mother chimed in. 'Did not he die and his sons, as well? I believe Lady Ferndale wrote me of it.'

'This is the new Lord Hale, Mama,' Joanna exclaimed. 'Everyone thought he would propose to Lady Sibyl—you know of Lady Sibyl, Mama. She is Crafton's daughter.'

'You remember Hale surely, Lizzie,' Susan said. 'He danced with you at our ball.'

Her mother's attention swivelled to her at that. 'Hmmm. A marquess, Lizzie.'

'But listen,' Susan insisted. 'Apparently he cried off. Francis told me that Crafton is threatening a breach of promise suit.'

'I cannot see how that would do,' Joanna said. 'Those so rarely are successful. It does seem so very bad of him, though. He seemed to be courting her. Everyone thought so.'

Eliza bit her tongue, although she yearned to defend him. He'd made no promise to Lady Sibyl, he'd said. She believed him, in this, at least.

Their mother's eyes widened. 'A marquess in need of a wife. That is a good thing. We must see that he becomes interested in Lizzie.'

'Mama!' Joanna scolded. 'Lizzie still is not mixing in society. She is not ready.'

Eliza was grateful Joanna leapt to her defence.

'That is right, Mama,' Eliza added. 'I have not accepted invitations, except for Lady Locksworth's ball. I could not refuse that one.'

'Refuse invitations?' their mother cried. 'That will not do. I insist you accompany me. It will look odd if your father and I accept invitations and you refuse them. You must go.'

She must, Lizzie thought, if only to keep her parents out of mischief.

Her mother turned to her sisters. 'And how are those dear children of yours? What do you hear of them?'

'Hear of them?' Susan exclaimed. 'Why, they are here. Joanna brought Basil to visit Edgar. They are in the nursery.'

Their mother clasped her hands in delight. 'Oh, have them brought to me! I long to see them.'

They all knew that having the children there would keep them from any of the topics their mother did not wish to discuss.

Chapter Twelve

That week Everly and Bentham had met Nate at White's every day for nuncheon. Nate thought it ironic that these two men who befriended him were so connected to Eliza. What's more, in the Lords that week their fathers, too, made a special point of including Nate in various ways. It helped a great deal in counteracting the ostracising Crafton seemed bent on.

Through Everly and Bentham Nate learned that Eliza had not left London as she'd told him she would, that the arrival of her parents prevented her from leaving. The two men also insisted that Nate attend Lady Ferndale's ball that evening, maintaining it was important for him to be seen in society, to show that he had not wronged Lady Sibyl, as she and her father made it be known. Better to be seen at some entertainments, they said, and to encounter both Lady Sibyl and her father with politeness. Even if they were not apt to be polite in return.

But it was not encountering Lady Sibyl or Crafton that concerned Nate. It was seeing Eliza. Oh, he yearned to see her, to see with his own eyes how she fared, but he had no wish to alienate her further.

So here he was, on his way to the Ferndale ball. On foot. It seemed foolish to bother Foster, his coachman, to drive him the few streets to Grosvenor Street where Lord and Lady Ferndale lived. Besides, the brisk evening air helped to ready him for what he always found unpleasant. The noise. The crowd. The nagging sense that he did not truly belong there.

But he was accustomed to walking into places where he was not entirely welcome. His entire school life had required it and many of his army postings. He'd served in regiments where some of the other officers cared more about family connections than skill on the battlefield. The impoverished distant nephew of a marquess was never lofty enough.

Some of those schoolmates and some of those officers attended the same entertainments as he these days. They mostly avoided him, not knowing how to treat him now that his title was higher than their own. Everly and Bentham were enough younger that they'd not known him in school. Perhaps that made it easier for them to befriend him.

Tonight, though, he did not care what the lot of them thought of him. Tonight he only cared about Eliza. That he do nothing to further set her against him. His goal was to be on friendly terms with her.

He reached Grosvenor Street and made his way through the crush of carriages to enter the door attended by a footman who gave instructions where to leave one's hat. As often happened at these festivities, there was a crush of people waiting to be announced to the ballroom and to shake hands with the host and hostess.

As Nate took his place in line, he spied Eliza with the man he recognised as her father and an older woman who must be her mother. Once finding her, he had great difficulty keeping his eyes off her.

She wore the same dress she had worn at the Locksworth ball, which pleased him somehow. It seemed practical. As if she, too, no longer cared much for society balls.

The crowd shifted a bit and Nate found himself even closer to her, close enough to hear snippets of conversation.

Her mother spoke. 'We really must get you to the modiste, Lizzie dear.'

He could not hear Eliza's reply.

Her mother looked bursting with excitement. Her father, impatient. Eliza, as if she wished to be anywhere else but where she was.

A few people greeted Nate. Several did not, but that was what he expected. Finally the line neared the door to the ballroom. He heard Eliza and her parents announced.

'Elizabeth, Viscountess Varden. Sir John Wolfdon and Lady Wolfdon.'

His turn came soon after. Eliza and her parents appeared to have left the receiving line just as he stepped up to the butler who announced the guests.

The butler raised his voice. 'The Marquess of Hale.'

Nate saw Eliza turn her head and quickly look away.

That was not a good sign.

Other heads also turned when he entered. Nate had no illusions. They wished to see the Marquess of Hale, not Nate. And he supposed they were eager to see if the Marquess who had jilted Lady Sibyl had suddenly grown horns. He heard Lady Sibyl's laugh and knew she'd deliberately ignored his arrival.

Lord Everly saw him, though, and approached. The two men shook hands.

'Hale, you did come! That is grand.' Everly did look pleased.

His wife stopped talking to Eliza and her parents and cocked her head towards her husband.

Everly leaned towards Nate's ear. 'That's a hint,' he said. 'She wants me to introduce you to Sir John and Lady Wolfdon.'

Nate could not refuse. He let Everly lead him to them.

And to Eliza.

Nate was most aware of her presence as the introductions were made. Then Everly was beckoned by his father and had to leave. Nate was alone with them.

Lady Wolfdon turned a broad smile on to him. 'I read of how you gained the title, Hale.'

'It was quite unexpected, ma'am,' he responded.

Her smile was replaced with an exaggerated look of sympathy. 'Oh, yes. How dreadful to lose both your uncle and cousins.'

'Knew your uncle slightly,' piped up Sir John. 'Cannot say I liked him.'

Eliza winced.

But Nate nearly grinned. It was refreshing to find someone in society who was not unfailingly correct. 'He was a difficult man.'

'Really, John! What a thing to say,' Lady Wolfdon scolded.

Her husband argued back, 'Why? It was the truth.'

They continued their exchange in sotto voce so as not to be overheard, but, of course, they could be.

Nate covered the awkward moment by greeting Eliza. 'Good evening, Lady Varden.' And her sister. 'Lady Jeffrey.'

'Good evening, Hale.' Lady Jeffrey glanced towards her parents. 'How nice you could meet our parents.'

He did almost grin, then. 'It has been my pleasure.' He bowed. 'Please forgive me. I am being summoned from across the room.'

Lady Jeffrey seemed to accept this little falsehood, but Nate knew Eliza saw right through it. He only hoped she understood that he left them for her sake, so she would not have to be in his unwanted company for long.

Everly stopped him as he was about to pass by. 'I am

certain we will talk later, Hale.' The man grinned. 'There is bound to be something happening to talk about.'

Nate returned the smile, feeling acutely Eliza's effort not to look at him. 'Let us hope it will not be about me.'

Everly leaned close for a moment. 'Or my in-laws.'

Nate nodded and walked into the crush of people in the room. Away from Eliza.

As soon as Nate walked away, Eliza's mother stopped her argument with her father and clasped Eliza's arm. 'You all but cut the man, Lizzie! What is wrong with you? He is a marquess!'

'Mama, leave her alone,' Susan chided. 'She hardly knows Hale.'

'Leave her alone?' her mother cried. 'I was merely trying to help.'

The two of them started arguing.

Eliza stepped back. Little did they know she knew Hale better than anyone in the room. She'd borne his child, after all.

Eliza was afraid he might attend this ball. A marquess of any sort was sure to receive an invitation and why wouldn't he come? Especially because Lady Sibyl and her father would likely be here. Her captain would be willing to face them, as unpleasant as that might be. Her captain had taught her to face difficult situations, so why wouldn't he do the same? It was in his character.

She was not at all sure she wanted to see her captain in this new Marquess. It made her decision to push him away more difficult to bear.

Eliza had to admit he looked splendid in his black trousers, black stockings and long-tailed coat, contrasted with snowy white shirt and neckcloth. Of course, many of the gentlemen in the room were dressed in a similar style, although some wore breeches instead of the more modern trousers. Somehow Nate outshone them.

According to Susan and Joanna, the *ton* was all abuzz with how Lady Sibyl was telling everyone Lord Hale had jilted her. Eliza believed him, though, that he'd never offered for her or mentioned marriage to her at all. He must have known he'd have to face Lady Sibyl here. And that everyone would be watching him.

She sighed. Nate's difficulties could not matter to her. She'd rejected him as thoroughly as any woman could reject a man's suit. Her bridges were burned.

It had been the right decision, though. She was afraid to trust him. He'd pushed her away! Like Henry had done. And could she really trust him with Natalie? Of course he would want Natalie to know he was her father. She was his only family.

No. Eliza was better off alone. And luckily she could be alone. She had wealth and independence enough to care for herself and for Natalie. She did not need anyone and no one but Natalie needed her.

Her father suddenly announced he'd spied Lord Blackburn and dashed off. Her mother immediately craned her neck to see where he'd headed.

'He's not looking for Burnie,' she huffed. 'He's off to chat up that detestable widow, Lady Holback. *Gwendolyn.*' She practically spat out the name. She straightened her spine and lifted her chin. 'Well, two can play at that game. See how he likes it if I flirt with Percy Fawlsley.'

'Mama!' Susan cried.

But their mother swept away.

There were her parents to worry over, though.

How much control did she have over her mother and father, really? They would dive headlong into disaster no matter what she did. At least everyone else in the family would not perish with them if they managed to make a shambles of their lives.

'Oh, goodness!' Susan cried. 'How will we ever keep an eye on them?'

'It is impossible,' Eliza replied in a resigned tone. 'But I am certain we will hear if anything goes awry.'

Susan groaned. 'Likely the whole room will hear it.' She gazed at Eliza and smiled. 'Well, we should try to enjoy ourselves. Shall we take a turn around the room? We can look for Joanna.'

As they strolled through the room, various friends and acquaintances greeted them. Susan was stopped by Lady Ferndale's daughter and the two carried on a lively conversation. Eliza stood by politely.

Suddenly Lady Sibyl approached, smiling sweetly. 'Lady Varden, how nice to see you again. I do hope you are enjoying yourself.'

Why was Lady Sibyl greeting her at all? They'd not even been introduced.

Eliza answered politely, though. 'We just arrived. The ball seems pleasant enough.'

'Very pleasant indeed.' Lady Sibyl looked her up and down. 'You do look lovely tonight, but then you also looked lovely in that dress at the Locksworth ball, did you not?'

Eliza almost laughed. What a charming insult!

'It is a favourite of mine,' she responded.

Eliza's gown was nothing remarkable. A pale blue overdress, with white muslin underneath and trimmed with lace. It was over two Seasons old, but it packed well and Lacy insisted she pack at least one ball gown, just in case.

Lady Sibyl's smile stiffened. 'It becomes you. Everyone says so.' She curtsied. 'Have a good evening.'

Eliza curtsied back. 'And you, as well, Lady Sibyl.'

To Eliza's surprise, Nate appeared at her side.

'I realise you would prefer I stay away,' he said, rather stiffly. 'But I was uneasy. What did she say to you, Eliza?'

He inclined his head towards Lady Sibyl, who was now turning her charm on someone else.

'Nothing of import, Nate,' she responded cautiously. 'But why would you ask?'

'I have lately discovered she has a biting tongue. I feared she'd abused you with some nasty comment or tale because of me.'

'Because of you?' she asked.

He shrugged. 'Well, perhaps she saw me greeting you and was jealous.' One corner of his mouth lifted in a wry smile. 'Or is that too vain of me to think I had something to do with it?'

She could not help but smile in return. 'Probably.'

A grin flashed across his face.

This was incredible. She and Nate were conversing comfortably, as if they were old friends. She'd thought he would despise her, not worry about her.

Eliza leaned forward in a conspiratorial manner. 'Lady Sibyl told me I *always* look lovely in this dress.'

He looked puzzled.

'She let me know she noticed that I've worn the same gown twice.'

'That was what she said?' He still looked perplexed.

Eliza could not help but laugh. 'Well, if you were a woman you would realise it was nasty. As insults go, though, she rather impressively clothed it in compliments.'

His mouth twitched. 'If she has something to say about your shoes, let me know. That I will not tolerate.'

Eliza laughed again.

Lady Sibyl swivelled around, but Nate had already walked away.

Eliza instantly relaxed. She might enjoy this ball after all.

Joanna and Susan descended upon her.

'Lord Hale spoke to you,' Susan said. 'Mother will be pleased.'

'I believe she is too busy with Lord Fawlsley to notice,' Eliza replied.

'Never mind Hale, what did Lady Sibyl want?' Joanna asked.

'To insult me for wearing the same dress twice.'

'How unkind of her.' Joanna glared at Lady Sibyl. 'She must be fancying you as a rival.'

'Goodness. He barely spoke to me.' But Eliza was grateful for every word.

'He did dance with you at the Locksworth ball, though. She would remember that.' Joanna leaned in conspiratorially. 'Francis told me that the gossip around town is false. That Hale never offered for Lady Sibyl and has made that clear to her. So this whole breach of promise thing is simply her saving face. Francis thinks the rumour that Hale would propose was started by Lady Sibyl or her father in the first place.' Joanna glanced over at Hale, who was some distance away, still conversing with Joanna's husband and father-in-law. 'If so, it failed miserably.'

Susan joined in. 'Jeffrey said the same thing. Seems she was intent on marrying a marquess.'

'Then she would not have to worry about ever wearing the same ball gown twice,' Eliza added.

Joanna and Susan broke into giggles.

'Oh, Lizzie,' Joanna said. 'I have not heard you joke in a very long time.'

At that moment Lord Lymond sidled up to them. 'Good evening, ladies. How are you all this fine night?'

Eliza's light heart fled.

'Lord Lymond,' Susan responded somewhat icily.

The orchestra stopped tuning their instruments and began playing something harmonious, signalling that the first set was about to begin. Everly and Bentham emerged from the crowd to collect their wives for the first dance, leaving Eliza standing with Lymond.

He leaned closer. 'Forgive me. I have promised this set to another, but I am certain other gentlemen will be lining up to dance with you.'

'I am unconcerned,' Eliza responded.

She backed away, making room for those who were taking their positions on the dance floor. Her father, she noticed, partnered Lady Holback and Fawlsley led her mother on to the floor. Lymond escorted Lady Sibyl.

Eliza glanced away, not wanting to see if Nate danced with anyone. She went in search of refreshment, feeling suddenly parched.

Eliza made her way to the refreshment room, where several other guests had also gathered. She picked up a glass of wine, intending to return to her quiet corner to wait out the ball, but still keep an eye on her parents. And Nate. She knew she could not help gazing his way.

Lord Crafton appeared at her elbow.

'Lady Varden.' His greeting seemed sinister.

'Sir?' she responded.

How many people knew she'd avoided marriage to this man? Her father, of course. Perhaps not even her mother, though. Ironic that both she and Nate had almost been trapped into marriage in this family.

'I noticed your parents are here,' he said. 'How very nice for you.'

Not nice at all, she thought.

He picked up a wine glass and sipped. 'I thought I'd see if Sir John was interested in a game of whist.'

Playing whist with Crafton had been precisely how Eliza's father wound up so in debt to him all those years ago. Before Henry married her.

'I believe my father is here to dance, not play cards,' Eliza responded.

At least that was what he'd promised to do. Her father had vowed on his honour never to risk more money than he carried in his pockets. He'd promised this in exchange for Henry paying his debts.

Her father had kept the bargain with Henry, but would he do so now that Eliza had inherited the control of his money?

'Well, that is a pity,' Crafton said. 'Sir John does so love a good game of whist. Or loo.'

Crafton was taunting her, Eliza realised. But why? Surely he could not hold a grudge against her all these years. She'd always felt she'd been offered as somewhat of a consolation prize and that Crafton had much preferred the money. Had she been mistaken?

In any event, she disliked the man. She was glad Nate would not be his son-in-law.

She curtsied to Crafton and walked away.

Nate was about to enter the refreshment room when he saw Eliza there. He stepped back, out of her sight. He did not want to assume their brief pleasant conversation meant she would want him by her side the whole night.

Crafton approached her instead.

What the devil? First Lady Sibyl, now Crafton? Was Crafton going to plague her like Lady Sibyl had done? Because of Nate?

Crafton's approach seemed very deliberate. And she'd seemed less than pleased with his company.

Odd how Nate now saw Crafton and Lady Sibyl both as false and opportunist when before he'd merely thought them helpful. In no way was Nate going to allow Crafton—or Lady Sibyl—to bother Eliza.

But he waited for Eliza to leave the room. Crafton fol-

lowed later. Nate got his glass of wine and stepped back
into the ballroom. He scanned the room until he found
Eliza in an inconspicuous corner watching the dancing.

He started to walk towards her when the set ended and
the couples scattered and suddenly he stood face to face
with Lady Sibyl on the arm of her dance partner, Lymond.

'Well, Hale,' Lymond said. 'Not dancing?'

'The ball has just begun,' Nate replied which was no
answer.

'Hale is a reluctant dancer, Lymond,' Lady Sibyl chimed
in. 'Not born to it, like you and I.'

'No indeed,' agreed Nate, feeling unfazed and damned
grateful he owed her no more attention than this. He could
not resist, though. 'Fortunately, my title and fortune make
the matter of dancing fairly irrelevant.'

Lady Sibyl gave him a haughty look. 'Come, Lymond.'
They walked away.

Bentham and his wife hurried to his side.

'Was that Lady Sibyl?' Bentham asked. 'How are you,
by the way.'

'It was,' he responded. 'And I am perfectly unscathed.'

'Oh, good,' his wife said. 'She was civil to you?'

He laughed. 'Almost civil. Just one minor jab at my lack
of an aristocratic upbringing.'

'The witch!' exclaimed Bentham.

'She is full of ill manners tonight, apparently,' his wife
added. 'Susan and I cannot for the life of us figure why
she would speak to Lizzie at all. I am not certain they were
ever introduced.'

It seemed clear to Nate that Crafton and Lady Sibyl's
sudden interest in Eliza was due the failure of their manip-
ulations to make Nate propose marriage. But could dancing
with Eliza once and conversing with her briefly—which
was all they could know of it—cause their spite?

It made no sense.

Chapter Thirteen

The ball dragged on for Nate and he'd not had a chance to catch Eliza alone. She seemed to keep herself in company or her sisters made certain she was not alone. But suddenly she rose and seemed to look around with a worried expression on her face. She left her seat and walked around the ballroom as if searching for someone.

Nate contrived to encounter her. 'What is it, Eliza?'

She glanced around. 'My father. I cannot find him. I am afraid he is in the card room.'

Everly and Bentham had told him of Sir John's gambling problem.

'Let us go look there.' Nate offered his arm.

He escorted her to the doorway of the game room where several gentlemen and a few ladies were deep in their cards and some others stood watching, Crafton among them.

Crafton watched one table with a smug smile on his face. Sir John played at that table.

Eliza started to enter the room. 'I must get him out of there.'

Nate held her back. 'Allow me, Eliza. If you go, it will only embarrass him. You do not want that, do you?'

'Maybe he deserves to be embarrassed,' she huffed. 'He promised he would not gamble!'

'Still, let me go,' Nate insisted. 'I promise I'll get him out of there. It is almost time for supper. I'll bring him to the supper room.'

She finally nodded.

Nate wandered over to the table where Sir John sat with four other players. The game was loo. Sir John did not look well at all. His expression was pinched and he swayed in his chair. A trickle of sweat slid down his face.

Crafton watched him intently.

Sir John gulped down a glass of wine as the last hand ended. He lost.

'Let us settle matters,' one of the gentlemen said. He was the clear winner and one by one the men paid up, most good-naturedly.

That left Sir John.

'Fifty guineas, Sir John,' the man said.

'Fifty…' Sir John turned pale. He stuttered. 'I—I—I do not… I—I—could possibly—'

Nate stepped forward.

'There you are, Sir John.' He made his voice jovial. 'I have been looking for you.'

Sir John blinked, obviously confused.

Nate went on. 'To pay my debt to you, sir. I said I would.'

'Debt?' Sir John's expression turned puzzled.

'Yes,' Nate responded. 'The sixty guineas?'

The older man's eyes widened. 'Sixty guineas?'

'I wonder if I could send the money to you tomorrow,' Nate continued.

'Send it to me?' The man was still baffled.

'I did not wish to carry such a sum on my person to-night,' Nate explained.

The man to whom Sir John owed the money, piped up. 'Sir John, perhaps Hale here can send me the fifty guineas directly. Save you the trouble.'

Perhaps he thought this was a more certain way of getting his winnings.

'Fifty guineas?' Nate pretended not to understand.

'My—my—debt of honour, sir,' Sir John managed to say.

'Ah, I see.' Nate nodded. 'That will be no trouble at all. Give me your direction. You will have your fifty guineas tomorrow.'

He and the other man made the arrangements. The man bowed and left them. Nate noticed Crafton backed away, as well.

Sir John collapsed in the chair and put his head in his hands.

Nate touched his arm. 'Shall I help you into supper, Sir John?' he asked quietly.

Sir John nodded and let Nate help him up. He leaned on Nate as they headed to the door.

Sir John stopped him before they left the room. 'Do you really owe me sixty guineas?' he asked.

Nate smiled. 'No, but you looked like you needed some help.'

'I could never have paid him back,' he said. 'I—I promised not to gamble. Not to gamble more than I could lose.'

'Perhaps you must not gamble at all,' Nate responded.

They walked further, but Sir John stopped him again. 'So...will you be sending me the remaining ten guineas tomorrow?'

Nate's lips twitched in amusement. 'Now what do you think?'

Sir John sighed. 'I think you will not.'

As they left the room Nate noticed Crafton watching with a frown on his face.

Sir John was unsteady on his feet, probably from drink, so Nate walked with him all the way to the supper room. The music had ended and everyone headed there. The supper room was really three rooms set with tables and chairs. They looked in two of the rooms for Sir John's family. Nate spied Everly and Bentham in the second room. And Eliza, seated with her sisters and mother.

Nate walked Sir John to the table.

When they reached it, Lady Wolfdon wheeled on her husband. 'Where were you, John? With *Gwendolyn Holback*, I suspect.'

Sir John straightened before lowering himself into the chair next to her. 'I was not in the game room, if that is what you think.' He sent a pleading glance to Nate, lifting a finger to his lips, the signal to keep quiet.

Eliza exchanged a glance with Nate, before asking her father, 'Were you gambling, Papa?' She, of course, knew he had been.

Her father looked at her defensively. 'Nothing's amiss, Lizzie. No harm done.' He turned to Nate. 'Is that not so, Hale?'

His gaze caught Eliza's again. 'No harm done at all.'

He bowed and turned to leave.

'Wait, Hale,' Everly said. 'Come sit with us.'

Nate glanced at Eliza again. He would not stay unless he was certain she would wish it.

She nodded almost imperceptibly. 'Thank you, Everly,' he responded. 'I would very much like to join you.'

The empty chair available was next to Eliza.

Eliza's senses heightened at Nate's nearness. The last time she'd sat next to him to eat had been in the cabin when they shared the small portion of bread and cheese he'd carried with him. Although he dressed like the wealthiest Marquess, he reminded her of that captain who'd handed her the last piece of cheese.

They hardly spoke to each other, but she learned her brothers-in-law met him for luncheon almost every day at

White's. Nate and her brothers-in-law conversed comfortably, as friends might do. How glad she was for Nate. To have such fine men as friends instead of the likes of Lord Crafton and Lady Sibyl.

She wished she had seen how Nate had extricated her father from the card room. Eliza was not surprised her father would break his promise about gambling. She was merely angry at herself that she'd lost sight of him for as long as she had. How much had he lost? she wondered.

She had not been able to keep her mother in sight either. She could not depend upon Nate's help for every scrape they got into.

After supper her mother settled in a chair, prattling with some other ladies, probably about the latest *on dit*. Which might have been about Nate. Her father seated himself near her mother and nodded off from all the drink he'd consumed.

At least he was not playing cards.

The next set was announced and the room was busy with gentlemen collecting their partners.

A voice sounded at her side. 'Lady Varden?'

She looked up.

It was Crafton. 'Will you do me the honour of this dance?'

She bristled. She had no doubt that it had been Crafton who'd enticed her father into the card room. Had he also plied her father with drink? Drink and cards was a lethal combination for her father.

'I am not dancing, sir,' she said.

He did not leave. 'Well, that is a shame, my lady. I was hoping to be your partner.'

She did not even attempt to sound cordial. 'How unfortunate for you.'

He laughed, a dry, wheezing sound. 'I will recover,' he

said. 'And may I presume to ask if I might call upon you tomorrow?'

Call upon her? No!

'Whatever for, sir?' she asked.

'A matter I wish to discuss,' he replied.

'Whatever would you need to discuss with me?' she retorted.

His smile turned slippery. 'Something I must see you about.'

Eliza was curt. 'It is not convenient for you to call upon me. Tell me here.'

Crafton smirked. 'Believe me, you would not wish this to be overheard. I will call tomorrow. Be available at ten.'

He bowed and sauntered away.

When he was far enough away she had a sudden need to escape the crowd and the noise. She headed for the door, as if escaping the ballroom would rid her of the ill feeling Crafton aroused in her.

What did he want with her? What could he possibly have to say to her?

When she reached the hallway, Nate caught up with her. 'Eliza?'

She turned to him.

He took her arm and pulled her into one of the rooms off the hallway.

'Nate! What are you doing?' she cried, but she was not unhappy to see him.

'Forgive me, Eliza,' he said. 'But what did Crafton say to you?'

She did not want to tell him, but she was unsure why. 'He asked me to dance and I refused. That was all, Nate.'

He peered at her and she knew he could tell she was not telling him the whole of it.

She turned the subject on to him. 'You should not have forced me to be private with you.'

He looked unchastened. 'I needed to warn you. Crafton can be a dangerous man.'

'I know how he is, I assure you.' She'd not tell him why she knew. 'But I am able to deal with him.'

If Crafton did call upon her on the morrow, she'd face him. Like Nate had taught her to face all unpleasant things.

'Let me help you,' he insisted.

She put up a hand. '*If* I need help, I will ask.'

How nice it would be to hand all her troubles over to her captain who would be strong and capable and wise. It did not help that the room was dark, lit only by glowing coals in the fireplace, too much like the lighting in the cabin. How wonderful it would be to simply lean on him and let him take care of Crafton.

But what would he expect of her in return?

No, better she stand on her own. Face her own problems, even the unpleasant ones like Crafton.

Her voice turned soft, though. 'I should leave now, before anyone discovers us together.'

'I've said all I needed to,' he responded. 'I'll wait a decent amount of time after you leave,'

She reached for the door latch, but turned back to him. 'I've not thanked you for helping with my father. I do appreciate it very much.'

Nate's gaze penetrated, even as he replied, 'It was a trifle. He needed only a little help.'

It had not been a trifle to her. Nate had been the rescuer again, this time of her father.

'You were able to remove him from the room without embarrassing him?' She had no doubt that was precisely what he'd done.

'I was. The hand was ending just as I walked up to the table, so it was not difficult.'

'Thank you, Nate. It was kind of you, a true gentlemanly act.'

'A gentleman,' he scoffed.

'Indeed a gentleman,' she insisted. 'I believe you always were, even more than most of the men here.'

He made a disparaging sound. 'They might disagree.'

They were conversing again, she realised, as if comfortable together, like they'd been in the cabin. As if he were her captain again and there was no risk in being so close and alone together.

'They would be wrong,' she murmured.

Her gaze caught his and held.

Eliza leaned closer to Nate. Inches away. Close enough to hear him inhale a breath, to see his lips so tantalisingly close.

'Eliza,' he whispered her name as if a plea.

It would be so easy to fall into his arms, to let him take over, to be weak against the allure of what they so briefly shared together and that her body craved still.

'I can't,' she answered in a strangled voice.

She forced herself to turn away and reach for the door latch. She opened the door and hurried out, not even checking first if anyone saw her.

Nate waited in the dark room until enough time had passed between her return to the ballroom and his own. The air in the room was still filled with her scent and the loss of her presence struck him all over again.

This encounter had not gone well—possibly because he'd been on the verge of taking her in his arms again, capturing her lips again.

And she'd called him a gentleman. How laughable when he'd come within a hair's breadth of quite ungentlemanly behaviour. Right when they'd been talking together almost like in the cabin.

Although she was holding back something, he was certain of it. Something to do with Crafton.

Perhaps Eliza would never want to be with him. Perhaps he was not meant to have a family with her and Natalie. One thing he knew, though. They were bound together. He could no more walk away from her when she was in need than he could do without air to breathe.

If Crafton caused Eliza trouble, he would have to answer to Nate.

Chapter Fourteen

The next day Eliza was indeed available to see Crafton at ten in the morning. It seemed the simplest thing to do. See him, discover what he wanted and send him on his way. It was also early enough that her mother and father were still sleeping off the rigours of the previous night's ball and Miss Gibbons had taken Natalie to church.

Promptly at ten, Barlow announced Crafton. Eliza saw him in the library, because, being on the ground floor, it was closest to the front door.

As Crafton entered the room and Barlow left, he executed an exaggerated bow. 'Good morning, Lady Varden.' He made the greeting sound sinister.

She did not return it. 'What is it you wanted to tell me?'

He smiled. 'So unfriendly, Elizabeth. Is that any way to speak to a man you almost married?'

How presumptuous of him to use her given name. 'The circumstances of that marriage were unacceptable to me,' she retorted. 'You were going to buy me, after all.'

He laughed. 'Buy you? That is an indelicate way to put it. I would say your father and I merely agreed on a somewhat unusual marriage settlement.'

Eliza waved a hand. 'Surely you did not come here to

talk of that. I told you it was inconvenient for you to call, so, if you would please get to the point.'

She had not invited him to sit, but he lowered himself into a chair near the fireplace. She continued to face him but remained standing.

He sighed. 'So much to explain…where should I begin?'

'A concise version, please,' she said.

He shifted in the chair. 'Well, there are two important issues at hand. The first—I intend to make a name for myself in the Lords and have found the perfect means…' He paused waiting for her to ask what it was.

Eliza merely glared at him.

He went on. 'I will resurrect the Society for the Reformation of Manners.'

'That means nothing to me,' she snapped.

He laughed again. 'Oh, it will mean a great deal to you, Elizabeth, my dear. You see, the society will be responsible for ridding the country of—how might I put this delicately—men who *fornicate* with other men. It will expose them and see they are punished to the fullest extent of the law.'

Eliza's insides twisted in anxiety, but she maintained her composure. 'And what has this to do with me? Do you expect a donation?'

'No.' He leaned towards her. 'I expect to show that there are such men even among the nobility. I expect to expose your husband—your late husband—as one of them.'

'My husband?' She did not have to pretend to be shocked. How had he discovered this? And why attack a dead man? 'That is preposterous!'

'Do not act coy, Elizabeth, dear. I suspect you knew of your husband's deviant nature.'

'Nonsense!'

Elizabeth had many years to consider her response if anyone guessed about Henry. Simply deny it, she'd concluded. Such total denial of the truth had often worked for her parents. This was her first opportunity to put her parents' ploy into practice.

'Oh, I assure you it is true,' Crafton insisted. 'I heard it on the greatest authority.'

'Who would tell such lies?' she cried. 'My dear Henry is dead. He cannot defend himself against such falsehood. This is outrageous!'

If Crafton truly knew about Henry, he would also guess who Henry's lover was. Henry might be beyond persecution, but what about Ryland?

Ryland would be destroyed and the lives of his family ruined as well.

Eliza's heart pounded. She and Natalie would face ruin as well, would they not? Was that Crafton's intent? To ruin her?

She levelled a gaze at him. 'What is this about really, Crafton? It cannot be simply to tell stories about a dead man.'

'But, you see, it serves my purpose,' he sneered.

She lowered her voice. 'I think you should leave now, sir. You are wasting my time with this drivel.'

'Oh, it won't be drivel if I tell certain people what I—and others—know.'

Would the *ton* not embrace such juicy gossip! She, Natalie, her parents and sisters would be tainted even if Crafton had scanty proof. And Ryland would be utterly destroyed.

This was cruel beyond measure. Her heart was pumping as hard as if she were facing a bull ready to charge.

Which in a way she was.

Her only recourse was to act unafraid. 'Please leave, Crafton. I am weary of this.'

But it was as if her words fluttered over his head.

He lifted a finger. 'Or I might be persuaded to keep Lord Varden's secrets. And yours.'

Her brows rose. Now she would learn what he really wanted.

'If you do something for me.' He smirked.

She responded in a scathing tone. 'Oh, extortion is it, then?'

He stood and faced her directly. 'You will reject any suit Lord Hale offers you. Refuse any association with him.'

'Lord Hale?' Eliza was stunned. 'Why would you think—?' No one knew about them. No one.

Crafton glowered at her. 'No denying it, Elizabeth, dear. You were seen leaving his house. He is suddenly a favoured companion of your brothers-in-law. And he stares at you. I saw him do so at the ball.'

'I assure you there is nothing—'

He raised his voice. 'He is meant to marry my daughter. If I see you flirting with him or consorting with him in any way, I will tell the world about your husband. In fact...' he spoke as if some new idea had just occurred to him '...if—if Lord Hale is not betrothed to my daughter in—say—two weeks' time—yes, two weeks' time—*everyone* will know the truth about your dear departed husband. I will ruin his memory. Ruin his lover. Ruin *you*.' He grinned. 'And make my reputation in the Lords at the same time.'

He stepped closer to her.

Eliza stood her ground.

'Of course, if you do as I say, bygones will be bygones. For old times' sake.' He was so close now she could see the spittle at the corners of his mouth. 'By the way, I'll wager that before the Season is out, your father will again be in debt. If so, however, I will no longer be buying. You are used goods, my dear.'

'Get out,' she said between clenched teeth.

He brushed past her and sauntered to the door, turning to bow before he left the room.

Eliza lowered herself into a chair. Her legs were trembling. How dare Crafton threaten her, then task her with something impossible? Oh, she could stay away from Nate. She needed to do that in any event, but how was she to ensure that Nate propose to Lady Sibyl?

He *knew* that could not be done. Even more, it *should* not be done. Nate must not marry Lady Sibyl! What a nightmare to be connected to such a family for ever!

If Eliza ever needed help it was now, but who could she ask? Nate? Tell him he must become engaged to Lady Sibyl merely to save Eliza's reputation and Natalie's? To be married under those circumstances— No. She would not do that to Nate.

Even though so many people would be hurt.

If only she could flee, run back to Sandleigh where the scandal might not reach, where she could keep Natalie safe… What, then, of her mother and father? Her sisters? Their families? Ryland? They would all suffer soon enough.

She groaned. All she could do was face it—would that not be what Nate would say?

In any event, Natalie and Miss Gibbons were due home soon from the church services and she'd promised Miss Gibbons an afternoon off and Natalie a walk to the park. She must press on.

Eliza rose and left the room.

When she entered the hall Barlow's bushy brows knitted. 'Is anything amiss, m'lady?'

Her stress must have shown on her face. She tried to smile. 'I simply dislike that man.'

Barlow nodded in agreement. 'Sir John came down, m'lady. For breakfast, I believe.'

Barlow knew of her parents' antics and that Henry had taken tight control over them. He knew how much mischief they could get into in town.

'Thank you, Barlow.' Eliza might as well seize this opportunity to speak to her father. She made her way to the dining room.

Her father had seated himself at the head of the table and was reading the *Morning Post*.

He stood as she entered. 'Good morning, Lizzie!'

How could her father be so in his cups one night and bright and cheerful the next morning? It was incomprehensible. How could he not realise that disaster was about to befall all of them?

She was well schooled in pretending so she walked over and gave him a peck on the cheek. 'Good morning, Papa.'

The breakfast was spread out on the buffet. She selected some bread and jam and sat near her father.

He poured her a cup of tea. 'What the devil was that Crafton fellow doing here this morning?'

'You saw him?'

'I was descending the stairs as he was leaving,' her father explained. 'Wasn't calling on me. Saw me. Didn't even give me a hello.'

She'd hoped Crafton's visit would have gone unnoticed.

'So why was he here?' her father pressed.

'Oh…' What could she say? 'He—he attempted to renew his acquaintance with me.'

Her father's face fell. 'I feared something of the sort.' He placed a hand on her arm. 'Lizzie. Do not involve yourself with him. He charms one minute, then strikes like a viper the next.'

She put her other hand over his. 'Do not worry, Papa. I sent him away.'

Her father's eyes filled with regret. 'I am sorry, girl. So sorry. I was desperate in those days when I tried to make you marry him.'

'I know, Papa.' She was touched. He'd never apologised before.

He clasped her hand and squeezed it before letting go and sitting back in his chair. 'It all turned out well, though, did it not?' The cheer in his voice returned. 'I mean, you marrying Henry and all—' He caught himself. 'Well, not Henry dying, of course.'

'Yes, Papa,' she responded, lifting her teacup. 'It all worked out well.'

They fell silent for a few moments while he read the paper and she nibbled on her bread. There was so much she could not say to him, especially about Crafton's threat that so preyed on her mind.

'Papa,' she said, though. 'I must speak with you about your gambling last night—'

He put the paper down, his expression ashamed. 'I ought not to have done, Lizzie. I never break my promises, you know that—'

He broke promises all the time. To her. Certainly to her mother. And, before Henry, to his creditors.

'That Crafton, you know. He gave me a drink. Chatted about some fool society he wanted to start and before I knew it I was seated at a table playing loo—'

She knew Crafton had set her father up! The evil man!

'Don't know what I would have done if that new fellow hadn't come along and paid for my losses. I fear I bet over my limit, Lizzie.'

'What?' Of course he'd lost. He always lost.

'That fellow. We were introduced. You know, Hale. Lord Hale.'

'Lord Hale paid your losses?' Nate had not told her he'd rescued her father by paying his debt.

Her father nodded. 'Don't know what I would have done.'

Eliza felt her insides twist in even more painful ways. 'How much, Papa?'

He looked sheepish. 'Fifty guineas.'

'Fifty guineas!' How could one man lose so much in so short period of time? She banked her fury at her father. 'I will pay Lord Hale back, Papa, but you must promise me no more gambling! None. I do not have so much money that I can afford to pay such sums. I need what Henry left me for Natalie.'

Her father looked contrite. 'I promise, Lizzie. No more gambling. And I'll pay you back the fifty guineas.'

He never would. Henry's man of business, who had taken control of her father's finances all those years ago when Henry had paid her father's debt to Crafton, was still paying off loans that settled his other debts. There was enough left over to maintain her father's estate and to provide comfort to her parents, but nothing more to spare. Especially after a terrible harvest the previous year.

'See that you do, Papa,' she said sternly, this new worry adding to everything else.

'And don't tell your mother,' he added.

'Of course.' What was one more secret to be kept?

At that moment her mother swept into the room, chatting about all the people she'd seen at the ball—and all the men who had flirted with her.

Eliza ate her bread and jam and sipped her tea and resolved to go to Coutts Bank on Monday to withdraw the fifty guineas from her account. But what to do about Crafton?

She feared there was nothing to be done.

It was near noon when Nate walked along Piccadilly on his way back from returning Pegasus to his stable when he spied a woman and child approaching, just as he reached Half Moon Street.

Natalie and Eliza.

His heart leapt at seeing his daughter again. He stopped to savour her every step, skipping ahead, then waiting for her mother to catch up to her. He could hear her chatter even before making out the words.

He ought to head to his house to avoid them, but how

could he give up this chance to watch Natalie, this flesh and blood of his?

As they got closer, Natalie looked his way and her face lit up with a smile.

She ran to him. 'Lord Hale! It is you!'

He crouched down to her level. 'Good morning, Miss Natalie.'

'We are on our way to the park!' She clutched a doll and spoke as if imparting important information. 'Miss Gibbons took me to church, but Mama could not go with us, but now Mama is taking me to the park instead of Miss Gibbons.'

'Is that so?' Nate said. 'I have just come from riding my horse in the park.' He'd given Pegasus a good run on Rotten Row, getting out both their frustrations.

Eliza caught up to them. 'Lord Hale,' she said, her tone wary. Because he spoke to their daughter, no doubt.

He stood and tipped his hat. 'Good morning, Lady Varden.'

'You have a horse?' Natalie asked him.

'I do.' He crouched down again. 'His name is Pegasus.' He glanced up at Eliza, who started in surprise.

'Pegasus?' she whispered.

Little Natalie piped up. 'Does he fly like the horse in the stories?'

'No, Pegasus is a very ordinary horse. He has no wings at all.'

'Then why is he named Pegasus?' the child persisted.

Nate knew from Eliza's tense posture that she wished him to disappear forthwith, but this moment was too charming, too precious for Nate to let go so easily.

'He is named Pegasus because he runs so fast, it is as if he is flying.' He put extra expression in his voice and relished the changing expressions on the child's face.

'So fast!' she cried so caught up in the story.

Eliza broke in, her voice on edge. 'Natalie, we must be on our way.'

What did she fear? That Nate would divulge the secret of the child's conception here on Piccadilly Street? Did Eliza think him so foolish, so reckless he might do such a thing?

He stood again, shooting Eliza a defiant glare. She looked as if she wanted to fly away like the mythical Pegasus.

'Mama says we must go to the park now,' Natalie explained, unnecessarily. 'Where are you going?'

'I am going home.' He pointed down his street. 'I live near here.'

'So do we!' Natalie said. 'We live on Clarges Street.'

Eliza took the child's hand. 'Natalie…'

How provoking that Eliza acted as if he were some sort of danger to the child. He might have no clue how to be a father, but he'd never hurt either of them. He'd die first.

He shot another annoyed glance at Eliza but smiled at Natalie. 'By all means, do not let me detain you.'

Eliza actually looked distressed as she led Natalie swiftly away,

But Natalie turned back to him. 'Goodbye, Lord Hale!'

He doffed his hat. 'Goodbye, Miss Natalie.'

Nate watched her skip away until she disappeared from his view, before turning on to his street and slowly walked to his town house.

What a mixture of emotions. Joy at seeing his daughter again and sorrow that she was gone. Sorrow, too, that the geniality he and Eliza had managed the night before disappeared again. Was she that fearful of him even talking to the child?

He closed his eyes and brought back every memory of how his daughter looked, how she sounded. But he remembered, too, how warily Eliza treated him, as if he were a threat.

Chapter Fifteen

Nate accepted the invitation to Lady Rothmore's musicale that evening because Everly and Bentham's wives insisted they attend. If Eliza's sisters attended, perhaps she would too.

He wanted to see Eliza, to confront her about their brief encounter on the street that morning. And he also wanted to be present if Crafton attended and approached Eliza again.

Nate had attended one of these entertainments in the last Season. But only one. He did not appreciate the musical performances. He'd noticed, though, that other gentlemen seemed equally as restless listening to one young debutante after another not quite sing on key.

This evening included some guest performers from the new Italian opera *Elisabetta*. Or at least that was what the programme said.

Lord Rothmore came up to him. 'Good evening, Hale. Will you be dreading this as much as I will?'

Nate smiled. 'You are dreading your own entertainment?'

'My *wife's* entertainment,' he clarified. 'I find it a dead bore. But I wanted to ask you. You know the man. What's all this Crafton's so puffed up about?'

'I probably know less than you,' Nate said. 'I am no longer in Crafton's confidence.'

'No?' Lord Rothmore looked surprised. 'Thought you were a favourite of his.'

Apparently Rothmore was not current with the *on dits* of the day.

'He did tell me about his proposed society,' Nate said.

Rothmore faced him. 'What do you make of it?'

Nate was surprised any of the Lords sought his opinion, but since asked, he would give it. 'I think the country has important problems to solve. This society of Crafton's is merely a waste of time. The men Crafton seems intent on persecuting do no harm that I can see.'

Rothmore gave a thoughtful nod, then sauntered off. Had Nate made an ally with his views or would Nate's opinion further separate him from other members of the Lords? He could not tell. He suspected most people in society would agree with Crafton.

Nate watched the door and saw the moment Eliza arrived with her mother and father. Everly and Bentham and their wives came soon after.

Then Crafton and Lady Sibyl walked in.

The music started shortly after. Nate stood at the back of the room to listen. To watch.

Perhaps he was imagining, but Eliza still seemed distracted, on edge. It pained him to see her so, as if her distress was his own. He wanted to pull her aside, wrap his arms around her, ask her what was wrong and do whatever needed to be done to make it right.

Unless, of course, he was what was distressing her.

But, no. This was something else. He sensed it.

And his senses told him Crafton had something to do with it.

During the intermission he happened to be next to her when she was at the refreshment table. He abandoned his plan to confront her, more concerned that she seemed upset.

'Eliza?'

'Oh, Nate!' Her voice trembled and her expression seemed to beg for his comfort, but she shook her head and turned away.

'What is troubling you?' he persisted. 'Is it Crafton?'

She glanced back at him in alarm. 'I cannot say. Oh, please, Nate. Just do not speak to me. I cannot be seen with you.'

What? 'Why not?' he asked.

'Please, leave me alone. Do not speak to me or call upon me or contact me or run into me on the street.' She fled from his side without even getting a glass of wine.

Nate's gaze followed her. Something was terribly amiss, he was sure of it.

Sir John spied him and broke into a smile. He sauntered over. 'There you are, young sir. Very good to see you again.' He picked up a glass of wine and drank it down quickly before picking up another. 'Haven't forgotten. I'm in your debt.'

'Do not concern yourself, Sir John.' Nate was more worried about Eliza than about money. He guessed her father would not discerning enough to think it odd if Nate asked him about her. 'Is something disturbing Lady Varden? She seems upset this evening.'

'Does she?' Sir John glanced over at her in surprise. 'I suppose she does. Probably because that devil Crafton is here.' He poured the wine down his throat.

'Why should Crafton disturb her?' Nate pressed.

'Don't know,' Sir John replied. 'Don't know why Crafton called upon her either.'

Crafton had called upon her? Then this was about Crafton. Nate would wager his fortune on it.

Sir John went on. 'Couldn't be he wants to marry her still. Only wanted that because I owed him a lot of money.'

'Sir?' Nate was not sure he heard correctly. 'Crafton wanted to marry her?'

'Oh, years ago, my boy.' Sir John picked up a third glass of wine and leaned closer, gesturing with his head towards his wife who laughed at something the gentleman next to her said. 'See that? My wife is after Fawlsley. Mark my words. Humph! See if she likes it if the boot is on the other leg!'

Sir John strode away but slowed his pace to a saunter. With a charming smile he greeted a gaudily dressed woman of a similar age who seemed quite delighted to see him. Nate glanced over at Eliza's mother. She glowered at her husband.

Eliza sat with her sisters, gripping her programme and looking as if she hardly knew where she was.

Why had she not told him about Crafton? That it had been marriage to Crafton from which she escaped by marrying Varden? She could have told him at the ball, if not before. How could she not have trusted him with this information? It angered and worried him.

How was Crafton involved now, though? His society, if she knew of it, would certainly offend her, but this must be something else.

The second part of the evening was announced, the part where the debutantes performed, the part Nate dreaded, but he would not slip out like a few other men had done. Not as long as Eliza—and Crafton—remained.

Everyone took their seats. Lady Sibyl walked to the front of the room and sat at the pianoforte. She was exquisitely dressed and groomed, as always.

Nate had heard her before. She'd sing on key, at least.

Lady Sibyl put her fingers delicately on the keys and started to play and sing:

George Collins came home last Friday night
And there he take sick and died;
And when Mrs Collins heard George was dead,
She wrung her hands and cried
Mary in the hallway, sewing her silk,
She's sewing her silk so fine,
And when she heard that George were dead,
She threw her sewing aside.

She brought her gaze directly to Nate.

Hush up, dear daughter, don't take it so hard,
There's more pretty boys than George.
There's more pretty boys all standing around,
But none so dear as George.
Look away, look away, that lonesome dove
That sails from pine to pine;
It's mourning for its own true love
Just like I mourn for mine.

Her voice really was as fine as the Italian soprano Lady Rothmore had hired. And her manner more captivating. The audience applauded in genuine appreciation after she finished. She curtsied prettily and walked back to her seat beside her father.

At the next break she approached Nate when no one else was nearby.

'Hale.' She looked up at him with her most endearing expression. 'Let me seize on this moment to apologise. I said some truly awful things to you.' She blinked. 'I am appalled at myself. I assure you I did not mean any of them. I hope we might be amicable. I would hate to lose you as a friend.'

Nate no longer believed a word she spoke, but he had to admit she was excellent at putting on the proper face for the words that came out of her mouth. No wonder he'd been fooled about her character.

'I see no reason not to be cordial.' He spoke without a smile, however.

She patted his arm, but her smile did not quite reach her eyes. 'Excellent! I am so gratified.'

She sidled away and others quickly engulfed her in accolades about her performance.

Nate glanced over to where Eliza had been sitting. She had a troubled look on her face, but she quickly turned away.

The next day Nate hardly attended to the debates in Lords with Eliza still on his mind. The sessions ended early and it was only half past seven when Nate returned to his town house.

Hawkins opened the door for him and took his things.

'Any mail today?' Nate asked.

No one wrote to him except perhaps his estate managers and correspondence from them usually meant problems.

'No letters, Major. Some invitations arrived and an envelope was delivered to you,' the butler responded.

'An envelope?'

'Delivered by a servant, sir,' Hawkins said. 'I put the lot on your desk in the library.'

Nate went directly there. He set the invitations aside without looking at them and opened the envelope.

It contained a bank note for fifty guineas. And a message from Eliza.

Dear Nate,
It was good of you to be so generous to my father,
but I am sorry I placed you in that position. My
father assures me it will not happen again.
  Here is your money back.
Respectfully,
E.

Nate folded the letter and sat back in his chair. He was
not going to accept this money. God knew he had enough
money to toss this bank note in the fire and not miss it. He
could send Hawkins with it to return it, but he suspected
Eliza would refuse it. Nate was determined to return it
himself. He wanted to speak to her alone.

But he could not call on her, not after she'd begged that
he not be seen with her. He'd see her, though, but not in
the usual way.

Nate put the bank note back into its envelope and put it
in his coat pocket. He left the library and took the stairs to
the lower level of the .own house. He passed the kitchen
and walked through the hallway to the back door, out into
the garden and through the back gate.

Eliza was in the nursery with Natalie, reading her *Will
Wander's Walk*, one of Natalie's favourite books. They sat
together on a sofa, Natalie leaning against her. The child
cradled her doll, the doll that went nearly everywhere with
her. Miss Gibbons was not back yet and Eliza's parents
were both out, who knew where, so she had a peaceful
moment alone with her daughter.

Lacy knocked on the door. 'Beg pardon, ma'am, but Mr
Barlow asked me to find you. There is someone here to see
you.'

Oh, no. If it was Crafton again… 'Who is it, Lacy?'

'Someone who came to the back door, Mr Barlow said.'

'The back door?' Who would call at the back door?

'That was what he said, m'lady.' Lacy sounded as puzzled as Eliza.

'Who would come to the back door?' she asked again.

'Mr Barlow said it was Lord Hale.' Lacy said his name as if she'd been careful to get it right.

'Lord Hale!'

'Lord Hale,' Lacy repeated. 'That is what Mr Barlow said. At the back door.'

Why was Nate at the back door? Why was he calling upon her at all when she'd told him to stay away?

'I suppose I must go.' Eliza closed the book. 'Natalie, can you amuse yourself while I see Lord Hale?'

'May I come, too, Mama?' Natalie asked. 'I could show Lord Hale my favourite book.'

Nate had obviously captivated the child. Did she somehow sense the connection between them?

'Not today, dearest,' Eliza responded. 'This is probably a matter of business.'

Matter of business had been a term Henry used often. Natalie understood it meant children should not be involved.

'Very well, Mama,' Natalie said agreeably. 'I will work on stitching my doll's new coat.'

Eliza's mother had found scraps of wool and helped Natalie cut it into a pattern for a new coat.

Lacy said, 'I have some things to do up here. I'll keep an eye on her, ma'am.' She smiled at the child. 'Won't I, Miss Natalie?'

'You can help me sew my coat!' Natalie said.

'Thank you, Lacy.'

Eliza descended the stairs to the lower level of the town house. Barlow met her in the hallway by the kitchen near the outside door.

'Are you certain it is Lord Hale?' she asked Barlow.

He walked with her to the door. 'It is, ma'am. I remember him. He is waiting outside for you. Said you'd prefer it that way.'

It was about the fifty guineas, she decided. Well, she would not take it back. Her father was her problem, not Nate's, and Eliza had money enough to cover her father's debt. This time.

She grabbed a cloak from a hook by the door.

'Do you wish me to accompany you?' Barlow asked.

'No.' Better to see Nate alone. 'There is no need.'

She walked outside and did not see Nate right away until he stepped from the shadows.

The evening sun lit his face and put flecks of gold in his dark hair. His light brown eyes looked almost feral, but, instead of menacing, her heart reached for him. There was so much to trouble her and all she yearned for were his strong arms around her, to give her strength, like he'd done in the cabin that rainy night.

But she knew she must temper her response to him. She needed to push him away, make Crafton believe they were nothing to each other.

She approached him slowly. He gestured for her to come stand in the shadows where they could not be easily seen.

'If this is about the fifty guineas, Nate—' she said.

He handed her the envelope. 'I can well afford to gift your father this money. Believe me, it is a trifling amount to me.'

'Gift him?' Did that mean there would be strings attached? She did not want to be beholden to him, not about money. 'I considered it a loan.'

'I knew when I offered he could not pay it back. It was my choice to give it to him.' He stood close.

The darkening shadows reminded her of the dim light of the cabin. He'd stood this close then, too. Closer.

'Why would you give him so much money?' she asked.

'Because he is your father,' he explained his voice low and smooth. 'Because I did not wish to see him shamed.'

Her heart ached. Nate was acting like her captain again. 'Oh, Nate.' She sighed sadly.

'It is not just the money.' His voice had an edge.

Her wariness grew. 'What is it then?'

His gaze seemed to penetrate. 'I recognised your distress, Eliza. Your altered manner towards me. I believe it has to do with Crafton. It must.'

'Crafton.' She spit out the name.

'He set up your father to incur that debt. I am sure of it.' But he waved a hand and leaned closer. 'More importantly, your father told me Crafton was the man you were supposed to marry.'

Her eyes widened. 'My father told you that? He had no right to—'

His gaze pierced even deeper. 'Why didn't you tell me, Eliza? Especially knowing my association with him? Did you not think that was something I might want to know?'

She averted her gaze. How could she explain? Keeping secrets seemed normal to her. 'It was so long ago.'

He seized her arms and made her face him. 'I know you do not trust me, but you must know I would never do anything to hurt you or Natalie. Or allow any harm to come to you. I saw your face when Crafton approached you at the ball, when you saw him at the musicale. Your father said he called upon you. Tell me. Is Crafton threatening harm to you in some way? Let me help you.'

She felt suddenly weak, as if his grip was all that held her up.

She could think of no way to avoid telling him…something. He would persist, like he'd persisted in the cabin until she'd told him everything.

She held his gaze. 'Crafton somehow learned about

Henry. He threatens to expose him to further the aims of his society.'

'Curse him,' Nate said under his breath. 'He *threatens*, you say?'

'Crafton will expose Henry unless—' She broke off. How could she tell him the impossible task Crafton required of her, one she would never pursue?

His grip tightened. 'Unless what?'

She took a breath. No need to tell him all of it. 'Unless I stay away from you.'

Nate dropped his hands. 'Stay away from me?' He looked puzzled. 'How does he even know we are connected?'

Connected. Yes. That was how it felt to her as well. She'd always be connected to Nate, even when she sent him away.

'Apparently someone saw me leave your house that day and assumed it was an assignation.' The half-truth would work, she hoped. 'I am now considered Lady Sibyl's rival for your affections.'

His gaze pierced hers and she felt his yearning.

He drew back. 'Damnation!' he cried aloud. 'Crafton would do such a despicable thing merely because he thinks you are Lady Sibyl's rival? He'd ruin you? You and Natalie?'

Nate had been so kind to Natalie, so patient with her on Piccadilly the previous morning. It made Eliza's heart ache to remember it.

But she still did not want him to speak to Natalie, did she? She needed to tell him so. Again.

No. Not now.

If only she could just take Natalie and go away. Away from Crafton.

Away from Nate.

A sharp pain pierced her heart at the thought.

She tried to look resolved. 'I want to simply return to the country. Perhaps that would appease Crafton. But I cannot think how to convince my parents to leave with me and I dare not leave them here alone. I cannot tell them. Believe me, I cannot trust them with Henry's secret.'

He listened to her without countering her and the floodgates of her emotions burst open wide. 'If Crafton exposes Henry, what will it mean for my sisters? Their families will be tainted, as well, will they not? And Henry's lover. My heavens, what if they hang him?'

'Crafton knows who your husband's lover was?' Nate asked.

'Oh, as soon as Henry is exposed, everyone will know. They were such friends. There could be no one else.' She felt a clench of fear. 'So many people hurt and I cannot stop it!'

He took her in his arms as he'd done in the cabin. 'Do not fear.' His low voice rumbled in her ear. 'I will call upon Crafton and deal with this. I will stop it.'

His embrace was so comforting, she almost felt safe.

But she pushed away so she could look into his face. 'No. Nate. You must do nothing. If you speak to Crafton about this, it will only confirm that—that—you and I are more than acquaintances. You must stay away from me. You must not even acknowledge me if you see me.'

He touched her chin and raised it. 'I will find a way.'

'No,' she insisted. 'You must do *nothing*. I am convinced Crafton will expose Henry no matter what. There is nothing to be done. Except stay away from me. Perhaps that will convince Crafton I am no rival.'

Nate must never know Crafton's ultimatum—that Nate betroth himself to Lady Sibyl. He must stay completely out of it.

How could she convince him? Her captain was a man of action. It was how he had plucked her from the rain storm, how he had convinced her to tell him about why she was running from Henry. No, she could not trust him. Because he would insist on doing something. About Crafton.

About Natalie.

'I cannot stand by and allow this to happen,' Nate said. 'I must do something to stop Crafton.'

She grabbed his arms. 'Listen to me, Nate. This is about *my* life. I know what is best. I will face this, horrible as it is.'

She still had some hope Crafton would not make good his threat. If her hopes failed, she'd warn Ryland. Her mind spun a plan, a plan that essentially meant running away.

She looked into Nate's eyes.

'I cannot see you hurt,' Nate said, his voice filled with pain.

She loosened her grip and he wrapped his arms around her, holding her close in his strong arms.

A flash of desire rushed through her and a flash of fear that he might again push her away, but suddenly she did not care. She needed his arms around her. She needed his strength. And she wanted what she'd so fleetingly had. Nate's lips upon hers. Nate's body against hers. His hands on her.

She rose on her toes and pulled his head down to hers, seeking and finding his lips. To her surprise, this time he clutched her harder against him and took possession of her lips.

She pressed herself to him, aching for that exquisite release from him she'd experienced only once before. She did not care that they were outside protected only by the shadow of the garden shed.

From a nearby house came the sound of water being dumped from a bucket. It woke her to where they were. Her garden. Almost visible. Eliza pulled away.

She gazed at him again. 'Nate.'

He took her in his arms again. 'Come to me, Eliza. Tonight. I'll meet you here any time you like.'

She should not. She should not tie herself to him any closer. But could she resist the unique joy joining with him could bring?

She could not.

And she so needed the illusion that she was not alone.

'I'll come at midnight,' she said. That was late enough for the household to be abed.

After one more kiss they parted and Eliza hurried back into house.

Barlow had waited for her. 'M'lady?'

'There is nothing to worry over, Barlow. Lord Hale simply wished to talk to me.' Of course if it had truly been simple, Lord Hale would have entered through the front door.

But Barlow would not question her. 'Very well, m'lady.'

As soon as Eliza reached the hall and started to climb the stairs to the first floor, doubts came flooding in.

She should keep her distance. Not climb into bed with Nate. How could she contain her emotions towards him afterwards? Would her passion not show on her face any time she saw him, even across a crowded ballroom?

She should send a message that she would not meet him. She climbed the stairs, still feeling his lips against hers. She should send a message.

But she would not.

Chapter Sixteen

The hours dragged by and Nate had found scant occupation to pass his time. He'd given most of his servants the day off. His butler, Hawkins, insisted on remaining, but Nate could trust him to keep mum. Cook and the maids who remained would be abed by midnight.

Nate had walked to the shops and purchased newspapers and pamphlets to read up on the unrest around the country, but he could not focus his mind on it.

He even tried to figure out why Crafton would threaten to ruin Eliza. Had the man felt scorned by her because she married another? The Crafton Nate had come to know seemed to have no interest in women, though. He doted on Lady Sibyl, but otherwise he seemed to be eager for the esteem of his peers, eager for power and influence. So forming this society of his made some sense, but ruining Eliza? That seemed an unnecessary cruelty.

Well, let him try to ruin Eliza. He would only fuel Nate's anger. And Nate had no doubt he could be a formidable enemy to Crafton.

Those thoughts merely swam through his mind. He shut them off. Crafton would not intrude on this night with Eliza, not even in thoughts. He ached for a repeat of the night they had shared together.

But he worried that he might lose control as he'd done in her drawing room. He spent a great deal of the hours dragging by talking himself into controlling himself. Eliza must direct how the night went, no matter what. No matter how he ached for her.

The clock chimed half past eleven. Nate could stand it no longer. He rose from his chair and made his way below stairs, through the darkened hallway to the back door. He delayed for a while on his own property before entering her garden and waiting some more.

More minutes crawled by until Nate finally heard a distant clock chime twelve times.

But still he waited. A minute or two passed. Five.

What if she didn't come?

His hopes weakened.

But then the back door to her town house opened and a hooded figure walked directly to him.

He wanted to take her directly into his arms, but she stopped an arm's length away.

He took in a breath and braced himself. 'Have—have you changed your mind, Eliza?'

She shook her head.

He held her arm more than she, his, and they walked side by side to his house, through the doorway and the dimly lit passages, up the stairs to his bedchamber. Once inside his room, he removed his coat and she her cloak. She wore only a nightdress and robe.

The coals in the fireplace—the only light in the room— illuminated her face and Nate was transported back to the cabin when he'd first spied her beauty lit the same way. His heart soared at the sight.

'This reminds me of the cabin,' she said, echoing his thoughts, though her expression was almost sad.

He attempted a smile. 'Except it is not cold and rain-ing, we are not dressed like farm workers and we have a marquess's bed instead of narrow cot.'

A returning smile flashed across her face but disappeared as quickly. She averted her gaze. 'It served us well enough, though.'

'It did indeed.' It had made her one with him, physically, emotionally. Connecting them. Dispelling his isolation. No matter what happened between them now, it had done all that for him once.

And by a miracle, it also created their daughter.

Nate yearned for her to be as eager for this as he was, but she seemed to be slipping away. He touched her chin and gently turned her face to him. He leaned down and, so like that first kiss in the cabin, touched his lips to hers.

He felt her tremble under his touch.

But she drew away. 'I—I have not done this since that night.'

Was she worried she would not please him? 'We managed well enough then, did we not?'

She nodded, looking into his eyes.

He gazed down at her, wanting her with every part of him. 'Eliza,' he murmured. 'I desire this above all things, but if you do not want it—'

She cut him off. 'I do want this.'

Then why her hesitancy? Why did it feel as though she would dissolve into smoke if he reached for her?

He chanced picking her up in his arms. She remained solid and warm and real even if not quite with him. He wanted to feel that connection with her again, even more than he ached for a physical release. Perhaps it would come. Perhaps this was merely nerves on both their parts—eager to recover that magical night they had spent together, yet fearful they could not.

Nate carried her to his bed covered in bed linens so fine they'd cost more than a month's worth of a lieutenant's wages. Such a contrast to the coarse fabric of the cot in the cabin.

Still he would prefer the rough linens of the cabin if it would bring back what they'd so briefly shared there.

In the cabin he'd felt as though they were joined together in a bond that surpassed time or distance. It was a bond like he felt as a child when his parents were alive, so needed like air to breathe, but noticed only in its absence. That feeling returned when he first saw Natalie, the beautiful daughter they had created. He instantly knew she belonged to him.

He wanted that feeling again with Eliza. To feel bound together. He wanted it so acutely it was akin to raw pain. Because, at the moment, it was absent.

Eliza watched Nate pull off his boots and stockings, momentarily paralysed.

So often she'd conjured up the memory of their lovemaking in the cabin. How perfect it had been. How it had comforted her all these years. How she'd yearned to experience it again. Now here she was—with Nate—and filled with uncertainty.

What was wrong with her?

Perhaps if she proceeded. Faced it, like he'd taught her.

She kicked off her shoes and pulled off her stockings, then untied the ribbons of her robe, acutely aware of Nate watching her. Clad only in her nightdress, Eliza turned to Nate and unbuttoned his waistcoat. He shrugged out of it. She untied his neckcloth and pulled it off and lifted her gaze to his.

He took her hand and brought her palm to his lips. The tender gesture made her heart ache so keenly she thought it would crack open. His white shirt gleamed in the dim light like some celestial garment. She reached for it and pulled it over his head. His muscled chest was firm to her touch, his shoulders broad. Strong. She stroked his skin, roughened by the hair on his chest and familiar to her touch. She stopped. Her fingers found a scar that had not been there all those years ago. She traced the scar nearly all the way across his abdomen.

She gasped. 'What happened, Nate?'

He shrugged. 'A Frenchman's sword at Badajoz.'

He made it sound like a trifle, but a wound like that— what if it had been a little deeper? What if it had festered?

What must it have been like for him to face swords and cannonballs and musket fire?

'Badajoz was a fortress, was it not?' Eliza had read all she could find about every battle, searching for mention of Nate's regiment, then searching the names of the wounded and killed, fearing she might find his. 'What did they call it? A siege?'

'Yes.' His voice was clipped and his eyes lost all emotion. 'A siege. Nasty fighting.'

He was withdrawing, she feared. The way she'd done earlier, except his were horrific memories from which he retreated.

She wanted him back.

She leaned down and touched her lips to his scar. As she looked closer, there were other marks of war on him, none so large but many of them. She touched some of them. She felt the pain of each of them, sensed the horror. 'You could have died,' she whispered.

He swept a lock of hair from her cheek, tucked it behind her ear and came back to her. 'But I didn't die, Eliza. I'm alive and I found you again.'

Suddenly her hesitation vanished. Like in the cabin, everything vanished but the two of them. Nate removed his trousers and drawers and Eliza threw off her nightdress.

She was naked underneath. His gaze intensified the fire now burning inside her.

'Lie back,' he murmured.

She lay against the pillows and he, beside her, resting on one elbow. His free hand pulled the ribbon from her hair, which tumbled down her shoulders. He combed it with his fingers, a glorious feeling.

He traced one finger over her forehead and down the side of her face to the sensitive skin of her neck.

But he stopped and looked into her eyes. 'If I do anything you do not like, tell me. I will stop.'

She gazed back at him. 'Don't stop.'

He flashed a smile and continued to stroke her skin. Her neck, down the centre of her chest, between her breasts, circling her breasts until his fingers touched her nipples, sending sensation straight down to where she ached for him.

She remembered vividly him stroking her in much the same way, that other time, even though seven years had passed. He was even gentler this time, more tentative, perhaps. She could not blame him. She'd been pushing him away ever since...ever since he pushed her away.

Was it wanton of her to want even more? She wanted that eagerness they'd both felt before, that sense of a one and only chance.

Before she could think too much she rose up and pulled his lips to hers, making her lips beg for that eager intensity of their first time.

He did not disappoint. He held her naked body against his and passionately devoured her lips. He released her against the pillows again and swept a voracious hand over her breasts and down between her legs. His fingers wrested sensation from that most private place that caused her to writhe with pleasure. He made the pleasure build until, to her surprise, he created that explosion of release. She could not help it. She cried out.

And fell back when the pleasure eased. Her whole body seemed to throb now, with yearning.

'Please, Nate,' she whimpered.

He moved off her. 'Stop?' he rasped.

She pulled him down again. 'No. No. Don't stop.'

He rose above her, hard and eager for her, and she thought she would perish from anticipation. She remembered! Remembered what was to come.

Unlike all those years ago, though, he plunged into her, but her body eagerly accommodated him, welcomed him, joined with him. She lifted her hips to him, moved with him. The sound of their breaths, their skin clapping together, the hiss of the fire, filled her ears and her need for him grew stronger and stronger with each thrust. She lost herself in the moment. She and Nate became one again in that primal way that took away all thought, leaving only sensation. Every nerve in her body fired, pushing her onwards.

This was more than she had dreamed of, more than she remembered. She and Nate together again. Her heart filled with joy as they moved faster and faster. Her need intensified.

Until the pleasure burst inside her again. Like fireworks at Vauxhall. A celebration.

As if he'd waited for her, his release came a moment later, joining her in that frenzy.

Of joy.

He leaned down for one more kiss, like putting a bow on a package. A gift. Then he collapsed on top of her, sliding to her side.

'Eliza,' he whispered, his lips close to her ear. He nestled her against him and held her close. His skin was warm and damp from the exertion. His arms strong around her.

As though they were still joined.

Somewhere in the room a clock chimed. Eliza woke with a jolt.

She must have fallen asleep. How many chimes had she heard? Two. Two in the morning!

She faced Nate, worried she'd woken him, but his face was composed in sleep, almost boyish. His arm draped around her shoulders. She dared not move.

Not until she sorted out the emotions rushing through her.

What power he had over her. He'd had merely to ask and she'd fallen into bed with him. Gladly. Yearningly. It frightened her. This had not been a good idea. It made everything so much harder.

Because now she had a new memory of making love with him.

Of loving him.

Yes. Loving him. Him. Nate. Not his memory. This man lying beside her.

And now he was always within her reach, not away at war, nameless so she could not even search for him.

She loved him.

And that gave him power over her.

She wanted so desperately to trust in him, believe *his* love was genuine and could last, but every time her life seemed perfect—or even simply untroubled—something snatched it away.

And now...how could this last?

She would wind up alone. She must wind up alone. Crafton had made it impossible for she and Nate to be together.

Nate's eyes fluttered open and before he could either reach for her or push her away, she sat up.

'I must go,' she said.

He sat up as well, sounding disoriented. 'What time is it?'

'Two.' She started to climb off the bed, but he stopped her.

'You are not running because of the time. What is it, Eliza?'

How could she tell him?

'It is just…' She hesitated, searching for words. 'Just every time my life seems settled or untroubled, something snatches it away. My parents' unceasing drama during my childhood. My father's debts when I was so full of hope during my first London Season. Then marrying Henry.' She touched his hand. 'Even meeting you—'

'And now it is Crafton?' he said.

'Yes.' But it was more than that. She brought his hand to her lips. 'I am afraid—'

He sat behind her on the bed, holding her, leaning her against his chest. His lips were close to her ear.

'Every time I've had someone who cares about me, they leave me or die,' he said.

She felt that pain. It was unbearable. She turned herself around so she faced him, both of them sitting cross-legged.

Her gaze dropped to his scar. How many times had he seen death? Cheated death himself?

He lifted her chin so she would look into his face. 'I do not want to give up, Eliza. I want to keep trying, no matter the risk.'

Her heart pounded and her fear grew.

A part of her wanted to stay with him, to never leave, but Nate was new to the *ton*, not quite accepted. What if he stuck by her and Crafton destroyed her? He would be destroyed, too, before he'd had a chance to show what a fine man he was, what a fine marquess he could be.

It felt like her house of cards was about to fall down upon her head. What chance was there to play any hand, winning or losing? Everyone she loved would be destroyed.

She inhaled a quick panicked breath. 'I must leave.'

Eliza scrambled off the bed and searched for her clothes. She found her nightdress and put it on over her head.

Nate came up behind her as she tied the ribbons at the neck of her nightdress. He hugged her from behind and placed a warm, arousing kiss on the sensitive skin of her neck.

'Meet me again tonight?' he murmured in her ear.

Her body tensed as if reflexively protecting her from saying yes again.

'No, Nate.'

He released her and she knew she'd hurt him.

She picked up her robe. 'I made a mistake in coming here.'

His voice lowered. 'Do not say this was a mistake, Eliza.'

She felt the pain of his words but forced herself not to react. Instead she put on her robe.

He pushed his arms through the sleeves of his shirt and thrust his feet through his trousers, his movements sharp. Angry. Hurt. 'Very well. As you wish it, Eliza. But there is still Crafton to deal with.'

'Crafton is my problem, Nate. Not yours. He will expose Henry no matter what.' Nate must stay out of it.

He seized her shoulders and turned her towards him. 'It is my problem too, Eliza. Anything that affects you and Natalie is my problem. You are who I care about. You and Natalie.'

Mentioning Natalie was like waving a red rag in front of a bull.

His anger at her was the only weapon she had. To protect him. To protect herself.

'Natalie? Was—was that what this was about?' She made her voice haughty. 'And since you mention it, no more of these *chance* meetings, Nate. You knew I did not want you to see her. But there you were. What was this about, then? Did you think by seducing me I would change my mind?'

'I did not seduce you!' he shot back. 'You know that, Eliza. You know a word from you and I would have stopped. And as to my encounter with *our daughter*, it happened by chance, as you yourself saw.'

'How do I know you did not contrive it!' she cried, shocking herself with the surge of emotion she suddenly experienced.

She knew Nate's meeting Natalie was accidental. She knew, too, that he'd not seduced her. She'd been more than willing.

But that did not stop her because she was truly out of control. 'Then this night was a manipulation. *Manipulating* me to get to Natalie!'

His eyes flashed. 'Are you mad? Of course it was not!'

What horrid thing might next come out of her mouth if she said another word?

Eliza quickly wrapped her stockings around her arm and shoved her feet into her shoes without them. She grabbed her cloak. 'I'm leaving.'

She dashed from his room and made her way down the stairs to the lower level, through the hallway and out the back door. She could hear him close behind her, but she kept going. Through her gate and up to her door.

She turned then, to see his silhouette at her gate. He stood there, coatless, perhaps shoeless, until she opened her door and stepped inside, but turned again before closing the door.

He'd gone.

She closed the door and leaned against it, closing her eyes as tightly as she could.

What was wrong with her? Was she indeed mad? She didn't really believe Nate would manipulate her merely to have access to Natalie, did she? She understood his need for Natalie.

Every sense inside her told her it was wrong of her to keep him from his daughter, but she was so afraid that Natalie would never heal from her grief—

Eliza was afraid of everything. Of Natalie not healing. Of her parents falling back into ruin. Of Crafton's scandal. Of Nate's becoming embroiled in it.

Most of all, though, she was afraid to trust that Nate loved her. She was afraid he'd again push her away. The moment she let herself believe he loved her, he'd push her away.

She was afraid that, like to everyone else—her parents. Henry. Even Crafton—that to Nate she was a mere means to an end, the way to get the family he craved.

The family he deserved.

She ran to her bedchamber, heedless of anyone hearing her. She closed the door and sank to the floor, burying her head in her hands.

Letting her tears flow.

Nate padded across the cobbles of the alley between Eliza's garden and his, a storm of anger, confusion and despair swirling inside him.

Did she not understand? Both she and Natalie were everything to him. They were his family. Natalie might have his blood in her veins, but Eliza had been his strength and consolation when enduring the bloodiest of battles, when raging fever from wounds threatened his life, when enduring cold, lonely nights. Here in London she'd brought him back to himself, to remembering who he was, no matter his title.

And he'd never felt more himself than making love to her this night.

Then why was she so intent on causing him pain? By so completely misunderstanding his motives? He was not manipulating her. Or seducing her—except that one time, but even then he'd stopped himself in time. Did she not know his character by now? That he would never do anything to harm her or Natalie.

There was something missing here. Something she was not telling him and it frustrated him to distraction.

When he again reached his room, Nate found the decanter of brandy Patterson always kept filled. He poured himself a glass and downed it in one gulp.

Eliza, Lady Varden, had not heard the last of him, though. He intended to help her with Crafton, no matter what she said. After that, he would see.

Chapter Seventeen

Midday Tuesday Nate went to White's as usual, not to meet Eliza's brothers-in-law, but in hopes he would see Crafton. Eliza did not want him to speak to Crafton, but Nate refused to sit by and do nothing.

He disliked all this secrecy, though. Except perhaps the secret about her husband. That secret that needed to be kept, in Nate's opinion, but only because Eliza—and Natalie—would indeed be ruined in polite society if that truth became known. It was Nate's duty to protect them at all costs.

If Nate could convince Crafton to give up this society idea, there would be no reason for him to expose Eliza's late husband. Nate could still avoid Eliza in public until Lady Sibyl found some other man to fix her sights on. He and Eliza needed time anyway.

And perhaps eventually she would return again to his house, his bed. Eventually.

Luck was with him. Crafton sat alone in one of the morning rooms off the front entrance. The room was bright with sunlight and Crafton was seated on one of the room's comfortable leather chairs reading a newspaper.

He looked up when Nate entered.

Nate pretended he'd not meant to encounter the man. 'Pardon me, Crafton. Would I disturb you if I also sat in this room? I was looking for a quiet place to read the papers, as well.'

Crafton gave him an assessing look. Trying to ascertain the truth of his statement, perhaps.

After a moment, Crafton said, 'By all means, sit.'

Nate sat and picked up a copy of the *Morning Post* left on the table for members. He acted as if he were reading for a while before he broke the silence and asked, 'How is that society of yours faring, sir?'

Crafton lowered his paper. 'I am still organising. Takes time for things like this, you see. Must gain support first thing before proceeding.'

'Are you finding support?' Nate asked.

'Enough,' the man responded uncertainly.

'Indeed?' Nate made himself sound surprised. 'I wondered if interest in such an issue had passed. It seems that you'd gain more notoriety by attacking a more timely problem like, say, unemployment or bread prices.'

Crafton folded his paper and leaned towards Nate. 'Here's the thing, Hale. Nobody knows what to do about unemployment or hunger or unrest or any of those issues we have been debating about.' He was in his element, instructing Nate about *how it is* in society. 'Nothing will be decided. It is too difficult a topic to be solved. But vice!' His voice rose. 'Vice, on the other hand, is something everyone can be against.'

'But are such men causing trouble? I cannot see that they are. It disturbs me that you might have executions on your conscience.' Nate doubted Crafton had much of a conscience, but he probably fancied himself having the finest one.

Crafton laughed. 'Dead men do not protest. Besides, who much cares if they die? They are breaking the law and the code of morality.'

Their lovers, family and friends care. But Nate did not speak that thought out loud.

Crafton continued his lecture. 'It is important to make one's name in politics, Hale. You have often heard me say so. By attacking vice I should be able to do so with relatively little effort and a big profit.'

No matter who was hurt, Nate thought.

He decided to become more direct. 'I would ask you to give it up, Crafton. Your skills are better used elsewhere.'

Crafton peered at Nate over the spectacles he wore for reading. 'You would presume to advise me?' His voice took a darker tone.

'Not advise,' Nate said, still attempting diplomacy over confrontation. 'But merely sharing my thoughts as one who used to, at least, think you a friend.'

Crafton's voice rose. 'My willingness to speak to you should not be interpreted as friendship, sir! You showed your true colours by treating my daughter shabbily, very shabbily indeed!' Crafton narrowed his eyes. 'Tell me... have you been conversing—or cavorting—with that widow of yours?'

Nate knew precisely who he meant. 'What widow? I do not get your meaning.'

'Oh, yes, you do.' Crafton laughed. 'Do not take me for a fool. I suspect you know very well what her late husband was. How honour demands I expose him. You think you can prevent a scandal that would ruin any chances of you making your mark in the Lords or in society if you keep it up with that widow.'

This was not going well. Nate had no other choice, though, than to continue his ruse.

'Late husband? Expose? What the devil are you talking about?' He feigned outrage.

'You know I mean Lord Varden. I suspect your paramour has told you all about it. Has she sent you to try to talk me out of my moral duty to combat vice?' It was Crafton's turn to sound outraged.

'You are mistaken, Crafton—'

Crafton cut him off. 'Am I?' He leaned towards Nate again and spoke in a low, sinister voice. 'You can tell *Lady Varden* that my offer still holds. I will keep her late husband's proclivities a secret, but only if you—' he pointed at Nate's chest '—only if *you* become betrothed to my daughter by Sunday after next.'

What? Was this what Eliza withheld from him? This crucial piece of information?

It was all Nate could do to hide his shocked reaction. 'Betrothed to your daughter? What has that to do with your society?'

Crafton leaned back again and crossed his arms over his chest, a smug expression on his face. 'Oh, the society is a mere bonus. I'd been looking for a way to distinguish myself in Parliament. It was brilliant that the idea fit so well to my main purpose. Which is that you must marry Lady Sibyl. Tell me, will my ploy work? I wager it will.'

The devil it would! It was a good thing no sabre was nearby or Crafton might never wager again!

Nate knew from battle that nothing put off an adversary more than dispassion. Unless it was murderous rage.

He chose dispassion. 'You, sir, have an odd way of negotiating a marriage settlement.'

He rose and sauntered out of the room.

He did not join Everly and Bentham for nuncheon, however. Nate strode out of White's and up St James's Street to Piccadilly to Clarges Street. He was about to charge up to her door and pound the Dionysus knocker when he changed his mind.

Better to come to the back door.

* * *

Eliza sat in the library, looking through bills that needed her attention, bills that her parents had acquired even in this short period of time. The bills were trifles, really, but unnecessary expenditures and were starting to add up. She had half a mind to contact her sisters and brothers-in-law. Why should she incur the total expense of their parents?

Why? Because that was what she'd always done. Taken on the responsibility for everyone in the family.

Barlow came to the door. 'Lord Hale calls, ma'am. Are you at home?'

Nate?

That usual surge of excitement rushed through her.

Then more rational thought. She'd told him to keep his distance. What was he doing, appearing at her door? He might have been seen. This was how he heeded her wishes?

She took a deep breath. 'I will see him, Barlow.'

'Here, ma'am?' the butler asked. 'Or in the garden?'

'He came to the back door?'

'He awaits you in the garden.' Barlow sounded incredulous.

Eliza felt guilty for assuming otherwise. She rose, intending to follow Barlow out the door, but she stopped. 'Barlow, are my parents at home?'

'Sir John left earlier, but I believe your mother is still in her room.'

Hopefully her mother would not show up in the library with an irresistible urge to read a book.

'And Miss Natalie and Miss Gibbons?' Eliza asked.

'In the nursery, ma'am,' he responded.

'Then I will see Lord Hale here.'

Barlow bowed. 'Very good, ma'am.'

Eliza's insides waged a war between excitement and anger. Why was he here when she had so clearly rejected him. Again? And why was her body reacting so to the thought of seeing him?

After what seemed ages, Nate stepped in and she thrilled at seeing him, as always. But she caught herself.

He walked straight up to her.

'Nate!' she said angrily. 'I did not want you—'

'Never mind that.' His eyes flashed. 'You kept something from me. I've seen Crafton—'

She felt herself go pale. 'You knew I did not want you to—'

'Do not fear. I did not mention you,' he responded. 'I merely attempted to talk him out of setting up his society. I thought if he gave it up, he'd have no reason to expose your husband.' He leaned closer. 'Do you know what he said?'

She knew.

He went on. 'His society is mere artifice, is it not? This whole thing is a ruse, a trick to force me to marry Lady Sibyl.' He pierced her with his gaze. 'That is the ransom he demands, is it not? I betroth myself to Lady Sibyl or he ruins you. How could you keep that from me, Eliza? It so directly involves me.'

Her anger flared. 'You did not need to know! You cannot marry her.'

'I have no intention of marrying her, but that was the crucial piece of information, was it not? You kept it secret from me.'

'This matter should not involve you!' she cried. 'It is all about Henry. Not you.' Why should this ruin his life when it was really all about hers?

'You are wrong,' he countered. 'It is all about me, Eliza. It is Crafton's way of forcing me to marry Lady Sibyl. That's the whole of it.'

They stood close—why did they always have to stand so close? It made it hard for her to think when she could reach out and touch him, when she longed for his touch.

The feel of his fingers on her skin, so recent a memory she could feel them still.

She stepped back.

He shook his head and averted his gaze.

After a moment he faced her again. 'Why keep this secret from me, Eliza?' His voice seemed to ache. 'You really do not trust me, do you?'

She gazed at him and could not answer. When she found her voice she lowered her eyes. 'I am afraid to trust you, Nate.'

'Afraid?' He sounded incredulous.

'How do I know what secrets you are keeping from me? Everyone else has something to hide. The only thing I know for certain is you want Natalie.'

That wasn't true, though. She also knew her captain would sacrifice himself to rescue her and Natalie. She did know that for certain and that is why she had not told him about Crafton's ultimatum.

His expression turned stony. 'To be precise, what is certain is that I want Natalie in my life. I would not take her from you, if that is what you fear—' He turned away abruptly and paced a few steps. 'But we do not have the luxury to argue this point at the moment, do we? In less than two weeks' time Crafton will ruin you unless I propose to Lady Sibyl. That is the gist of it.'

'I've made my decision about this already, Nate. After Crafton exposes Henry I will leave London with Natalie. My parents will undoubtedly wish to leave with us. I'll tell my sisters to disown us. They might be able to weather the storm that way.'

But what of Ryland, though? And his family? All she could do was warn them.

'Or,' Nate countered in a defiant tone, 'I propose to Lady Sibyl. Then it all goes away.'

She went to him and clutched his arms. 'No, Nate! You

must not do that!' Why should he alone pay the price? 'What sort of marriage would that be for you? A terrible one. You deserve more.'

To her surprise he wrapped his arms around her and held her close. 'There must be another way. We must not surrender so easily. We fight back. We must find another way.'

With his arms around her she almost believed him.

But she murmured, 'There is no other way.'

Nate wanted to hold her for ever and never let go. He was bound to her. He had no doubt of that.

He'd find a way out of this. He must.

How Nate wished they could start over. Find another cabin, one that could shelter from a storm outside, but also the storm that raged inside between them.

He forced himself to release her, needing something to calm his senses and clear his brain. 'Do you have some drink here? Port or claret or brandy?'

She looked as shaken as he was by their embrace. 'I can call for Barlow to bring some,' she said. 'What would you prefer?'

'Port, I think.'

Had he made such a request to Lady Sibyl she would have instructed him, albeit in a teasing tone, as to how a guest simply *does not ask* for refreshment, but must wait for it to be offered.

Eliza merely summoned her butler. 'Some port, Barlow, please.'

'Very good, ma'am,' the man replied. 'One or two glasses?'

She glanced over at Nate and back to her butler. 'Two, please.'

When the butler left she turned to Nate. 'I could do with some port as well.' She gestured to a chair. 'Shall we sit?'

He lowered himself into the chair she'd offered and she sat across from him. He rested his head in his hands and tried to think.

What to do? What to do?

The butler brought a decanter of port and poured two glasses. Eliza thanked him and he left.

Nate took a long sip.

If Eliza's butler wondered about his lady drinking port so early in the day, especially with the strange Lord Hale, he had not let on. The butler seemed watchful, though, maybe even protective of her. Nate could not tell for certain. Of course, such men were supposed to appear impassive. How was anyone to guess his butler, Hawkins, had been a hardened soldier? Except when Hawkins slipped and called him *Major*.

There were always clues about a man if you looked hard enough.

Nate glanced up at Eliza. She looked forlorn. Defeated. It tore at his heart.

He was not that ready cede the battle. He had an idea, but first he needed to investigate if it could be done. No sense worrying her before he knew.

He finished his port in a gulp and stood. 'I should be going.'

She rose, too. Her eyes were sad. 'Nate, please do not do anything. I do not want you to. And do not even consider marrying Lady Sibyl. Not under these circumstances.'

Maybe under *these* circumstances he'd be forced to, Nate thought. But he might just have another way. And he was determined to see it through.

Nate did not attend the Lords that day. Instead he went back to his town house, through the garden, of course, and called for Hawkins.

He explained the whole to Hawkins—well, almost the

whole. He did not tell Hawkins of his attachment to Eliza. Hawkins might have guessed, though. Nate supposed the old soldier had been perfectly aware of Eliza's visit to Nate's bedchamber the previous night.

Nate asked him, 'Do you know if any of our soldiers are here in London? Any who might be interested in being hired to follow Crafton?'

'Smith and Yates are out and about, sir.'

Clever men, Smith and Yates. Not inclined to follow rules particularly, but fearless in battle and generally game for anything.

'Do you know where to find them?' Nate asked.

Hawkins grinned. 'I've been known to drink with them at the Lamb and Flag. I believe Patterson was there last night, sir. Shall I ask if he's seen them?'

Patterson was Nate's valet, but he'd been Nate's batman before that.

'By all means,' Nate said. 'Let us find them today. If they agree, I'll pay well.'

Hawkins nodded. 'I expect they will be pleased to hear that, sir.'

Chapter Eighteen

It was nearly the dinner hour and Eliza had no idea where her mother and father were. Her mother had gone out on morning calls shortly after Nate had left Eliza. She did not know if either her mother or father intended to dine at home.

One added anxiety she did not need at the moment.

She sat at the desk in the library, quill pen poised, trying to write a letter she did not wish to write. A letter to Ryland. To warn him.

But she could not compose it and could not turn her mind away from Nate. Had she convinced him to do nothing and to stay away from her? It seemed as if she tried over and over to do so and he did not listen.

Even acting as a crazed woman had not been enough to make him despise her. He came back, but now it was so much worse. He knew that he could stop Crafton's threat by marrying Lady Sibyl.

She put the pen down.

How she wished it could be all different! How she wished she could wake up in his arms again. Fall asleep after making love with him. Feeling him moving inside her—

She shook her head. It did not help to dream of that.

She had a mere twelve days before her world would tumble down on her. And on Natalie.

And the rest of her family.

And Ryland.

She must think of that.

Or how everyone would react when they learned the truth about her marriage.

She must not think of any of this! Just press on as if her world were not about to crash in on top of her.

Tomorrow she'd take Natalie to the Egyptian Hall. At least the child would see some of the sights Eliza had promised to show her. That should take Eliza's mind off Crafton.

And Nate.

She heard Barlow open the front door and her mother's voice sounded in the hall. A moment later her mother swept into the library.

'Oh, Lizzie, dear!' she exclaimed. 'I had the loveliest afternoon. Lord Fawlsley took me for a drive in the Park. Everyone was there. Simply everyone.'

Eliza was a little shocked. 'Did you wish to be seen? Will Papa not find out?'

'I do not care, I assure you!' she exclaimed, then she leaned towards Eliza and shook her finger at her. 'But do not say a word to him! This is just between you and me.'

As always.

Her mother turned and headed towards the door. 'I know. I know. I must change for dinner. I'll be down directly.'

She was gone.

This was all so familiar to Eliza. Her parents had been taunting each other with these old paramours ever since they'd arrived.

Barlow knocked and entered. 'A message from your father.' He handed Eliza the sealed note.

She broke the seal and read it.

Eliza,
I'm dining with Lady Holback tonight. If your mother
asks, tell her I'm with Blackburn.
Yours,
Sir J.

She would do no such thing. If her mother asked, she'd
say to ask her father when next she saw him.

Eliza crumpled the paper. Lies. Secrets. Manipulation.
Putting her in the middle of it. She was sick of it.

'Bad news, m'lady?' Barlow asked.

'No,' she admitted. 'Usual tomfoolery.' She rose and
threw the note in the fire. 'Tell Cook my father will not
be dining with us tonight.'

Barlow bowed and left and Eliza tried to compose a letter to the housekeeper at Sandleigh, saying to expect their
return in two weeks' time.

The words would not come for that letter either.

After several tries and more crumpled paper, Barlow
again came to the library door. 'Ma'am, Lord Hale has appeared at the back door with two other…fellows. He asks
to speak with you. What do you wish me to do?'

She could not help it. Her heart beat faster. Why was he
back so soon? Had he done something else foolish?

She could not receive him and his companions here in
the library. Her mother had just shown she'd breeze in at
any moment.

'I'll come down.'

Barlow walked ahead of her. The lower floor ought to
have been busy preparing dinner, but the curious faces of
the kitchen maids peeked out in the hall. No doubt Cook
was right behind them.

Nate and two men, dressed like workmen, stood at the
end of the hallway near the door, where Barlow must have
asked them to wait.

Imagine asking a marquess to wait at the back door. Poor Barlow.

'Barlow, is there somewhere I may talk privately with Lord Hale and his companions?' she asked.

'The servants' hall, ma'am?' he responded uncertainly, gesturing to a door near her. 'I'll make certain you are not interrupted.'

'That will do.'

Barlow approached the group and ushered them in to the servants' hall. Nate glanced at Eliza as he passed her and their gazes caught briefly.

Before Eliza followed them in, Barlow's brows knitted in concern. 'Do you wish me to stay, ma'am?'

How dear of him to worry. 'No, Barlow. It will be fine. But stay nearby, if you do not mind.' Just in case she needed protection from Nate, her protector.

He closed the door.

Nate began introductions immediately. 'Lady Varden, may I present Yates and Smith.' He gestured to them in turn. 'They were soldiers in my regiment. Good men.'

'M'lady,' Yates said.

Smith made an awkward bob of his head.

'Thank you for seeing us,' Nate said. 'We will not take up too much of your time.' His formal tone saddened her when their last contact had been a kiss.

'What is it, sir?' she asked in kind.

'Smith and Yates have agreed to help with Crafton.'

She glanced at the two men, not sure she'd ever seen any as rough. What did Nate expect them to do? Use their fists on him?

'I've hired them to follow Crafton,' he explained. 'But I wanted you to know their faces so if you see them, you will know who they are. And, of course, you can turn to them for help, if ever you need to.'

She shook her head. 'I do not understand this—'

'What we will do,' Nate said, 'is fight Crafton's fire with fire of our own. He must have something to hide, some secret he does not want revealed. These men, and others if need be, will follow him and try to discover what that secret might be. When we discover it, we bargain with Crafton. If he keeps your secret; we will keep his.'

She'd told him to do nothing. Instead he's devised a whole plan?

'You think this will work?' she asked. It sounded like grasping at straws to her.

'It has to.' Nate's expression was resolved. 'We will find something. A man like Crafton will be hiding something.'

How dare Nate make this plan, this impossible plan, and hire men for it when she'd asked him to do nothing? Even now he was not giving her the option to say no. He was merely informing her, that much was clear.

But somewhere inside her a tiny ray of hope glimmered. Would he rescue her one last time?

She turned to Yates and Smith. 'Did Lord Hale tell you why Crafton wishes to blackmail me?'

Nate answered for them. 'They know about your late husband.'

'Begging your pardon, ma'am, two lads in our company were like your husband,' Yates said. 'Good lads, they were.' He paused. 'Died together at Quatre Bras. We'll do our best in honour of them.'

She was touched—and surprised. 'I am very grateful to you.'

The two men nodded and looked uncomfortable.

'Well,' Nate said, apparently noticing their discomfort—or her coolness towards him. 'That is all. We will take our leave.'

'May I speak to you alone a moment first, Lord Hale?' she asked, keeping her voice even with effort.

'Of course.' He turned to his companions. 'I'll meet you outside.' Yates and Smith bid farewell and left the room.

Nate turned to her. 'I know you said I must not help, Eliza, but I will not stand by and do nothing.'

'You might have asked me first,' she said.

He smiled ironically. 'You'd have said no.'

He was right.

'And it seems a great deal of effort for a slim chance of success.' Time was running out, as well. 'Expensive, as well.'

Nate shrugged. 'The expense is a trifle. And we'll find something.'

'And if you don't?' She glared at him. 'Have your men assault him?'

He rubbed his face. 'No. Although I admit I've felt like showing him my fists. Or my sabre.'

She was horrified. 'You cannot do that.'

He shook his head. 'I'll not stoop lower than Crafton.'

She spoke in a serious tone. 'Report back to me, Nate. No more secrets. I mean it. I don't want to be kept in the dark about this. It involves my life and Natalie's more than anyone else.'

'I will. I promise,' he said, but Eliza knew better than to trust promises.

But she nodded as if she believed him.

'Shall I call upon you tomorrow?' he asked. 'If I have something to report?'

She'd be shocked if he had something to report so soon.

'Not in the morning,' she replied. 'I'm taking Natalie to the Egyptian Hall tomorrow morning.'

His expression was etched in pain. 'That should be enjoyable.'

She was sorry she'd mentioned Natalie, knowing it hurt him.

'I must go,' she said.

He nodded and moved to the door, opening it for her.

'Goodbye, Nate,' she said as she passed him. She hurriedly fled down the hallway before she said or did something she should not.

Like fall into his arms again.

The next day Nate met with Yates at a spot in Hyde Park they'd agreed upon. It was early enough that Crafton was most likely still abed. Nate's previous association with Crafton gave him some knowledge of the man's routine.

'He did not leave his house,' Yates said.

It was too much to expect he would expose himself the first night, Nate knew.

'I am not surprised,' he said.

There were few entertainments on nights Parliament was in session. But then, Nate was not expecting them to discover some vice at a society event either.

'You spoke of needing more men. Any luck on that?' Nate asked.

'Smith went to the public houses while I watched Crafton. He found three more of our men who were glad to help us. Patterson and Hawkins said they would take the watch while we organised. I'm meeting them after this.'

'Give them my regards,' Nate said. 'And tell them they will all be well paid.'

'Already did so, Major.' Yates touched his hat, almost like a salute. 'Best be on my way now.'

It felt natural to be called Major and to be saluted, Nate thought. 'Good job, Yates.'

Yates hurried off.

Nate wished he could have gone with him to see the other men, but it was best to leave them to their assigned duties.

He laughed at himself. *Assigned duties?* He was back in command, in his role as Major, as natural as breathing air.

He walked out of the park and reached the corner of Piccadilly and Half Moon Street. He paused, remembering this was where he'd last seen Natalie. His daughter. His flesh and blood, the flesh and blood of his mother and father. And Eliza.

With any luck he'd see her again today. He planned to wait until he saw Eliza and Natalie on their way to the Egyptian Hall. He knew he shouldn't, but he planned to follow them without them knowing so he could glimpse his daughter's reaction to the many specimens and artifacts to be seen there.

He waited almost three-quarters of an hour before he saw them. Eliza and Natalie. Natalie holding Eliza's hand. They were walking up Piccadilly towards the museum.

He followed them. All he intended to do was keep them in sight and not show himself, because he knew Eliza did not want him near.

Soon there it was, the Egyptian Hall, Bullock's Museum of curiosities, its façade made to mimic an Egyptian temple with pilasters and hieroglyphics and two huge statues of Egyptian figures above the entrance.

Eliza hoped that a Wednesday morning might find the museum uncrowded. Natalie had been reasonably excited about the adventure—as soon as she knew she could bring her doll with her—her Henry doll as Eliza thought of it.

Natalie oohed and ahhed at the ornate, Egyptian-inspired entrance.

'Maybe we will see an Egyptian cat!' Natalie cried.

Miss Gibbons had taught her that ancient Egyptians revered cats.

Perhaps when they returned to Sandleigh, Eliza would find a kitten for Natalie. There always seemed to be a kitten or two among the cats that lived around the stable.

She paid their two shillings and entered the great room of the museum.

Natalie stopped just inside the room.

It was an impressive sight. The walls of the spacious room were lined with glass cases of specimens of birds, shells, artifacts of all kinds. In the centre of the room were the largest displays. Full-sized beasts from mostly Africa, Eliza guessed. An elephant, a hippopotamus, zebra, birds larger than a man, all posed as if in their natural state.

Natalie slowly approached them and circled around them, not speaking a word, until she'd seen them all.

She looked up at her mother with tears in her eyes. 'They are all dead, aren't they?' Before Eliza could answer her, her voice rose. 'They are all dead. They're dead!'

'Natalie!' Eliza cried.

She leaned down to her distraught daughter, but Natalie pushed away from her and ran for the door, crying, 'They're dead. They're dead!'

She ran straight into a man's arms.

Nate.

He scooped her up and when she saw who he was, she sobbed. 'Lord Hale, all the animals are dead!'

Eliza stared at him in shock.

He gazed back with what she could only describe as a shared look of parental worry.

'There, now, Miss Natalie,' he murmured to her. 'The animals died a long time ago. The museum simply made them this way so we can know what they looked like. But you do not have to look at them if you do not want to.' He looked over at Eliza. 'Is that not right, Lady Varden?'

'Yes,' she managed to say.

Nate carried their daughter out of the building. Still grasping her Henry doll in one hand, she buried her face in his shoulder. Out on the pavement, he put her down and crouched to her level.

'There,' he said. 'We can no longer see the animals, can we?'

Natalie hugged her doll and shook her head.

Nate stood. 'I followed you, Eliza, but I assure you, I had no intention of making myself known to you.'

She was too upset about Natalie to spare anger at him. 'I should have realised…'

'Do not blame yourself,' he said.

She snapped back, 'Who else is to blame?'

He responded with comfort, 'Sometimes things just happen.'

His comfort upset her more. It was so much easier to be angry at him.

She took Natalie's hand. 'Shall we go home then, Natty?' Natalie pulled her little hand away. 'Mama! You said we could go to Gunter's and have an ice!'

Nate laughed.

'I did say that, did I not?' Eliza responded.

Still smiling Nate said, 'Allow me to get you a hackney coach. It is several streets to Gunter's.'

'Mama! Can we ride in a hackney coach?' Natalie asked.

'I suppose.'

He left them to find the nearest coach stand. Soon a coach pulled up to them and Nate disembarked. 'Here you are, ma'am.'

'Thank you, Nate,' she murmured as he helped her in and handed Natalie up to her.

'Enjoy your ice, Miss Natalie,' he said.

Natalie grabbed his coat sleeve. 'But you are coming, too, are you not, Lord Hale?'

The look he gave Eliza nearly broke her heart. So full of yearning.

She nodded. 'If you wish to.'

He climbed in. Natalie positioned herself between them,

her doll on her lap. She turned the doll to face her. 'This is Lord Hale, Henry. You have seen him before when we were on the way to the park.'

'Your doll is named Henry?' Nate asked her, darting a glance to Eliza.

'Henry was my papa's name,' Natalie explained. She turned to Nate. 'Did you know my papa, Lord Hale?'

Eliza was having a hard time holding back tears.

'I never had that pleasure,' Nate responded. 'I have heard he was a very good man, though.'

'The *best* man,' Natalie said emphatically. 'He loved me.'

Nate's gaze met Eliza's again and held for a moment longer than before.

This was excruciating, to hear Natalie talk of Henry to Nate, the man who had fathered her. Enough light came through the windows of the coach to see that Nate and Natalie had the same eyebrows, the same shape face, the same dark curly hair. Would other people also see the resemblance?

The coach pulled up to Berkeley Square near the tea shop.

'Shall we eat our ices inside the coach?' Nate asked.

'Oh, yes, please!' cried Natalie. 'I've never eaten ices in a hackney coach before.'

Eliza released a tense breath. At least no one would see them together and report back to Crafton.

'What flavour, Miss Natalie?' Nate asked.

'Elderflower!' she responded.

'I'll have the same,' Eliza said.

A few minutes later a waiter appeared at the coach window and took their order. Nate added, 'Ask the coachman what he would like, as well.'

Eliza wished Nate would not be so flawless. It made pushing him away so much more difficult. He was perfect with Natalie and did nothing that deserved Eliza's reproach.

Except for following them in the first place.

When their ices came Natalie chattered through each spoonful, with Nate's complete attention. When the hackney coach finally pulled up to Nate's door first, to lessen the chances they'd be seen together, Nate climbed out, but turned and, looking directly in Eliza's eyes, mouthed, 'Thank you.'

Chapter Nineteen

When Nate met Yates in Hyde Park on Friday morning, he was losing hope. So far the observations had led to nothing.

'We watched your man closely yesterday,' Yates told Nate. 'Just like usual we always have two men on him, so's one can get messages to us as to where they are or if anything big happens. Tuesday and Wednesday nothing, as you know.'

'And yesterday?' Nate asked.

'Last night was more promising. After his house went dark, we thought it would be more of the same, but then his door opened and out he comes. His carriage shows up and we follow it.' The man smiled. 'To Covent Garden.'

'To Covent Garden?' Nate asked. That was promising.

'He seemed to be looking for something or someone around the arcades, but then it started to rain and he left. Took his coach back to his house.'

'Hmmm.' Nate knew one could find prostitutes in Covent Garden. 'I wonder what that was about.'

'He seemed pretty set on being there,' Yates said.

Would Crafton return to Covent Garden tonight? Most of society planned to attend the Theatre Royal this night to see Kemble in *Coriolanus*. Nate had originally been invited to share Crafton's box for the performance. Unlikely he could count on that, but he might be able to find a seat somewhere.

'Good work, Yates,' Nate said. 'I'm going to attend the theatre at Covent Garden tonight. So is Crafton, I believe. Perhaps he will go to the arcades again.'

'We'll be on him, Major,' Yates assured him.

Nate nodded. 'I'll observe him while he is in the theatre and I'll find you and Smith after. I'd like to see for myself what he was looking for in the arcade.'

'Very good, Major.'

They parted and Nate walked on to White's where he met Everly and Bentham for drinks before they needed to return home for dinner. The more time he spent with these men, the more he liked them, even though they were more like the aristocratic boys of his youth with their impressive lineage and would not have any reason to know him without his title. Now he outranked them.

When the opportunity afforded itself he asked them about the theatre.

'Good God,' cried Everly. 'I could not get out of attending if I tried. My wife has been talking of it all week.'

'Just one week?' scoffed Bentham. 'I've heard of nothing else for a month.'

'I was planning to attend,' Nate said. 'At Crafton's invitation, but you can bet that invitation is rescinded.'

'Well, come with us,' Everly said. 'My father would welcome you, I am certain.'

'You had an extra seat?' Bentham exclaimed. 'How did you keep from giving it to Sir John or Lady Wolfdon?'

Everly smiled. 'I said we had no space.' He turned to Nate. 'So you see, I need you to come, Hale. If they've found some other box to sit in and see an empty chair in ours, it will be hell to pay.'

'In that case, I will accept your offer. I will meet you at the theatre.'

Everly gave him the number of the box.

If Eliza's parents were begging seats, maybe Eliza would not be attending. He wondered if he dared attempt to meet her in her garden ahead of time to ask. If he did meet her, he could thank her for that precious time with Natalie.

Likely there was no time to do so, however. He'd chance that she'd pass up the theatre.

That night Nate found the theatre box and rapped lightly on the door and was given entry. Lord and Lady Locksworth greeted him warmly, as did their son and their daughter-in-law, Eliza's sister. Among the other guests was Eliza. They greeted each other with a mere nod, but Nate did not miss the irritation in her eyes.

In another box within easy sight were Crafton and Lady Sibyl. Lady Sibyl would have been appalled not to have a full box, so the chairs were filled with her particular friends. And Lord Lymond whose purpose was probably to admire her. Lady Sibyl did bask in admiration. Nate once thought the admiration was deserved.

Eliza's sister manoeuvred him into a seat right next to Eliza, though. When no eyes were on them Eliza glared more openly at him.

He leaned over and spoke quietly. 'I did not think you would be here or I would not have accepted the invitation.'

'It can do no good at all for me to be seen with you,' she whispered.

'We are far enough in the back that Crafton and Lady Sibyl cannot see us,' he assured her. 'I am here only to watch Crafton.'

But he could not ignore they sat close, close enough to whisper together, close in the darkness. Just what he needed. To be close to Eliza in a dark place.

There was enough light to see that Eliza looked as beautiful as usual. She wore the same dress she'd worn to the ball and that somehow gratified him. Made him feel as if she, too, did not take all this society nonsense seriously.

He gazed over at Crafton's box. What if he could discover something useful from Crafton? Nate thought about Lady Sibyl's effort to be 'cordial' to him at the musicale. Maybe that wasn't such a bad idea.

If Nate acted friendly in return, perhaps she and Crafton would think their plan was working and maybe he could learn something. Maybe Crafton would let his guard down. Had he not learned in the army to study the enemy? The more you knew, the better your strategy.

The curtain opened and the play began.

Even if there had not been the usual buzz of conversation blocking the actor's oratory, Nate would have had difficulty attending to it. His mind was on Eliza. Every slight change in her posture. Every whiff of her scent. Any change of expression as the play progressed.

The play, from when Nate could attend to it, was all about an outsider trying to break into the power of Rome. He knew the ending. Coriolanus succeeded but was killed. He'd sacrificed himself.

All this came too close to home for Nate.

At the intermission the noise grew louder as members of the audience left their seats. This was the time for visiting other boxes, for some, the whole purpose of attending the theatre.

Nate whispered to Eliza. 'I am going to pay my respects to Lord Crafton and Lady Sibyl.'

'No, Nate!' she whispered back.

'Do not fear. I am merely making Crafton think I am coming over to his side. We're following him tonight. Might have something to report after.'

She returned a sceptical look.

Everly had about the same reaction as Eliza when Nate told him he would visit Crafton's box.

'Say you are not!' Everly countered. 'Why ever would you do that? Were they not trying to trap you into marriage?'

Nate responded. 'They were. I suspect they still are, but Crafton's Society for the Reformation of Manners troubles me. I want to see if I can influence him to give it up.'

Everly scoffed. 'Like promise to marry Lady Sibyl? I dare say that will do it.'

Everly unknowingly guessed the gist of his and Eliza's plot. How clever of him.

'I'll not go that far,' Nate assured him. That was a last resort.

In the corridor Nate spied Eliza's mother on the arm of the same gentleman Sir John so objected to at the musicale. Was Sir John with Lady Holback, then?

When Nate appeared at Lord Crafton's box, Lady Sibyl looked genuinely astonished, but characteristic of her, she did not lose her composure. In fact, the only time Nate saw her lose composure was when he told her he would not marry her.

'Hale,' she said brightly. 'How good of you to call.'

'I thought I might pay my respects,' he told her. 'Repay your cordiality to me.'

She stepped forward and shook his hand.

Lymond also stepped forward. 'We did not notice you were here,' he said, his smile pasted on his face.

Nate nodded to him. 'I was invited to share Lord Locksworth's box.'

'Lord Locksworth?' Lymond repeated.

Lady Sibyl's eyes narrowed.

'He's been quite decent to me of late,' Nate went on, but he was not here to converse with Lymond. He turned to Lady Sibyl. 'And how are you liking the play, Lady Sibyl?'

She clasped her hands together. 'I think Kemble is divine. How the theatre will miss him!'

It was the popular opinion, of course. She always knew the right thing to say.

Nate kept an eye on Crafton, but he was surrounded by his cronies and engrossed in conversation. He chatted for a few more minutes with Lady Sibyl and took his leave. At least Crafton noticed he was there. Even if he somehow realised Eliza was in the same theatre box as Nate, perhaps he would not put much stock in it.

He returned to the Locksworth box and resumed his seat. Eliza pretended to look at the play's handbill.

Somehow Nate endured the rest of the play but rose as the last scene concluded.

He said a swift goodbye to Everly and left the box.

He positioned himself nearby the door to Crafton's box so he would be able to see and follow him after the play. He waited while he presumed Crafton was saying his goodbyes to his guests.

Finally Crafton emerged, accompanied by his daughter and Lord Lymond. Nate followed them to the line of carriages waiting.

Nate heard him say, 'Lymond, will you see Lady Sibyl home for me? I agreed to meet someone.'

'My pleasure, sir,' Lymond responded.

'Will you be late, Papa?' Lady Sibyl asked. It was already one o'clock.

'Might be. Might be.' He patted her hand. 'Do not wait up for me.'

Nate watched Crafton step back from the carriage when someone took his arm.

It was Eliza.

'I'm coming with you,' she said.

'You are not,' he responded. 'Go home with your sister.'

'She thinks I'm riding with Joanna.' She tightened her grip. 'I'm going with you.'

Lymond helped Lady Sibyl into the carriage and Crafton looked as if he was ready to dash away. Nate did not have time to argue with her.

'Come on.' Crafton started off towards Covent Garden's square. Nate refused to lose him. 'Keep up. We don't want to lose him.'

Keeping Crafton in view was difficult in the dark of night with so many men dressed nearly alike. Nate could not afford to take his eyes off him.

'Blast it, Eliza!' he said, though. 'This is no place for a woman.'

'Even if it is your plan, you cannot order me about,' she retorted. 'I am finished with others telling me what I must do.'

Eliza's decision to accompany Nate was impulsive, made in the instant he left the box early. She'd grabbed her cloak, said a quick word to Susan. Before Susan could ask or protest, Eliza had dashed off.

She felt exhilarated. Like finally she was doing something she chose to do, even if it was merely following Nate.

She'd found him near Crafton's box door, but stayed out of his sight, only coming to his side when he was watching Crafton and Lady Sibyl at the carriages. How could he leave her then, unaccompanied in that crush of people?

Her excitement grew as she and Nate followed Crafton to the square. Crafton suddenly slowed his pace, stopping as if taking his bearings. Nate pulled her into the shadows of a storage shed where they could still see Crafton.

'What is he doing?' she whispered.

'We do not know yet,' Nate whispered back, his tone angry. 'And you are a complication we do not need.'

'A complication?' How dare he call her a complication.

'Again, I remind you I have the most right to be here. Just stop being so overbearing.'

'Overbearing?' he huffed. 'Did no one tell you that Covent Garden at night is a dangerous place?'

'But I have a soldier to protect me,' she countered.

There was a sound behind them and Yates and Smith emerged from the shadows.

'Three soldiers,' she corrected smugly.

'Beg pardon, Major, but what is the lady doing here?' Smith asked.

'She insisted,' Nate responded.

'I will be no trouble, gentlemen. I assure you.'

The night was cool and Eliza was glad she'd worn her hooded cape and glad it was a dark fabric that blended with the night.

Crafton moved and they turned their attention to him. He sidled to a less conspicuous space, but they could still see him.

Yates inclined his head. 'This is where he was last night. Before it rained.'

They stood and watched. The cacophony created by the carriages picking up the theatregoers quieted to an occasional sound of hoofbeats and wheels. Crafton had not moved and neither had Eliza and her companions.

Until a lady's voice cried, 'I will not go with you! Not to some filthy place!'

They all turned to see a gentleman pulling a lady's arm. The pair were dressed as if they'd just come from the theatre.

'Come with me now,' the man said.

'I will not!' She wrenched her arm out of his grasp. And the hood of her cape fell back. There was just enough light from the new gaslights on the street to show her face.

'Goodness! It's my mother!' Eliza said.

And a man who looked like Lord Fawlsley. He was trying to force her to go with him somewhere.

Fawlsley waved his hand. 'As you wish. I am leaving.'

'No,' her mother cried. 'How shall I get home?' She tried to hurry after him.

But he was too fast and he soon was out of sight. Crafton must have also heard the commotion. He left his chosen perch and looked as if he wanted to cross the square, but did not want to be seen by her mother.

'What am I to do!' her mother wailed. 'What am I to do?'

'I have to go to her.' Eliza started towards her.

Nate held her back. 'No. I'll go.' He turned to the soldiers. 'Yates, you take Lady Varden to my carriage. Foster is waiting nearby. You'll find him. I'll take her mother in a hackney. Smith, you stay with Crafton.'

'Yes, sir!' the two men said.

'Wait here until I get her away.' Nate crossed the square to where she was wringing her hands. 'Lady Wolfdon?' he asked when close.

She spun around as if being accosted but flung herself into Nate's arms as soon as she saw who he was. 'Oh, it is you! I am so very happy to see you. I am in desperate need.'

'Of course, my lady, I will assist you.' He extricated himself from her grasp and took her arm. 'Would you like me to see you home?'

'Oh, yes! If you would be so kind.'

Nate turned towards Crafton, who stared at Eliza's mother and Nate, but as soon as they were out of sight, Crafton hurried across the square. Smith left to follow him.

'Come, m'lady,' Yates said.

They walked back to where the carriages picked up the theatregoers and quickly found Nate's carriage.

'What?' Nate's coachman said.

'It is too hard to explain,' Yates responded. 'Major says to take the lady to Clarges Street.'

'Will we arrive there before Lord Hale?' Eliza asked Yates as he helped her inside.

'We should. Foster knows how to drive the horses.' He closed the door and climbed up next to the coachman.

Nate's coachman did drive the carriage at a good speed and it helped that the streets were nearly empty of other vehicles.

She rapped on the roof when they reached her house and Yates appeared to help her out.

'Thank you, Yates,' she said. 'And thank the coachman for me.'

She hurried to the door.

Barlow opened it immediately.

She handed him her cloak. 'Barlow, has my mother arrived yet?'

'Not as yet.' He looked at her in somewhat of alarm.

'Excellent,' she replied. 'Can you quickly bring me some wine or brandy or something? My mother will be here in any minute. I'll wait in the library.'

She'd hardly paced the length of the library twice when Barlow returned with a decanter of brandy and two glasses. A second glass for her mother? Not likely her mother would tarry to share a glass with her.

He returned to attend the hall and Eliza poured herself a glass of brandy and sank into a chair to drink it.

How exciting it had been to be with Nate, spying on Crafton, like she was finally acting instead of reacting to what someone else did. And how ironic that he should rescue her mother this time. Was he working his way through the entire family? First rescuing her from the rain—and from running away—next her father and now her mother. She could argue that he'd also rescued Natalie from the hall of death that had been the museum.

Why did Nate have to be so wonderful, so perfect at times? It made leaving him even more difficult.

Chapter Twenty

It took some time for Nate to find a free hackney coach since most had not returned yet from taking theatregoers home, but one eventually pulled up to the stand. All the while Lady Wolfdon clung to his arm and declared that she did not know what she would do if he had not come along. Over and over.

When he finally had her seated in the coach, she seized his arm once more, anxiety in her voice. 'You will come with me?'

'I will,' Nate assured her.

He gave the jarvey the direction and climbed in beside Lady Wolfdon, who had not questioned why he knew precisely where to take her.

'I cannot believe Fawlsley is such a cad!' she cried as soon as the coach moved into the street. 'To think I would be willing to go with him to some disreputable tavern he knew of! Why would he think such a thing?' She did not pause for a response even if Nate could have thought of one. 'I mean, I am not above an assignation, but in a filthy tavern?'

'Lady Wolfdon—' Nate attempted to interrupt. She should not be taking him, a virtual stranger to her, into such intimate confidence.

Unheeding, she went on. 'I was delighted when he invited me to share his box to see Mr Kemble—not that I could follow that play at all. Never could comprehend anything Shakespeare wrote. Now Sheridan is different. Did you ever see *Duenna*? A libretto, you know. I always adore the music. I once heard Lord Byron call it the best opera ever written and one can always value his taste, if not his morals.'

A year ago, Lord Byron was all but run out of England in a scandal that included cruelty to his wife and extra-marital sexual escapades including a supposed affair with his half-sister.

Lady Wolfdon paused for a breath and seemed to find her way back to the topic of Lord Fawlsley. 'I tell you, though, I have never been so shabbily treated. That Fawlsley is no gentleman, I assure you.'

Nate had heard that some taverns around Covent Garden were places gentlemen took ladies for assignations, places they could be private and unlikely to be seen by wives or anyone else who might know them. Of course some of the more expensive ladies of the night might use those same taverns.

Had Crafton been in the square at Covent Garden to meet a prostitute? Nate might have expected such behaviour from other men, but Crafton never gave Nate any indication of such interests. An assignation with a prostitute would not be enough to use as blackmail, though. Too many aristocrats frequented women of the night.

Whatever it was, Lady Wolfdon had interrupted it.

Lady Wolfdon kept up her chatter as the hackney made its way down Piccadilly to Clarges Street.

As Nate helped her out of the carriage she whispered, 'You, of course, will say nothing of this. I cannot have it reach the ears of my husband.'

'You can trust my discretion,' Nate replied.

He paid the coachman and walked Lady Wolfdon to the door, which flew open.

Eliza and her butler were standing in the doorway.

'Mama!' Eliza exclaimed. 'Where have you been? I have been frantic with worry.'

Eliza knew precisely where Lady Wolfdon had been.

'This gentleman, Lord...' Lady Wolfdon waved her hand. She still did not remember his name.

'Lord Hale,' he supplied helpfully.

Lady Wolfdon brightened. 'Oh, the Marquess. How silly of me to forget.'

Eliza spoke. 'Lord Hale. Mama. Do come in so we can close the door.'

Nate was glad to do so. He had some words for Eliza.

After the butler closed the door behind them, Eliza turned to her mother. 'Where have you been? We expected you ages ago.'

Her butler raised his brows at that statement. She would, of course, only have arrived a few minutes before them.

Her mother handed the butler her cloak and dramatically placed her forearm on her forehead. 'Oh, I am too fatigued and distressed to go into it tonight. Be a good daughter and wait until tomorrow. Tomorrow I will tell you all.' She started up the stairs but turned. 'Do not say anything to your father. *He* does not need to know a thing.'

When she disappeared Eliza faced Nate. 'Would you care to come to the library, Lord Hale?'

He followed her to her library which was right off the hall. As soon as they entered, she poured him a glass of brandy and one for herself.

'Was what happened with my mother what I think it was?' she asked.

'A failed assignation, do you mean?' he responded. 'Fawlsley was apparently planning to take her to a room in a tavern,' he said. 'Your mother did not wish to go.'

She gave a dry laugh. 'Yes. She would have been offended. A room in a tavern would not suit her at all.'

He finished his brandy and put the glass down on a table. 'That is all beside the point, Eliza. It was dangerous out there for your mother and for you. I will tend to this. You can trust me on that.'

Her eyes flashed. 'Trust is not the issue, Nate. It is control. If I wish to do something, I will do it. You have no say in it.'

'Of course I have a say in it,' he shot back. 'It is my plan.'

'A plan I expressly asked you not to make,' she pointed out. 'I asked you to do nothing about Crafton. Nothing. It is my life he is trying to ruin. I should have the say on what was done about it.'

'But you planned to do nothing!' he countered. 'To just let him ruin you!'

'That was my choice!' she cried. 'I choose to do nothing. Since it is my life at stake, I ought to be the one who chooses.'

'Since the ransom to be paid is my betrothal to Lady Sibyl, I would say I also have a stake in it. Not to mention the damage it would do to our daughter.'

She straightened. 'Our daughter? Oh, that is another thing. You followed us to the Egyptian Hall. You admitted it. You knew I did not want you to see her and you deliberately went against my wishes.'

He stepped closer to her and his voice got very low. 'You know very well why I wanted to see her, Eliza, and you know what that encounter meant to me.'

Eliza felt his words like a dagger to her heart. Yes, she knew. She knew he treasured that afternoon with his daughter.

She faced him, lowering her voice as well. 'Yes, Nate. I know. But it doesn't necessarily mean my wishes can be discarded. I must determine my own life. And Natalie's. You witnessed how vulnerable she is. I must protect her.'

He still looked wounded. 'Do you not see I want to protect her, too? Both of you. Not control you.'

She held his gaze. 'I know you do not understand what I am saying. Even at the beginning, you insisted on taking me on your horse when you found me in the storm, even though that was one time I was acting on my own—'

'You were running away,' he corrected.

He was right. 'Perhaps I was running away, but that was what I decided to do.'

'And you decided to return to your husband after that night,' he added.

She shook her head. 'You showed me I had no choice, really. And now you've decided we should marry. Because of Natalie. And you decided on a plan to stop Crafton when I decided to do nothing. I told you not to see Natalie and you followed us—'

His eyes flashed. 'I do not deserve this set down, Eliza. Look who is controlling here. You will not allow me to get to know my own daughter. You decide to handle Crafton all by yourself even though it is my life he wishes to manipulate. Helping you is not controlling you, Eliza. But you are too busy taking everyone's problems on to your own shoulders to recognise help when it is offered.'

Their gazes held. He stood close to her, so close she had only to take a step and she'd be enfolded in his arms.

'Goodnight, Eliza,' he said in clipped tones.

He turned on his heel and walked out of the room and, once again, she experienced the pain of him leaving her.

She heard him speak to Barlow in the hall, then the door opened and closed again and she knew he was gone.

He was wrong, wasn't he? About not accepting help? He must be wrong. He simply could not understand.

She hated herself, hated that she'd had to push him away

with such angry words, even if the words she spoke were true. Her resolve almost crumbled when he had stood so close to her in the dark room lit so like the cabin. Her chest ached. She would never feel his arms around her again.

That was what she gave up. Gave up because she was afraid he would take over her, like everyone else. She loved him, but she did not trust him. How could she?

Everyone—her parents, her sisters, Crafton, society itself—expected her to do as they wanted her to do. Even Nate. Her impulsive act to follow Nate this night was her doing as she *wished* to do. The excitement of that moment returned. She'd taken the reins of her life into her own hands.

Her exhilaration dissipated quickly, though, and she sank into a chair.

Why did the price of her freedom have to be paid at the cost of hurting Nate in such a fundamental way? She wanted to hold him and never let go. She wanted to lead him to her bed and make love with him again, share that exquisite pleasure they could create together.

But giving him what he most desired—her and Natalie—meant relinquishing her life. She'd already lived in the shadows of another man's life. She could not bear taking the risk of doing so again. Not when her widowhood gave her freedom.

Eliza took in a deep bracing breath.

She'd undoubtedly see Nate again at the society entertainments. At least the ones that occurred before Crafton brought down scandal on her head. And Natalie's. And her family's. And Ryland's. Nate's plan of catching Crafton in something nefarious seemed impossible.

No matter her newly discovered resolve, at the moment Crafton controlled her destiny, not she. But once he exposed Henry, once he ruined her, she would be free of him. Because there was nothing else Crafton could do to her.

* * *

The next day Eliza's internal turmoil subsided. She felt in control for once. She also felt incredibly sad.

She'd hurt Nate, the finest man she'd ever known, the only man she dared love. He'd been strong for her. He'd rescued her in so many ways. He'd even rescued her father and mother. His kindness to them was remarkable.

But it was his tenderness towards Natalie that made her ache inside. How could she keep such a wonderful man from her daughter? Was she being unfair?

Unfair or not, it hurt him. *She* hurt him.

It did not bear thinking of.

She breakfasted alone, which did not surprise her. Her mother was probably avoiding her and avoiding having to explain to her why Lord Hale had brought her home at that late hour. Her father had staggered in from wherever he had been an hour after Nate left.

Being alone with her thoughts was not a good thing at the moment, so she ate hurriedly and went upstairs to the nursery.

'Mama!' cried Natalie when she entered the room. Natalie bounced up from where she sat with Miss Gibbons, a slate and chalk in front of her. 'I was practising my computation.'

Eliza gave her daughter a hug and a kiss. 'That is very fine. Will you show me?' She turned to Miss Gibbons. 'Good morning.'

'Good morning, ma'am.' The governess smiled. 'Natalie is doing quite well as you will see.'

Natalie sat down again and used a cloth to wipe her slate. Eliza stood next to her chair.

'Give me two numbers,' the child said confidently. 'Not as big as one hundred.'

'Very well.' Eliza would not make it too difficult. 'Twenty-two and forty-five.'

Natalie scribbled the numbers on her slate and carefully wrote the answer. *Sixty-seven.*

'Well done!' Eliza exclaimed.

'See?' Natalie pointed to the slate. 'First, I add the two and the five, then I add the other two and the four!'

'How clever of you,' Eliza said. 'I am quite impressed.' And she was glad Natalie was excited about something besides her doll, even though the Henry doll was seated on the table in front of her as if overseeing her lesson.

'Miss Gibbons taught me.' Natalie said.

Eliza gave the governess an approving smile.

'She learned quite quickly,' Miss Gibbons said.

Eliza pulled up a chair next to Natalie. 'Show me more.'

Conjuring up numbers for Natalie to add and making certain they not too difficult almost kept Eliza's mind off Nate. And Crafton. And the scandal that seemed inevitable.

Soon, though there was a little rap on the door which burst open.

Her sister Susan swept in.

Natalie again jumped up from her chair. 'Aunt Everly!'

Susan engulfed Natalie in a hug. 'Good morning, sweet girl!'

When she released her, Natalie picked up her doll and thrust it towards Susan. 'Aunt Everly! Have you seen my new doll!'

With a quizzical glance to Eliza, Susan properly oohed and ahhed over the male doll. Then Natalie went on to fuss over placing him back on the table just so before writing more numbers on her slate.

'I am delighted to see you, Susan,' Eliza said. 'But surprised.' It was still early for morning calls.

Eliza's sister grinned. 'I am here on a mission!'

This did not bode well. 'A mission?'

'I know you, Mama and Papa all received invitations to Lady Lansdowne's ball tonight and I came to make certain you do not wear the same gown you have worn three times before.'

'It is the only gown I brought,' Eliza protested. 'So perhaps I should not attend.'

Avoiding the ball meant avoiding Nate, Crafton and Lady Sibyl. That seemed most desirable.

'Nonsense!' cried Susan. 'You must come with me now to my house. Let us see if one of my gowns might do.'

'Really, Susan, it is not necessary—'

Her sister interrupted her. 'I insist!'

Natalie looked up from her computations. 'A ball, Mama! You must go to a ball and wear a pretty dress.'

'Indeed she must.' Susan hugged Natalie again. She turned to Eliza. 'See? Even Natalie agrees.' She took Eliza by the arm and pulled her towards the door. 'I've sent a message to Joanna to meet us there.'

'Goodbye, Mama,' Natalie cried cheerfully. 'Pick a pretty dress!'

Nate's morning found him more restless and agitated than he could stand, thinking incessantly of what Eliza accused him of. It had kept him from sleep, from any productive activity. Even a bruising ride on Pegasus shortly after dawn had not helped.

Eliza was wrong. Surely she was wrong. He did not try to control her or ignore her wishes. He protected her. *Loved* her. He would do anything for her or their daughter. He'd *die* for them if necessary. He wanted only their happiness, their safety.

That was not controlling.

When he left his house again to walk back to Hyde Park to meet with Yates, he strode in determined steps as if his boots pounding on the pavement would pound the disquiet from his heart.

He arrived at the meeting place early, which left him

more time to think, to wonder if his scheme to stop Crafton was futile. He was still determined to stop the man, to keep Eliza's reputation safe, to ensure an untainted future for his daughter, no matter what Eliza said she wanted. He was right in this. He was certain he was right in this.

But what if he did not discover anything disreputable about Crafton? What if he was unable to protect his family?

He heard a man approach, but it was not Yates, but Smith.

'Morning, Major,' Smith said. 'It is me this morning, because I was the one to follow Crafton.'

'What have you to report?' He sounded more like the Major than the Marquess even to his own ears. Was that how he sounded to Eliza?

Smith shrugged. 'There is not much. The man caught a hackney and went to his town house. Unless he left when I was coming here, he's still there.'

Nate's spirits sank even deeper. 'That was expected, I suppose.' If only Lady Wolfdon had not shown up when she did.

Would it have made any difference?

'I did see something,' Smith added. 'Don't know if it was anything.'

'What did you see?' Nate asked.

'Looked like some man left the house after Crafton went inside. Not Crafton, though.'

Nate nodded. Might have been a footman. 'Well, we simply keep up the watch,' he said to Smith. 'Tonight there is a ball that I am certain Crafton will attend. I will be there as well. I'll try to join you afterwards to follow him. See if he returns to Covent Garden.'

'We'll look for you, sir,' Smith said. 'Yates and I will be on the night watch.'

'Good. We'll meet up tonight, then. After the ball.' Crafton needed to show his true colours soon. Nate wanted to be present when he did.

'Yes, sir!' Smith replied.

He turned to leave, but Nate called him back. 'Get some sleep, Smith!'

'Yes, sir!' Smith even saluted before hurrying off.

Nate certainly acted the Major with Smith, he realised. He might have asked the man if it was wise for him to meet up with them or if he thought any of this was worth it. He might have asked what Smith thought they should do next instead of merely barking orders. Had he been that way with Eliza?

No. Surely he was different with Eliza.

Nate rubbed his face and started for White's.

Her sister Susan's home was the very large town house of her husband's parents, Lord and Lady Locksworth. It was also the place where she'd first seen Nate again at that first ball her sisters dragged her to. Before then her memories of Nate had been confined to a stretch of road between Henry's and her parents' country houses and a cabin where she and Henry used to play. Now so many places would remind her of him.

Susan's carriage left them off in front of the town house, where Joanna was waiting for them. They were soon in Susan's bedchamber, where Susan's lady's maid had strewn several gowns across Susan's bed and stood aside, ready to assist.

Susan gestured to the bed laden with silks and muslin and gauze and lace of all colours. 'My mother-in-law contributed some, as well.'

The two sisters pulled one dress after another and made Eliza hold them against her body while her sisters decided whether the dress warranted trying on. All the dresses were beautiful, as finely made as the best London modistes could produce, but Eliza did not really care. At first she wanted something that would make her as inconspicuous as possible. Her sisters, though, talked of her making a great splash.

And Eliza suddenly thought of the ball in a different light.

She could use the ball to show Lord Crafton and his daughter that she was not intimidated by Crafton's threats. She'd been running scared, wanting to hide. Better to face them, was that not what Nate would say? Face them with courage. Take some control.

'How about this one?' Susan held up a confection made of a gold silk underdress and gold gauze overdress, trimmed with gold beads. 'As I recall, Lady Locksworth never wore it.'

The gold dress glittered in the daylight from the windows. Candlelight in a ballroom would make it incandescent.

Joanna inspected it carefully 'It might do.'

Her heart beating with excitement, Eliza said, 'I'll try it on.'

Chapter Twenty-One

Saturday evening finally came. Patterson helped Nate dress for Lady Lansdowne's ball. Patterson had been on Crafton's watch part of that day. The activities he reported were all benign. Crafton had walked to the shops and home again. He'd not met anyone.

The night offered the next best chance to catch Crafton in some vice. Vices flourished in the dark.

After he finished dressing and descended the stairs, Nate's thoughts drifted back to Eliza. He would not approach her though.

He'd see her at the ball. He wished he could speak with her there. Renew their discussion. Convince her he wanted only what was best for her and Natalie.

What was the use? She would not give him another chance. He was not certain she even should. Perhaps he was precisely how she described him. Overbearing. Controlling.

Nate would also see Lord Crafton at the ball. Lansdowne was known to invite lords from both sides and Crafton would not miss an opportunity to mix with both Tories and Whigs to try to interest them in his society. Nate would watch him and follow him after the ball. With luck they'd discover why he visited Covent Garden so late at night.

In the hall, Hawkins helped Nate into a cloak which

he wore more as a disguise in case Crafton glimpsed him later on. The night was chilly and breezy, though, so the cloak might also be welcome for warmth. Besides the chill, the weather was fine. Clear skies, bright moon, a perfect night for whatever Lady Wolfdon had interrupted before.

'Good luck, tonight, Major,' Hawkins said. 'Remember. Third time's a charm.'

'I hope you are right,' Nate said. He stepped outside to his waiting coach.

Ordinarily Nate would have walked the four streets to Berkeley Square, but this night his coachman Foster drove him in the curricle, a vehicle more suited to afternoon drives in Hyde Park, but more nimble to pursue Crafton wherever he might go.

The curricle dropped him off a street away from the Lansdowne town house.

'I'll be watching,' Foster told him. 'I won't let you down, Major.'

'I know you won't,' Nate responded.

He walked the rest of the way, through the gate and across the front garden that allowed the Duke of Devonshire to have an unobstructed view of Berkeley Square from the back of his mansion on Piccadilly.

Nate was admitted by a footman tending the door at Lansdowne House. There was already a crush of guests in the hall waiting to enter the ballroom. Nate was greeted by some of the Whig lords to whom he had suddenly become agreeable.

He finally reached one of the arched doors to the ballroom and was announced. In the receiving line Lord Lansdowne welcomed him with seeming pleasure and introduced him to his wife whom he'd seen at the various entertainments but had never formally met.

'I have heard fine things about you, Lord Hale,' she said to him.

Fine things? Nate could not imagine what that could be. 'I thank you, my lady.'

Nate walked into the ballroom, trying not to gape. The room was a wonder of beauty, an expanded version of the formal rooms in the Hale town house which looked miniature by comparison. The colourful and ornate plasterwork was matched in the chairs and sofas pushed over to the walls. The room and all the areas of the house he'd just walked through were a grand reflection of generations of wealth. Clearly his own ancestors had limited vision in comparison.

'Hale!' a cheerful voice called.

Bentham strode over to him, hand extended.

'Good to see you, Bentham.' Nate shook his hand.

'Come join us.' The man brought him over to a group that included Everly, their wives—Eliza's sisters—and their parents, the Locksworths and the Winbrays.

How ironic that the friendliest acquaintances he'd experienced since inheriting his title were Eliza's family and, before them, Crafton, her most dangerous enemy.

Bentham turned towards the doorway and commented to his wife, 'Oh, blast. Your parents have arrived.'

Nate glanced over. Framed in the doorway, though, was Eliza, her parents behind her.

'Elizabeth, Viscountess Varden,' the butler announced. 'Sir John Wolfdon and Lady Wolfdon.'

Nate was struck dumb. Eliza was a vision. The dress she wore looked as if it had been spun out of gold and lit from within.

Others were also staring at her. Nate heard several murmurs of approval. Indeed, there was nothing to do but admire her.

Eliza's sisters made sounds of delight.

Lord Locksworth commented, 'Elizabeth looks remarkably well tonight.'

'Indeed she does,' his wife agreed, turning to toss a conspiratorial smile at Eliza's sister who returned like smiles.

Nate needed to avert his gaze lest Eliza see him gaping at her. He scanned the room and saw Crafton and his daughter taking in Eliza's entrance with less enthusiasm.

By the time Nate dared to glance back at Eliza, she and her parents had already been through the reception line. Her parents stepped away from her and were whispering to each other, each looking very vexed. They parted and went their separate ways, leaving Eliza standing alone.

Her sisters soon remedied that, rushing over to her and bringing her over to join the group. Nate withdrew to the outskirts of it and engaged Lord Locksworth in conversation, merely nodding a greeting to Eliza, who nodded back.

Soon after, Lord and Lady Lansdowne left the receiving line and the orchestra tuned their instruments, signalling that the dancing was about to commence. Everly and Bentham quickly engaged the partnership of their wives for this first set. Nate knew he had to slip away lest he and Eliza be placed in a position where they had to dance together. She noticed his departure and looked…approving.

To his surprise, though, Lymond approached Eliza and, with a look less than pleasure, Eliza seemed to accept his invitation. Nate glanced over at Lady Sibyl who was trying not to appear distressed at being partnerless. Nate made a quick decision.

He walked over to her. 'Are you engaged for this dance, Lady Sibyl?'

'Not as yet,' she equivocated.

'Perhaps you would accept an old friend as a partner?' He held out his hand.

A moment of suspicion flickered in her eyes, but she recovered and assumed her most charming façade. 'With pleasure, my lord.'

Lady Lansdowne had chosen a country line dance for

the first set, which Nate appreciated. He was often not equal to the more elaborate, livelier dances.

While he and Lady Sibyl awaited their turn to dance down the line, she did the socially correct thing and engaged him in conversation.

'How do you do these days, Hale?' she asked. 'Since I so rarely see you.'

'Except at the theatre last night,' he responded. He was not likely to tell her what really consumed his time and energy these days. And his thoughts.

'Oh, that is right,' she responded with a sweet smile. 'I had quite forgotten.'

Nate fell silent.

Lady Sibyl undoubtedly felt compelled to converse. 'I see you have been befriended by Everly and Bentham. How nice for you.'

'They have been quite cordial to me, that is true,' he said.

She turned her smile ironic. 'Have they persuaded you away from my father's companionship, then?'

Nate felt she was fishing for information. About what? Was she trying to decide if he was coming back to her?

He decided to tell her a version of the truth. 'I must admit that your father's idea for this society of his has put me off.'

'Oh?' Her brows arched in interest, then she gave him an amused look as if imparting the cleverest joke. 'Do you have a *tendre* for such people then?'

He answered seriously. 'I see it as an issue that does not need addressing. Especially where the country has much bigger problems.' He composed his expression into a patronising one. 'But I would not bore a lady with a discussion of such matters.'

He noticed her attention caught further up the line. Eliza

and Lymond were approaching. Lady Sibyl's eyes narrowed. Nate pretended not to notice.

Eliza only now saw that Nate had joined the line of dancers. With Lady Sibyl. What was he about? Partnering with Lady Sibyl for the first dance?

Still, Eliza reacted as she always did at the unexpected sight of him. Unable to breathe. She managed to dance past him, trying not to show how her whole body came alive when she brushed past him in the dance. Much too close.

Lady Sibyl looked exceptionally beautiful this night in a pink, gauzy gown that floated around her like a cloud. Perhaps even Eliza's gold gown paled in comparison.

She shook off the thought. This was a night for courage, not self-doubt.

Eliza and Lymond reached the end of the line and she would have to converse with him again. She'd seen him in Lady Sibyl's company often enough to make her especially suspicious of him. Why ask her to dance at *this* ball when he'd not done so before?

'Gracious!' he exclaimed. 'Did you see Lady Sibyl with Lord Hale? I wonder if romance has been rekindled.'

'Was there a romance between them before?' she asked in a polite tone as if merely doing her duty to converse with him.

'Everyone was certain they would be betrothed before the Season was out,' he replied. 'Perhaps it is still true.'

Now Eliza realised why Lymond asked her to dance. He'd wanted an opportunity to taunt her about Lady Sibyl.

'Perhaps,' she responded in a uninterested tone.

Lymond glanced back at Lady Sibyl. 'I do believe she outshines every lady here tonight.' He faced Eliza again with a smirk. 'Except for you, of course, my dear.'

What possible stake did Lord Lymond have in this

drama? He was certainly attempting to fuel her jealousy towards Lady Sibyl.

More concerning, what were Nate's motives? Nate, she knew, would not do something so spiteful as try to make her jealous. He was angry with her, but he'd never be vindictive.

Lymond changed the conversation. 'And how are your parents enjoying the Season?'

Lymond was working very hard to dispirit her. 'I believe they are reasonably entertained.'

Eliza's father had not gone into the game room. That was a good thing. And her mother had cut Lord Fawlsley and was seated with some of her lady friends. So far her parents were both behaving themselves.

At long last the excruciating dance was over and Lymond returned Eliza to her sisters who immediately pulled her aside.

'Why on earth did that man dance with you?' Joanna asked.

'There can be only one reason,' Susan said. 'He is after Eliza's money.'

Eliza was very certain it was not her money Lymond was after.

Joanna leaned close to Eliza and spoke earnestly. 'Under no circumstances should you become involved with that man. He is a rake and a fortune hunter.'

Eliza laughed. 'Do not worry on my account. He holds no appeal.'

Her sisters breathed a collective sigh of relief.

'We do worry, Lizzie,' Joanna said. 'You are so very eligible and, I tell you, all eyes were on you when you walked in. I dare say you will not want for partners tonight.'

Except she did not really *want* dance partners. She much preferred being at home. But she was at this ball to put on a show of bravado and put on a show she would.

It seemed to be working. Lord Crafton kept glancing her way, a frown on his face. Had he expected her to cower in fear of him? She'd face him with courage, as Nate had taught her.

Susan nudged her. 'Eliza, here comes young Darrow. Mark my words he's going to beg an introduction. You need to know he's poor as a church mouse and barely out of leading strings.'

Eliza stifled another laugh. 'Do not worry. I assure you I am not in the market for marriage.'

Darrow did get his introduction and Eliza danced the next set with him. As she performed the figures, she glimpsed Nate trying not to look at her and Crafton glowering at her. For Crafton's benefit, she acted as if she was enjoying herself. Indeed, Darrow was a sweet young man. She wished him well, but she was glad when the dance ended.

Afterwards, Eliza stepped out of the ballroom, looking for some relief from the crowd. As glad as she was of her newfound strength, the ball was tedious and she wished she was home.

And away from the pain in Nate's eyes whenever their gazes met.

She was about to enter a nearby room when she heard a woman's laughter and a man's voice inside.

She heard the woman say, 'You naughty man', then more laughter.

As Eliza stepped away from the doorway, Lady Sibyl and Lord Lymond emerged, his arm around her. They did not see Eliza.

Lady Sibyl was receiving some consolation since Nate had broken with her, apparently. It did seem that Lymond was often around Lady Sibyl.

Eliza abandoned her quest for a quiet moment alone and returned to the ballroom.

Crafton walked in her direction.

Eliza lifted her chin. She refused to be intimidated by him any longer.

He approached close enough she could smell his revolting perfume. 'May I engage you for the next dance, Lady Varden?'

She looked him directly in the eye. 'If you must.'

As he led her to where the line for the dance was forming, Crafton looked her up and down. 'Your appearance is vastly improved, my lady.'

Eliza smiled disdainfully. 'Is it? It must be the gown. Do you find it pleasing, Crafton? Others have told me so.'

He looked her over again and his gaze made her skin crawl. 'Ah, yes,' he agreed, returning a cold smile. 'It is the gown.'

Crafton tried other ways to deride her, but Eliza never rose to the bait. When the dance was over, he escorted her to a secluded spot where no one could hear what he said to her.

'You are aware of your time limit, are you not, Lady Varden?' he sneered. 'One more week. One more week and I will tell the *beau monde* all about your dear late husband.'

She straightened and she realised she was as tall as he.

She glared directly into his eyes. 'How cowardly you are, Crafton.'

He laughed. 'And you are pretending to be brave, are you not? But I've noticed Hale seems to have renewed an interest in my daughter. I am glad you took my threat seriously, but you must hurry him. Only a week, you know.'

Her gaze did not waver. 'I have asked nothing of Lord Hale. How could I broach such a subject to a man I hardly know? If he is interested in Lady Sibyl, it is his own idea, foolish as that may be.'

'Foolish?' His face turned red. 'There is nothing foolish about courting my daughter! I swear to you, Lady Varden,

I would relish ruining the memory of your husband and you in the process!'

So Crafton fancied always having power over her? No. He could only hurt her once.

So Eliza did not flinch. In fact, she almost smiled. 'Will you? I wonder...'

With that she turned and walked away.

Nate noticed the exchange between Crafton and Eliza. Eliza looked as if she'd held her ground. Nate was proud of her. Her newfound strength was very appealing.

Although he ought not to think of how appealing she was.

Crafton certainly seemed disturbed this night, but perhaps that was because he seemed unable to interest some of the lords in discussing his society. More than once he walked to the ballroom windows and peered out as if contemplating an escape.

Nate saw his posture change. Crafton then strode over to Lady Sibyl and whispered something in her ear.

He was saying goodbye, Nate realised. He was leaving the ball.

Nate made a quick decision. He hurried over to where Eliza stood, momentarily alone.

'Crafton is leaving,' he said to her in a low voice. 'I'm going to follow. Do you wish to come with me?'

She gaped at him in surprise. 'Yes. I'll catch up to you in the hall.'

Crafton approached Lord and Lady Lansdowne, saying his goodbyes probably. Eliza spoke to her sister and turned in Nate's direction. Nate's anticipation grew. Perhaps tonight would be the night Crafton revealed himself.

Nate reached the hall right as the footman attending the door was closing it, behind Lord Crafton probably. Nate was not too late.

'My cloak, if you please,' he said to the other footman. 'And Lady Varden's.'

By the time the footman retrieved both garments, Eliza had reached Nate's side. They threw the cloaks over their shoulders and hurried out the door.

The street was lined with carriages whose lamps helped light the street. Nate saw Crafton several carriages away, climbing into one of them. As that carriage pulled out of the line, a man dashed after it and climbed on to the back unseen. One of Nate's men, no doubt.

Another vehicle appeared in the street right in front of him.

'Major!' a voice cried. It was Foster.

Nate lifted Eliza into the curricle beside his coachman and climbed in himself. They were off, Foster keeping within sight of Crafton's carriage while still casting curious glances at Eliza.

'Lady Varden, this is Foster,' Nate said.

Foster's brows rose knowingly.

'Foster is another of my former soldiers,' he explained to her.

'A pleasure,' she responded breathlessly.

Nate could not help but ask, 'What did you say to your sister?'

She took a breath. 'Only that I was leaving and to see Mama and Papa got home. I suppose I will have some explaining to do later.'

As expected, Crafton headed directly to Covent Garden and in no time Nate and Eliza joined Yates and Smith in the same spot where they'd watched Crafton the night before. The two men nodded politely to Eliza.

'He's standing in the same place,' Smith told them, keeping his voice low.

They waited and gradually other figures appeared, disappearing into the shadows under the arches. Crafton crept closer and appeared rapt by some activity there.

'I'll see what it is,' Yates whispered.

Remaining in the shadows, he moved around until Nate could no longer see him, but they could easily make out Crafton remaining spellbound. Then a figure left the archway and Crafton retreated to a lighted spot. He pulled a notebook and pencil from his pocket and made a notation. After replacing both in his pocket again, he walked off in the direction of the hackney coach stand.

Yates returned to Nate's side. He tapped Smith on the arm. 'We'll follow him,' he said to Nate and the two were off.

Nate and Eliza stood alone in the shadows of Covent Garden where obviously men were meeting other men beneath the arches.

'I'll take you home,' Nate finally said.

Chapter Twenty-Two

Eliza walked in silence with Nate back to the curricle, the weight of disappointment slowing their steps. Eliza never dared to believe Nate's plan would yield results, but it was crushing to realise she'd built up hopes just as strong as his. Because now they were dashed. Nate would discover nothing useful against Crafton. Crafton would expose Henry in a week's time.

When they reached the curricle, the coachman asked, 'Back so soon, Major?'

'There was nothing to discover,' Nate said in a depressed voice.

The coachman shrugged. 'Where to, then, Major?'

'We take Lady Varden home,' Nate replied.

When they reached her street, Nate turned to her. 'Will you meet me in the garden in a half-hour?'

She should not, but she nodded. They needed to talk about this. She wanted him to know she appreciated him for trying…to *help* her.

The curricle stopped in front of her house and Nate helped her down. She did not wait for him to walk her to her door but ran up to it and sounded the knocker once.

Barlow opened it immediately and she entered. He noticed the curricle drive away.

'Is there anything amiss, m'lady?' he asked.

'Oh, Barlow!' She sighed. 'So much is amiss! And you have been so kind as to not question me about it.' But he deserved some sort of explanation. 'Lord Crafton found out something about my late husband and he threatens to disclose it to the world. Lord Hale has tried to help me stop him, but there is nothing we can do.'

Barlow looked concerned, but unsurprised. 'May I be of assistance in any way?'

Eliza hugged him. 'You already have. You have been so discreet about Lord Hale's comings and goings. I must ask for your discretion again. I am going to change my clothes first, but must meet him in the garden in half an hour. I'll need my cloak.' She threw it over her arm and hurried up the stairs.

Lacy jumped out of a chair when Eliza opened her bedroom door. 'Beg pardon, ma'am. I must have fallen asleep.' She glanced at the clock. 'But are you not home early?'

'Yes. Help me into another dress, will you, Lacy?' Eliza dropped her cloak on the bed. 'I must go out again. I—I must meet someone in the garden.'

'Lord Hale, ma'am?' Lacy asked.

Eliza swung around to her. 'Yes. Lord Hale.'

'The kitchen maids said he came from the garden with two ruffians before.'

'He—he is helping me with something.' Eliza probably would explain more to Lacy as well. But not tonight.

And Lacy did not ask her more. She helped Eliza change into the walking dress she'd worn earlier in the day. Eliza picked up her cloak again and ran out.

Nate already waited in Eliza's garden, where he'd met her before. The night they'd made love.

This night, though, was not filled with that anticipation, that eagerness, that feeling that he'd truly come home.

But this must not be an ending. Nate might have lost this skirmish with Crafton, but he'd not admit defeat. In a battle one strategy might fail, then one retrenched and tried a new tactic.

The door opened and Eliza emerged.

He stepped into her view. 'Will you come into my house? We can talk there.'

She nodded.

They walked side by side through her gate, entering his and crossing the yard to his door. He'd told the servants to retire for the night so they would be alone. He brought her up to the library, the room where she first came to accuse him of deliberately seeing Natalie.

What next for them?

If Crafton made good his threat, Eliza would leave and take Natalie with her. Unless Nate changed the battle plan.

'Please be seated, Eliza.' He walked over to a cabinet and opened it. 'Brandy?'

'Please,' she responded.

He brought out the decanter and glasses and poured for them, handing her a glass before taking a seat himself.

'I'll keep Yates and Smith on Crafton,' he said. 'But it is clear to me it will be useless. Watching men at Covent Garden and taking notes about them is distasteful, but nothing he'd need to hide.'

'I am forced to agree,' she replied in a soft voice. 'So there is nothing left to do. It was good of you to try, but there was never anything to be done. When Crafton makes good his threat, I'll retire to the country where Natalie and I can live away from the scandal.'

'There is something else we can do,' he insisted. 'Marry me. My rank will offer some protection, will it not?'

She shook her head. 'Then you will be ruined, too.'

'That does not matter to me,' he insisted. 'I'd prefer the retired sort of life you are facing. In the country. Away from town.' He'd prefer any life that kept her with him.

She gave him a shocked look. 'You cannot simply leave, Nate. You have responsibilities. To your estates, and the people who depend upon you for their livelihood. To your country, even. As a marquess—'

'A marquess.' He spoke the word with disgust. 'I was never meant to be a marquess. I know nothing about being a marquess.'

'You do so.' She spoke earnestly. 'You know how to command. I've seen it. I've *experienced* it. What is a marquess but a leader in command?'

'Then retire with me to my estates,' he said. 'My principal seat is grand enough for Natalie to run as far as she wants.'

Her brows twisted in confusion.

'Never mind,' he said, waving his words away. 'Just marry me. I can direct everything from wherever you wish to be.'

'But you cannot help enact laws unless you come to town. You have a duty to your country, too, Nate. The other lords are starting to listen to you. I've noticed it. They are seeking your opinion. My sisters' husbands esteem you enough to call you friend.'

He sank down on the sofa and reached for his brandy. He drank it down. 'I have been an outsider among such men all my life. Now you tell me I am one of them and, because I am one of them, I cannot be a part of you and Natalie?'

The ache inside him was nearly unbearable. Why could she not see reason? It was all so clear to him that they could work it out if she would only agree to try. He was ready to stand by her, no matter what. Why did she not feel the same?

Unless...

He looked up at her. 'What you speak is all nonsense, is it not, Eliza? About me needing to be a marquess. You say so merely because you are afraid to trust me. You do not believe I would be good to you. Good to Natalie. You do not believe that I would do anything to see you both safe and happy. You think I wish to control you or I only want you because of Natalie. You believe anything but that I love you.'

He hardened his gaze at her.

She lowered her gaze.

He went on. 'I have tried in every way I know how to prove to you I will do anything for you and Natalie. Sacrifice anything. And you do not believe me. You do not trust me.'

He said he'd sacrifice anything and he meant it. There was one more thing he could do.

Nate had one final hand to play and in this hand he held all the cards.

Nate's words pierced Eliza's heart. They stung because they were true. She was afraid, afraid that the moment she fully trusted him, all would change. As it had before. With Henry.

If she said goodbye to him now, he could remain for ever the Nate of her fantasies. Her captain.

Besides, she did not need rescuing any more. She finally felt strong, strong enough to conquer whatever life threw at her. She was strong enough to make her own decisions, her own choices. She had enough wealth to take care of herself and Natalie. She did not need Nate overwhelming her life, commanding her.

She would be safe alone.

But he was not commanding her now. He was *asking* her. He was saying he *wanted* to be with her, with Natalie. Precisely what she yearned for.

And what she was most afraid to do.

So she'd hurt him instead. What sort of person was she?

He lowered his head in his hands.

She sat down beside him. 'I—I am sorry, Nate.' Her words seemed feeble. 'I simply can't.'

Can't overcome her fear, she meant.

He was so right about her.

He turned his face to hers. 'Then this is goodbye. We cannot be together.'

Her insides fluttered in panic. Goodbye? Never to be with him again?

He stood.

She rose, too, feeling shattered inside, but still unable to summon the courage to do what he'd asked. Trust him. Marry him. Put her life in his hands.

He was right. She was all nonsense. She had no courage, not really. She was simply afraid.

'Then—then I should go.'

He walked with her through the library doorway, through his hall and down the stairs to the back door. He walked her all the way across their gardens to her back door.

And then he left her, backing away into the night until she could not see him any more.

It had been hard for Eliza to fall asleep after the events of that night. The disappointment. The despair. The self-loathing. The being too afraid to venture into the unknown with Nate.

She finally dozed off when dawn crept over the horizon, but a voice broke through her slumber. 'Mama! Mama!'

Eliza opened her eyes. Natalie had climbed on her bed and was looking directly into her face. 'Mmm…' she said. 'Good morning, Natty.'

It was a good thing she was well practised in hiding her misery.

'It is Sunday, Mama,' Natalie said. 'Will you come to church with Miss Gibbons and me? I want you to.'

Eliza rose.

The church was St James's Church, a short distance down the street on Piccadilly. It was not the most fashionable church in Mayfair, but it was closest and the early service suited Eliza well enough. The skies were blue and the air clear. It would make a lovely morning walk for Natalie.

Eliza could at least make her daughter happy. She must console herself with that.

The street was usually busier but, being Sunday morning, many of the residents of Mayfair were still abed, recovering from the various entertainments of the night before. Like the Lansdowne ball. Eliza had yet to face any repercussions from leaving that ball so early.

With Nate.

She tried to walk briskly, disguising her low spirits.

Eliza, Natalie and Miss Gibbons walked past Devonshire House, so elegant and massive its property reached all the way to Berkeley Square, to where she had been the night before. Next came Burlington House, equally as impressive. They stopped in front of Albany, the gentlemen's residence, waiting for some slowly moving wagons laden with goods to pass so they could cross the street.

The sound of laughter behind them made Eliza turn. A woman in a hooded cloak emerged from an Albany door. The woman pulled a man out with her and gave him a very passionate kiss.

'Oh, my!' Miss Gibbons exclaimed.

Luckily Natalie's interest was taken by the horses passing by and she did not see the man fondle the woman intimately. When he released her, Eliza had a glimpse of his face before he disappeared into the building.

Lord Lymond. Dressed only in a banyan.

Eliza regarded the woman more closely. She appeared to be wearing dancing slippers. Her cloak blew open a bit, revealing a gown of pale pink. But the woman covered her face with her hood as she headed away from the building.

Eliza took a chance. 'Lady Sibyl?'

The woman froze and turned her way, undeniably revealing precisely who she was. Her eyes were wide with alarm, then panic as she reversed her course, rushed up to Eliza and clutched her arm.

'Lady Varden,' she pleaded. 'Please say nothing of this! It—it—is not what you think—I mean, it will ruin me. No gentleman will have me. It—it—was just one mistake. Surely you will understand.' She started to sob. 'Please. Please. I am begging you.'

Eliza knew the feeling. Like the whole world would come crashing down upon her. She could not help but feel sorry for the younger woman.

Eliza shook her. 'Compose yourself, Lady Sibyl. Leave before someone else sees you.'

Lady Sibyl nodded and turned on her heel, but turned back, tears staining her cheeks. 'Please, ma'am. Please do not ruin me!'

She hurried away, covering her face again.

'Who was that lady, Mama?' Natalie asked, her little brows knitted. 'Why was she crying? Did somebody die?'

Eliza's attention turned fully to Natalie. Was death so often on her mind? 'No, dearest. Nobody died. The lady was just somewhere she was not allowed and she does not want anyone to know.'

Natalie's face lit with comprehension. 'Oh, like when I ran away from Miss Gibbons in the park and Lord Hale talked to me.'

And Eliza had chastised him for it. 'Yes, dearest. A little like that.'

Natalie turned her attention back to the passing carriages. 'Look, Mama. Two white horses.'

An expensive carriage pulled by a beautiful, matched pair rumbled by and the street cleared enough for them to cross. They dashed to the other side and continued on their way to the church, Natalie running ahead.

Lady Sibyl's terrified expression would not leave Eliza's mind. Nate was already lost to Lady Sibyl, but this would make it impossible for her to make any respectable match.

'My goodness,' Miss Gibbons exclaimed when Natalie skipped far enough ahead of them to be out of earshot. 'I can hardly believe I saw what I saw. You know her, obviously.'

'I know who she is,' Eliza responded.

'An unmarried lady?' the governess guessed.

'Yes,' Eliza replied.

Miss Gibbons shook her head. 'That would be a scandal. An unmarried lady visiting a gentleman in his private apartments.'

'It would be ruinous for her,' Eliza agreed.

'She sounded so frightened.' Miss Gibbons lowered her voice, even though Natalie still was too far away to hear her. 'Are you going to keep her secret?'

Eliza thought about it. The means to wreak revenge on Crafton and Lady Sibyl had fallen into her hands. Eliza could do to Lady Sibyl what Crafton was going to do to her.

Did she want to create such misery for his daughter? She knew precisely how it would feel. 'How can I not keep her secret? I do not want to cause the ruin of anybody.'

Not even Lady Sibyl.

Besides, who would she tell? Nate? He already knew what sort of person Lady Sibyl was. To tell anyone else would merely be malicious gossip.

Some secrets were better kept.

Chapter Twenty-Three

Nate spent Sunday holed up in his library alternating between depression and anger—and wretchedness—and fruitless searching for some other way out of his dilemma. Out of what he feared he must do.

Both Hawkins and Patterson tried at various times to cajole him out of the room. Or to encourage him to eat, but he was having none of it. The only companion he desired was brandy. Or whisky. Or anything to shut off his emotions.

Nate heard his butler and valet discussing him outside the library door. At times other voices joined them. Foster, for one. Even Yates and Smith.

Why hadn't Hawkins gathered the whole 2nd Battalion of the 30th Regiment while he was at it? Let them all fret about him.

Nate wanted to be alone, as he'd always been, to rage about the decision he'd made. Once done there would be no going back.

After his men finally abandoned standing sentry over him, Nate made his way up to his bedchamber and a fitful night's sleep.

In the morning he acted as if nothing happened. He rose at dawn. Rode Pegasus on Rotten Row. Returned to change clothes and eat breakfast. At his usual time, he met Hawkins in the hall.

'I am bound for my meeting with Yates,' he told Hawkins. 'I trust he will be there.'

'Did not say otherwise, Major,' Hawkins responded.

Nate nodded and left his house. When he reached the corner, he stopped, recalling the moment his little daughter had charmed him in this very place.

And Eliza had hurried her away.

It was still true. Nate lost anyone he dared love.

Nate shook his head and trod on, entering the park and following the path to where he and Yates met.

The former soldier was waiting for him, pacing back and forth. When he heard Nate approach he looked up, an expression of concern on his face.

'Wasn't sure you'd come today, Major,' Yates said.

Nate shrugged. He'd not made their meeting the previous day.

'Have you anything to report?' Nate already guessed the answer.

'Nothing, Major,' Yates started to walk with Nate on the path they usually walked. 'Crafton left his house after noon. Called upon some other lords who live around here. Didn't stay long any place. Went home again then out to what looked like a dinner at what we were told was Lord Bathurst's house. Then he went home.'

Lord Bathurst was a powerful Tory, a close friend of Wellington and Castlereagh, Nate had heard. A worrisome alliance for Crafton to have. If Bathurst came around to support Crafton's society—

Nate must stop that cursed society as well, but, at the moment, Eliza was his priority.

'As I expected,' he said to Yates.

'If you will pardon me saying so, Major,' Yates continued, 'this Crafton fellow does his mischief among the likes of you and the lady. That's bad what he wants to do to the lady, but I doubt you lords will blink an eye at any of it. Not against Crafton, that is.'

Nate nodded. 'I agree. I cannot see making you men continue this surveillance. I'll pay you for the rest of the week, though. Have the men come to the house tomorrow.' He'd try to find other employment for them, if he could.

Nate walked next to Yates in silence until they reached the place where they usually parted.

'What will you do about the lady, Major?' Yates asked.

Nate gave an ironic laugh. 'Get married.'

Yates broke out in a grin. 'To Lady Varden, Major?'

'No.' Nate could not even force a smile. 'To Lady Sibyl. Lord Crafton's daughter. I'm on my way to call upon them now. If I see the man watching Crafton, I'll tell him he can leave.'

'It is Smith, sir,' Yates said.

'I'll tell him,' Nate walked away, heading to Crafton's house on Dover Street.

Nate could not make himself call upon Crafton right away, though. He detoured a street out of his way to Berkeley Square and sat on one of the shady benches where diners at Gunter's often ate their ices. A child and her governess played at the far end of the square, reminding Nate of Natalie. About the same age.

Would it not be fine to witness Natalie growing up? She was so little now, but she would grow taller and smarter and he would not be a part of it.

He turned his gaze away from the little girl and watched a man and woman open the door of Gunter's Tea Shop. Nate closed his eyes and relived when, parked in a hackney coach on this very square, he, Eliza and Natalie ate ices together like a family. At least he had that memory to savour. That wonderful day.

At least he was ensuring that Eliza and Natalie would never again be threatened by Crafton.

He'd said he'd do anything…

Nate sat there for what might have been a whole hour before rising again and walking over to Crafton's town house. He found Smith easily enough and sent him on his way before sounding the knocker.

It was early. Much too early for morning calls, but Nate wanted no delay.

Or he might lose his nerve.

Crafton's butler opened the door and looked surprised to see him. 'Lord Hale. It is so early. I fear Lord Crafton and Lady Sibyl have not quite risen.'

Nate pushed past him and stepped inside. 'I'm here to see Crafton. Rouse him. He will want to see me. I'll wait in the drawing room.'

'Yes, m'lord.' The butler squirmed but did not question Nate's authority.

Apparently Nate's commanding nature had its uses.

Nate cooled his heels in the Egyptian-inspired drawing room that now looked to him as more of a contrivance than the latest in decor. He waited nearly half an hour before Crafton entered, a little out of breath.

Crafton went on the attack. 'Hale. By God, you are not a gentleman. No gentleman calls upon another at this early hour.'

Nate fixed him with a cold glance. 'Would you have me wait until a more decent hour? I am here to end this threat of yours.'

Crafton's expression changed. 'Oh? Does that mean my requirement will be met?'

Nate did not blink. 'That largely depends upon you, sir.'

'Upon me? No. No. No. I believe I have made myself very clear…' Crafton's voice was suddenly eager. 'But I will hear you out. Never say I am not a reasonable man. However, I am not asking for much, am I?'

Only for the rest of Nate's life.

Eliza was finishing breakfast when Barlow appeared at the door.

'Several…uh…fellows ask to speak with you, ma'am,' he said. 'I believe two of them called here before with Lord Hale.'

Yates and Smith, did he mean? Why ever would they call on her?

Unless something happened to Nate.

She rose quickly. 'I will see them.'

She followed Barlow to the hall where he'd left them to wait, hats in their hands, and he stood behind her as she approached them.

She blurted out, 'Lord Hale. Is he—?'

Yates responded quickly. 'Oh, he is not hurt, m'lady.'

Now she was puzzled. 'Then, why—?'

Along with Smith and Yates were two more finely dressed men.

One of them spoke. 'Permit me. I am Hawkins, m'lady. The Major—I mean Lord Hale's—butler.' He gestured to the other like-dressed man. 'This is Patterson, his valet. We are all the Major's men from the 30th—'

Yates interrupted him. 'The thing is, we talked it over and came to it that we must come and tell you.'

Eliza was becoming impatient. 'Tell me what?'

Hawkins spoke again. 'We think the Major—Lord Hale—has gone to Lord Crafton's house—'

Smith interrupted this time. 'He has gone there. I saw him myself.'

Hawkins gave him an annoyed look. 'He told Yates he was going there to marry Crafton's daughter.'

'He did not seem happy about it, m'lady,' Yates added.

Eliza felt the blood drain from her face.

No. Impossible. Nate could not do this. Not for her. Not to rescue her. He must not.

'I must stop him.' She turned to Barlow. 'Tell my parents, Miss Natalie, tell them I've gone out.'

Barlow gave her an encouraging look and moved to open the door. 'I'll tell them.'

She rushed out the door followed by Nate's men. 'I do not know where Crafton lives.'

'We know,' said Smith, gesturing for her to follow.

At the end of the street a familiar curricle pulled up beside them.

Foster, Nate's coachman, called down to them, 'I got the message. Climb in, Lady Varden. I'll get you there post-haste.'

One of Nate's men lifted her up beside the coachman and he signalled the horses to pull away and to run faster than seemed prudent.

Eliza's mind was in a whirl. Would she be in time? Would Nate listen to her? Would she convince him? What could she do?

In a flash of clarity, Eliza knew precisely what to do, how to defeat Crafton and remove his power over them all. Of course, she'd warn Ryland first. By messenger, if need be, but it would solve everything.

Why had she not thought of it before? Oh, yes, she'd been raised to make this the last thing she'd think of.

Ironically, it had been Nate who knew the answer all the time and the answer certainly did not entail him marrying Lady Sibyl.

It meant simply facing the truth.

'Here is what I require.' Nate stood over Crafton who remained seated in the chair. 'First and foremost, you are to do nothing to interfere in Lady Varden's life. You are not to hold this story about her husband over her head ever again.' No need to admit to the truth about Lord Varden. 'Or anything else.'

Crafton nodded. 'If you agree to marry my daughter, I will say nothing about her late husband.'

'You will forgive me if I do not automatically trust you, Crafton,' Nate retorted. 'Any man capable of such a threat must also be capable of lies and deceit.'

Crafton laughed. 'You wound me, Hale.'

'There is more,' Nate said. 'You must give up this society of yours. Give up the idea of persecuting people who are not doing you or anyone else any harm.'

'Give up my society?' Crafton shot to his feet. 'Never! It is a grand idea. It will make my name—.'

'What is more important to you, Crafton?' Nate pressed. 'That your daughter marries a marquess? Or your society? Because you may not have both.'

'This is an outrageous request!' Crafton shouted.

'It is not a request,' Nate stated. 'It is a demand.'

There was a knock on the door and Crafton's butler poked his head in. In an incredulous voice he announced. 'A Lady Varden to see you, m'lord.'

'Lady Varden?' Crafton cried. 'Tell her I am not home!'

Eliza was here? What the devil?

The butler made a helpless sound and Eliza pushed past him, hatless, gloveless, cheeks flushed and eyes lit with resolve.

She looked magnificent.

'I am really here to see Lord Hale.' She turned to Nate. 'I won't let you do this, Nate.'

'It is already done!' cried Crafton.

Nate glanced back to him. 'You have to agree to my terms first, Crafton,'

Eliza ignored Crafton. She faced Nate instead.

'I know what to do,' she told him. 'It was in front of us

all the time, but we did not see it.' She took his hands in hers. 'It is so simple. I will tell the gossip first! Before Lord Crafton. Of course, I will warn anyone who needs warning so they can prepare, but, you see, if I tell the truth and it is already known, Crafton has no power over us at all.'

'No, Eliza. The scandal—'

The gossip could get vicious. It undoubtedly could follow her and Natalie for the rest of their lives. She must not appreciate this, because she looked so completely calm, radiant even.

'Don't you see, Nate?' she said. 'The scandal can only hurt me once. I will lose the hand I was dealt, but I'll play it. I won't leave the game.'

The door opened again, but this time it was Lady Sibyl dressed in a nightdress and robe. 'I heard voices. I was *trying* to sleep,' she snapped.

But then she noticed Nate and her expression lit with pleasure.

Until she also saw Eliza.

Lady Sibyl advanced on Eliza, grabbing her by the shoulders.

'You!' She shook Eliza. 'You told them, didn't you? How could you!' She pushed Eliza away and looked from Nate to her father. 'You mustn't believe her! She is lying!'

She started to attack Eliza again, but Nate caught her and held her back.

'Enough, Lady Sibyl,' he demanded. 'Control yourself. Lady Varden has not been talking about you.'

'Not talking about me?' Lady Sibyl paled for a moment, then shook her head. 'I do not believe you! She told you! She must have!'

Nate looked to Eliza. 'What does she think you told us?'

Eliza didn't answer him, though. Instead she addressed Lady Sibyl in a calm, patient voice. 'I did not speak of— of what you fear I did. I never intended to tell anyone. Do you not think I, of all people, would know how devastating the threat of scandal can be?'

Lady Sibyl lowered her gaze.

'I need to know what happened,' Nate said. If it was something so important that Lady Sibyl turned into a raving witch, he needed to know. 'You have to tell us now.'

Eliza cast a regretful glance at Lady Sibyl. 'I would have kept silent, but I will not lie for you.' She turned to Nate and Crafton. 'I saw her walk out of Albany early Sunday morning still dressed in her ball gown. She left Lord Lymond, who stood in the doorway wearing only a banyan. She kissed him and he fondled her.'

Eliza certainly did not mince words, Nate thought.

'Lord Lymond!' Crafton shouted. 'You were with Lymond?'

Nate almost laughed out loud. He had been right all along about discovering something nefarious to counter Crafton's threat. But he'd looked in the wrong place. He ought to have had his men follow Lady Sibyl.

Lady Sibyl fussed with the lace on her robe. 'It was not what she thinks, Papa.' She glared at Eliza. 'Lymond and I were merely…talking. We were talking! I—I met him on the way to church—'

'Dressed in your ball gown?' Crafton's voice rose even higher. 'Fondling you!'

Lady Sibyl's expression turned maniacal. 'She wants Hale! That is what she wants. She knows I am a rival! She wants to ruin me!'

But Lord Crafton was having none of that. He was apoplectic. 'You? With Lymond? How could you be so foolhardy? No respectable gentleman will want you now. You've ruined yourself!'

Crafton was right. Lady Sibyl, expert in all the nuances of society, had broken one of society's strictest rules.

Her father raised his fist. 'I ought to throttle you!'

'No! Papa!' Lady Sibyl wailed. 'You are going to make Lord Hale marry me.'

'Not now, Lady Sibyl.' Nate could not keep the sarcasm from his voice. 'As your father said, now no respectable man will marry you. And neither will I.' He flashed a quick smile at Eliza. 'But I do have a proposition.'

Crafton glowered at him. His daughter dabbed at her tears with the sleeve of her robe.

Nate used his most commanding voice. 'Lord Crafton. You will give up your society and all plans to persecute those it would affect. Neither you nor Lady Sibyl will say anything against the late Lord Varden or Lady Varden. In return Lady Varden and I will say nothing of Lady Sibyl's…indiscretion.' He turned to Eliza. 'Do you agree to this?'

She nodded. 'If Crafton agrees, I will agree.'

Nate turned to Crafton. 'Do you agree?'

Crafton's face went bright red with fury. 'You give me no choice.'

'I do know how that feels,' Eliza murmured just loud enough for Nate to hear her.

He faced Lady Sibyl next. 'You also must agree.'

Crafton piped up. 'She will keep her mouth shut. I will see to it.'

Lady Sibyl sniffed loudly.

'Very well, then,' Nate said. 'You will write out the agreement now for us to sign. I want your seal, as well.'

'What about your seal?' Crafton challenged.

'You cannot require it,' Nate told him. 'You have to trust us.'

Crafton made a growling sound like a dog ready to attack, but suddenly his shoulders sagged. 'Come to my library.'

He slunk to the door and opened it. Eliza and Nate followed him. Lady Sibyl dragged behind.

Her father turned and jabbed his finger in her direction, his energy momentarily returned. 'Not you, Sibyl. You go to your room. Not another word out of you or *I* might tell the world you are no better than a common strumpet!'

Lady Sibyl wailed and fled to her room.

Chapter Twenty-Four

In the library Eliza watched Nate direct Crafton on the wording of the agreement. He made the man make two more copies.

She felt lighter. No wonder. An incredible burden was off her shoulders. She and Natalie were safe from scandal. Nate was safe from a loveless marriage. Ryland was safe. His family was safe. Her family, too. Countless men like Ryland and Henry were safe as well—at least from Crafton and his society. Their lives must still be lived in the shadows, in secrecy.

Eliza wanted nothing more to do with secrets, although she must keep Henry's secret still, because of men like Crafton. She must keep it because society did not understand men like Henry and Ryland. What they did not understand they condemned to death.

At least, after all this, the secret lost its power over her.

Nate turned to her, a quill in his hand. 'Will you sign, Eliza?'

She stepped forward, touching his fingers as she took the quill from him and signed her name on each sheet.

Nate handed Crafton his copy.

Crafton snatched it from him. 'How do I know that *you* will keep this agreement?'

Eliza watched Nate meet his gaze. 'Because we are honourable people, sir.'

Crafton sputtered and strode out of the room, clutching the paper.

Eliza and Nate were left alone.

He turned her with a puzzled look. 'How did you know to come?'

She gazed into his handsome face and her heart fluttered as she suspected it always would.

'Your soldiers,' she responded. 'They came to tell me.'

He blinked in surprise. 'My soldiers?'

She nodded.

Before he spoke another word, though, she took his arm. 'I want to leave this place.'

'So do I.' He folded their copies of the agreement and put them in his coat pocket.

They hurried out of the room and into the hall where Crafton's butler was ready with Nate's hat and gloves. A moment later they were outside in the fresh air, greeted by four men loitering on the pavement and one in the street holding the horses of a curricle.

Hawkins stepped forward. 'Well? What happened? Were you in time, m'lady?'

She took his hand and swept a gaze over the others. 'Thanks to you all, I was in time! Crafton backed down. All is well.'

She'd keep the agreement. That was all she would ever say to anyone.

Nate stepped forward and the pleased laughter of the men ceased abruptly.

Hawkins spoke in a defensive tone. 'Beg your pardon, Major, if we spoke out of turn by telling the lady, but we could not—'

Nate shook his head. 'The lot of you never could follow orders.' He smiled and clapped them each on the back.

Foster, still holding the horses, asked, 'May I take you and the lady anywhere?'

Nate looked to Eliza.

'I'd rather walk,' she said.

Nate reached in his pocket, took out some coins and handed them to Hawkins. 'You all go and have a pint or two on me. And come see me tomorrow. I'll settle up your wages.' He added, 'There will be bonuses for all of you!'

Foster climbed on to the curricle. 'Save me a pint, lads. I'll see to the horses first. Will you be at the Lamb and Flag?'

Yates nodded. 'The Lamb and Flag.'

Foster rode away and the others headed off to celebrate.

Nate offered Eliza his arm. 'Where to now?' he asked.

Where to, indeed? she thought.

'Let us just walk,' she responded.

With her un-gloved fingers she relished the strength of his arm evident even through the cloth of his coat. Of how he shortened his natural stride to match hers. Of how tall he was.

Of how he almost sacrificed his future happiness merely to protect her from scandal. What had he been thinking?

She imagined the conversation, so rational and sensible. They'd discuss how Crafton thought his threat would work. Did he think that once Eliza spurned Nate that Nate would naturally form an affection for Lady Sibyl? Lady Sibyl and her father did not know of Nate's and Eliza's connection to each other, though. They could not have known their attachment to each other to be the reason Nate was willing to sacrifice himself for her.

But why was she thinking about Lady Sibyl and Crafton? Why even consider talking about them? She'd had more than enough of Crafton and Lady Sibyl. They would not intrude on this walk with Nate.

'Eliza?' Nate spoke so quietly she was not certain she'd

heard him, not through her own rambling thoughts. 'All I really want is your happiness and well-being and Natalie's.'

'Oh, Nate,' she responded. 'You proved that, certainly.'

He went on. Determinedly, she thought. 'No matter what form your happiness takes. It is all I want.'

Even if it meant she'd run away to Sandleigh? Alone? She could ask that, but she already knew the answer. Of course it meant that. No matter how *she* hurt *him*, he still wanted her happiness.

Instead she said, 'You were right, you know, Nate.'

'About what?' he asked.

'I was afraid. Afraid to trust you. I am so accustomed to being afraid, I could not see it.'

He stopped walking and gazed down at her. 'What you did today—what you were prepared to do—that was not fear.'

'Oh, it was, though,' she countered. 'I was afraid you would marry Lady Sibyl.'

He cocked his head.

She waved a hand. 'But I do not want to think of them! Lady Sibyl and Crafton! They have caused us enough grief. What I meant to say was, it was you who taught me what to do. You taught me to face my problems head on, to play my hand even if I lost. You taught me not to be afraid of the truth.'

'I taught you all that?' He smiled wryly.

She nodded. 'In the cabin.'

'Good God, I was wise.'

She laughed out loud.

They reached Clarges Street and stopped, but Nate could not bear to say goodbye to her so soon.

'Would you consider a walk in the park?' he asked. 'We can stop by your house if you wish to get a hat and gloves.'

She gazed up into his face, the morning sun illuminating her features. Her beauty. He must remember her face at this moment of relief and uncertainty.

He tried to smile. 'See? I am asking, not commanding. I took what you said to me to heart, Eliza. I realise how easily it is for me to assume command, but I do not need my way. I need your happiness.'

She did smile at him and finally responded. 'I would love a walk in the park. Forget the hat and gloves. No harm will come if I do not wear them this one time.'

They walked in silence but in relative ease past his street and on to the Hyde Park Corner gate.

They entered the park and came to a fork in the path.

Nate stopped. 'You must choose the path, Eliza.'

She giggled. 'Do you realise you are commanding me to do what I choose?'

He felt like kicking himself. 'I apologise. I cannot seem to help it.'

She squeezed his arm. 'I noticed.' She gestured ahead. 'Let us walk to the Serpentine.'

As soon as they turned a bend in the path, a small figure spied them and ran towards them. 'Mama! Mama!'

It was Natalie, Miss Gibbons hurrying behind her.

Natalie, clutching her doll, ran straight to her mother. 'Mama! I fed the swans this time.'

'Did you?' Eliza picked her up and gave her a hug.

'Where is your hat?' Natalie asked in a scolding tone.

'I forgot it,' Eliza responded.

Nate stepped back, ready to retreat entirely.

'Look who is here,' Eliza said to her daughter as she placed her back on the ground. 'Lord Hale.'

Natalie smiled in delight. 'Lord Hale!' She thrust her doll towards him. 'I have my doll with me. See?'

Nate, his heart aching, squatted down to her height. 'Hello, Henry,' he said to the doll.

Natalie was delighted. 'Henry likes the swans. Do you like the swans, Lord Hale?'

Swans. He'd read swans mate for life. 'I do like swans.'

'You should feed the swans,' Natalie said. 'They like that.'

'A very good idea.' He stood again.

Miss Gibbons looked from him to Eliza, her face pensive. 'Miss Natalie, we should be on our way.' She took the girl's hand.

'Mama,' Natalie asked Eliza. 'Are you taking a walk with Lord Hale without your hat?'

Eliza laughed a little. 'Yes, I am. I will be home later, though.'

Natalie lifted her doll up to Nate. 'Say goodbye to Lord Hale, Henry.'

Nate crouched down again, looking directly at the doll. 'Goodbye, Henry. I hope we've done well by you.'

Miss Gibbons looked puzzled, but Natalie seemed to think it nothing strange to say. Eliza's eyes glistened.

He stood again and watched his daughter walk away—no—skip away, still holding her doll securely against her little chest. Only when he noticed Eliza looking at him quizzically did he offer his arm again and they walked on.

As they walked she spoke. 'I think there is something we must do.'

Something more about Crafton? He thought all those strings were neatly tied.

'Feed swans?' he asked.

She flashed a smile. 'No. At least I did not mean that.' She took a breath. 'I think we should start again. Courting, I mean.'

He stopped and faced her. 'Do you mean that, Eliza?'

She glanced away. 'Well, not at the pace we've previously set. Slow, perhaps. Getting used to each other.'

Nate's spirits soared. There on the path in Hyde Park

where anyone might see, he forgot about going slow. He took her in his arms and swung her around.

'As you command, my lady,' he said. 'As you command.'

Epilogue

Hale House, Surrey, 1822—five years later

Lady Natalie Page ran the entire length of the garden behind Hale House. She was out of breath and hot, but exhilarated, as always. Ever since she was a little girl and she felt pent-up energy or agitation or frustration she would run. Her Papa Henry taught her to do that.

Poor Papa Henry.

She still remembered him, how he'd smile at her and toss her in the air. How he taught her to run.

She still missed him. She still had her Henry doll, the doll that she carried everywhere with her when she'd been six. She even played with it sometimes, although at eleven years old she'd added several other dolls to her collection. A whole family of them.

Natalie walked back to where her mother sat in the shade of a tree. Her two brothers, three years old and two, played with a ball nearby. Natalie's younger brother was named after Papa Henry, the older after Papa Nate's father. Natalie's baby sister, Miranda, whom Mama held in her arms, was named after Papa Nate's mother. Papa Nate's mother and father had died when he was only a little older than she had been when Papa Henry died.

Of course, to the world she must say they were her half-brothers and half-sister, because her father was Papa Henry and theirs was Papa Nate. When she turned eleven, though, Mama told her she was old enough to know what must be kept secret from everyone else. How Papa Henry really loved a man more than Mama, but she met Papa Nate and they made a baby that was her. Mama and Papa Henry pretended Natalie was his daughter because Papa Nate went off to war. And that Papa Henry loved her very much. Natalie remembered that part. And she remembered when Mama and Papa Nate found each other again.

Oh, Natalie did not understand it all, though, and Mama promised to explain more when she was older, but she was old enough to know this much and old enough to keep the secret. She promised.

Natalie sat down next to her mother and reached for the baby. 'I'll hold her, Mama.'

Her sister was the dearest creature! So pretty with her dark curly hair and blue eyes. Mama said Natalie looked very much like Miranda when she was a baby.

Her mother handed the baby to Natalie, closed her eyes and leaned back to let the sun warm her face. 'I wish your father would come back.'

She meant Papa Nate, of course. He went out riding alone and Mama always worried a little when he did that.

'He is back, Mama,' Natalie said. 'He just walked through the gate.'

Mama opened her eyes and her whole face lit up with happiness. 'Yes. There he is.'

Papa Nate smiled as he approached. Mama straightened and looked like she was ready to fly off the bench to meet him. They always looked like that when they saw each other after being separated for a while. They loved each other, you see.

'Hello, Family!' Papa Nate called when he came close enough.

He always greeted them that way. *Hello, Family.*

Her brothers toddled towards him, their arms reaching up. Papa Nate scooped them up in his arms. He could carry both of them at once, because he was strong. Soldiers were very strong.

When he got close to Mama, though, he put the boys down. She rose from the bench and embraced him. Papa Nate kissed her and the boys clung to his legs. He kissed her a long time, which always made Natalie smile.

When she grew up she wanted to marry someone exactly like Papa Nate, because he loved her mother so very much.

After he kissed Mama he leaned down and kissed Natalie on the cheek and Miranda on her soft curly head. 'And how are my girls?' he asked.

'I just ran the whole length of the garden,' Natalie told him.

'Good for you,' he said, putting his arm around Mama again.

Natalie took it all in. Her mother and Papa Nate arm in arm, her brothers demanding their attention, her dear little sister sleeping through it all.

How lucky she was—how lucky they all were—to be a family.

* * * * *

*If you enjoyed this story, be sure to check out
Diane Gaston's exciting miniseries
Captains of Waterloo*

Her Gallant Captain at Waterloo
Lord Grantwell's Christmas Wish

*And why not read about society's most notorious family
in The Scandalous Summerfields miniseries?*

Bound by Duty
Bound by One Scandalous Night
Bound by a Scandalous Secret
Bound by their Secret Passion

Love Harlequin romance?

DISCOVER.

Be the first to find out about promotions,
news and exclusive content!

Facebook.com/HarlequinBooks

Twitter.com/HarlequinBooks

Instagram.com/HarlequinBooks

Pinterest.com/HarlequinBooks

You Tube YouTube.com/HarlequinBooks

ReaderService.com

EXPLORE.

Sign up for the Harlequin e-newsletter and
download a free book from any series at
TryHarlequin.com

CONNECT.

Join our Harlequin community to
share your thoughts and connect
with other romance readers!
Facebook.com/groups/HarlequinConnection

HARLEQUIN
PLUS

Announcing a **BRAND-NEW** multimedia subscription service for romance fans like you!

Read, Watch and Play.

Experience the easiest way to get the romance content you crave.

Start your **FREE 7 DAY TRIAL** at
<u>www.harlequinplus.com/freetrial</u>.